QUEEN TAKES CHECKMATE

THEIR VAMPIRE QUEEN - BOOK 5

JOELY SUE BURKHART

QUEEN TAKES CHECKMATE

THEIR VAMPIRE QUEEN, book 5
Published by
Joely Sue Burkhart

A Reverse Harem Vampire Romance

The god of light has met his match. But whose life will the red serpent claim?

Killing the queen of New York City has added a million new responsibilities to Shara Isador's list. The former queen's Blood must be dealt with before they turn thrall. The queens Keisha Skye coerced into sibling relationships must either be formally sworn to House Isador or freed. Though Shara can't in good conscience allow anyone into her house who took part in the rampant torture in which House Skye indulged.

While every single day, Shara feels the weight of the red serpent coiled around her throat. The goddess's gift grows heavier with every passing moment. If she doesn't act, the serpent will consume everything she loves. But if she goes after Ra as promised...

Someone she loves very much will die.

Any of her Blood will gladly pay that cost, but Shara loves them too much to even consider losing one of them.

Who will survive the epic showdown with Ra, the god of light, and will this be the end of Shara Isador's story?

For my Beloved Sis.

Thank you to my comma warriors and beta readers:
Mads Schofield, Shelbi Gehring, Alyssa Muller, Meagan Cannon West,
Sherri Meyer, Laura Walker, Briana Walker, Stephanie Cunningham,
Kiersten Wukitsch, Kaila Duff, Amber Lynn Hamblin, Karmen Vele,
Heather Hollmann, Ashley Strom, Kristy Atkinson, Monica Skee, Kee
Robinson, Lydia Simone, Ashley Carlson, Bibiane Lybæk

SHARA

I wanted to see the body.

I couldn't help but fear that Keisha Skye had died too easily. In my rush to get to Rik and save him from the demon child, maybe I'd missed something. Maybe Keisha was faking her death or had some secret power that we'd never seen before. I'd died and come back. Maybe she could too.

I hadn't even changed out of the ruined dress, but I couldn't rest back at my own home until I'd checked the body. I had to be sure.

Waiting for the service elevator to arrive, I tried to remember the young woman I'd been before I learned of my power and Isis' heritage. Life on the run had been hard and exhausting. I never stayed in one place for more than a week or two. I had no one to even talk to, let alone depend on. I didn't want to go back to that lonely, dismal life.

Yet that Shara had never killed anyone.

I'd killed Keisha Skye with my own hands. My Blood had pinned her for me despite her struggles. I'd locked my mouth to her throat and drained her life force, leaving a husk of a body behind. I could have spared her, but I *chose* to kill her.

Because of my actions, more people might die. I had to figure out what to do about Keisha's Blood before they turned into thralls, like the monsters that had hunted me all of my life. I had no idea how many people my dragon and gryphon had killed in the turmoil following Keisha's death. I'd been in the basement, trying to break a demon's blood circle to save Rik.

Several hundred people were missing from the Skye registry. I hoped to goddess they'd simply fled and could find a new life with a new queen somewhere safe.

The elevator doors finally opened. Xin and Llewellyn stepped inside, Xin pressing the button to hold the doors open. Nevarre, Itztli, and Tlacel guarded our rear. Guillaume and Mehen had already taken the elevator down to the basement and waited for us to join them. Daire and Ezra were using their prior Skye contacts to smooth feathers and organize those who wanted to stay, along with Gina and Madeline, the consiliari.

To be honest, that work was mostly being accomplished by Daire, but Ezra was willing to help, and his gruff, no-bullshit attitude was actually helping people realize that I wasn't the same kind of queen as Keisha.

I wasn't sure if I could trust Skye's former consiliarius, but I trusted Gina implicitly and she was willing to work with the woman. To a point, I agreed. Madeline Skye would know the ins and outs of Skye's legacy. She could help us determine how to slice and dice the properties, treaties, and funds as needed for better management.

I stepped onto the elevator with Rik glued to my side. In fact, he hadn't stopped touching me since the ordeal. I wasn't complaining, far from it. I couldn't wait to get away from all the curious, prying eyes so I could cuddle with him.

And yeah, I'd probably bawl like a baby. I'd come so close to losing him.

The elevator was painfully slow and crowded with so many Blood. Again, not that I was complaining about them being pressed against me. I wanted—needed—them close. Always.

I tapped my bare toes with impatience. I'd ditched the stupid heels hours ago.

Rik slipped his arm around my waist, pulling me in even closer to the protective heat of his body. "You really think she might not be dead?"

I shook my head. "I don't know. She was the fucking queen of New York City. Could she really have been that easy to kill?"

"She didn't die easily," Xin said. "You drained her. Most queens wouldn't begin to have enough capacity to drain a queen in one feeding. That alone was a remarkable way to kill a powerful queen."

"Think of Mayte," Rik added. "She could only take a small amount of your blood at once, because she couldn't handle the power. Your capacity is much greater. You absorbed Keisha easily."

So easily that my stomach quivered with dread. I'd drained

her to *death*. Worse, I could easily retire with my Blood and feed from all of them again. In fact, I'd need to do exactly that soon. My hunger was never satisfied, not even by all the blood in the former queen of New York City.

"She also attacked you during the presentation," Xin said. "That was no small spell she threw at you. She'd probably devastated many visiting queens that way, or at least scared them into surrendering before they were all killed."

"Plus her child," Rik whispered. My prime, badass alpha didn't shiver or flinch from what he'd endured in my service, but Tanza Skye had scared the crap out of all of us.

Rik had been in the fucking circle with her while she hurt him with the kind of torture that didn't leave external marks. Even after I'd healed and fed him, he still had tender spots deep inside that would need more attention. We Aima healed quickly, but I feared the wounds Tanza dealt him would never ease unless I continued to give him my blood as often as possible.

"I had her bond inside me," Rik continued. "I felt her spreading like worms through me, and her power... It was crushing. You're the closest I've ever felt to that level of power, my queen. I think that Keisha was pumping everything she had into Tanza, who fed off her as much as she fed on the pain and torture of alphas. Keisha probably didn't have much left to fend you off."

That made me feel a little better, until Rik set me down and I saw her body.

Xin had brought her down to the same place her daughter died. I'd already blasted Tanza's body into a pile of ash. Keisha had only been dead a couple of hours, but she looked and smelled like she'd been dead a week.

Her body was bloated and decaying. Her eyes were already gone. Something wriggled beneath her skin, and I caught a flash of what might have been the hard shell of a beetle.

I recoiled, clutching my stomach. Bile churned. I had to will myself not to throw up.

I'd fed on her. I'd drank her blood. Was that corruption inside me now? I'd been so careful to burn Tanza's tainted blood out of Rik and Ezra, but I'd never thought to check myself. My heart pounded so hard I swayed, my vision swimming.

Rik closed his hands around my upper arms and squeezed, breaking through some of my panic. His bond surged through me like a giant searchlight, shining on every nook and cranny inside me.

"There's nothing." He dragged me up in his arms. "You're fine. She didn't contaminate you."

"Are you sure?"

I hated the quiver in my voice, the tears on my cheeks, and the burn of acid in my stomach. I hated being afraid.

"I'm sure. Whatever's wrong with her isn't inside of you."

I breathed deeply, dragging his scent into my body to help ease my panic. Hot rock and smoke, a tang of iron and steel. His rock troll hovered just beneath his skin, ready to surge out and defend me to the death.

I turned my head, keeping my cheek on his chest, and looked at the body again. "Do all Aima decay so quickly?"

Guillaume squatted down beside the body, completely unaffected by the smell or creepy crawlies. "Thralls can decay like this while they're still alive, but I've never seen an Aima do this before, let alone a queen."

Mehen let out a disgusted hiss and averted his nose. "I've seen this fucking shit before. That's not demonic taint. That's what Ra's touch does to an Aima queen once he's got hooks in her."

She had gone to Ra to try and sire a child with a god, the same as my mother. But how could the god of light make her rot like this?

"It's a perversion of the old vampire myths," Mehen said. "If she'd died in sunlight, she would have burst into flame and disintegrated into dust and ash, but there's no sunlight down here. I can shift and blast her with fire, if you like, my queen."

"No, thank you, Mehen. I'll take care of it."

Rik's chest rumbled against my ear. "There's no need for you to get closer to her or do this yourself. We live to serve in any way possible, and there is no restitution or punishment you need to put yourself through. You saved me. You saved us all."

I forced my feet to start moving toward the body. No, toward Guillaume. I focused wholly on my Templar knight as Rik moved with me so smoothly that I didn't even have to move my head. I held my hand out to Guillaume and the flash of silver told me he'd cut me. I didn't feel the pain of his knife. "I killed her. I should make sure she's taken care of."

He must have made a fairly large cut, because it didn't take long for me to bleed the full length of her body. I made myself watch as I coated her in blood. Blue-black beetles moved beneath her skin, devouring her from the inside out. I swallowed hard. "Are these scarab beetles?"

"Looks like it," Guillaume agreed. "Knowing your heritage, and his, it makes sense."

"Can they report back to him in some way? Or infiltrate the rest of the nest?"

They looked at each other and shrugged. "I'm sorry, my queen, but anything is possible," Rik finally said. "Keisha was able to use ants before. Maybe these beetles carry the same magic. Maybe that was Ra's power all along."

Fuck. I needed to be sure that I blasted them all to be safe. The last thing I wanted was a beetle horde spying on us.

I bled on Keisha's body until my tongue felt like a wad of cotton and my knees wavered. Even if I thoroughly destroyed her and these beetles, I didn't know if I'd ever feel safe enough in this building to sleep. Though sleep sounded heavenly right now. I must be near the end of my reserves. I didn't want to wipe myself out for weeks again.

Something Mehen said earlier tickled in the back of my mind. "There's no sunlight down here."

Guillaume's brow creased with concern, and Rik picked me up in his arms, cradling me carefully in his arms. "Enough, my queen. You have to rest."

"No, not yet. This is important."

He paused mid-turn to the elevator. "Do what you must, my queen, but then I'm taking you back to the Isador house."

"It's dark, here. Complete darkness. My mother said I should always work my greatest magic in complete darkness. Can someone turn out the lights, please?"

I closed my eyes and breathed deeply, relaxing fully into his arms. My alpha had me. My Blood were here. My loved ones were safe and close. There wasn't anything in the darkness that could hurt me.

I'd rarely ever gone outside at night. It wasn't safe with the thralls constantly hunting me. My bedroom at home in Kansas City had been pitch dark like this, because I couldn't sleep in a room with windows. Glass wasn't enough to keep the monsters out.

I let my mind drift for a moment, resting in that darkness. Ra couldn't touch me. He had no power here.

This power is yours.

My mother's voice whispered in my head, so familiar, even though she'd died shortly after my birth. She'd given me to her sister to raise far from the Triune political games and any nest or queen who might influence me. She'd loosed me on the world on purpose.

Controlled chaos. Spreading change, reveling in blood, and now, drawing on the powers of the dark.

There *was* power here. Not like the ancient earth energy of my grove back home in Eureka Springs, but a vibrant energy despite the darkness. With my eyes closed, I focused on the internal tapestry of my mind. Deep purple flowed around me like I'd jumped into an indigo river. Strands of power swept on either side of me, some softer lavender and others as dark as a shadowed bruise. Where were the streams going? Where had they come from?

I couldn't be sure without doing some investigation. Power eddied and flowed here in the basement, maybe connecting to

QUEEN TAKES CHECKMATE | 9

other underground tunnels and access points like subway routes under the city. I wasn't sure if this power was everywhere, or only here in New York City. I couldn't recall ever being in complete darkness—and looking at the tapestry like this.

All darkness is yours. A male voice I'd never heard before rasped in my head, each word stretched out as if from a great distance. *My daughter.*

Oh. Fuck.

Typhon. The father of monsters. *My* father.

Something rustled deep in my mind, as if I'd opened up a basement door and peered inside.

She gave you the Great One's legacy. I give you dominion over any creature of darkness. The breath of the night wind. The darkest shadow slipping silently through the trees. The silent music that rises from the earth as it cools from the punishing light of day. The paths of death that lead to life. The ways are open to you, Daughter.

The rustling sound came closer, and I finally recognized the sound as scales rasping over concrete. I saw him for a moment, at least in my mind. He filled the space around me, his head bent down toward me. His shoulders rose almost to the ceiling. Long black serpents flowed around me. He had arms and a bare, muscular chest, but no legs. Just the snakes, each as thick as one of Rik's massive thighs.

Typhon's eyes glowed like molten magma at the earth's core. Liquid rock, unimaginable heat. He cupped my cheek and his palm was even bigger than Rik's rock troll.

Be not afraid of any creature that hides from the light of day, for Ra is merciless and has hunted our kind through the ages.

"The demon child, Tanza. Was she not of the dark?"

We have our demons of darkness. We have our thirsts, our needs for pain and blood and pleasure. We are monsters and revel in that need. But Tanza was no child of darkness. She was wholly a child of Ra—a vile, evil creature of his own creation. Not the vilest, and certainly not the evillest.

Great. Just fucking great. Something worse than Tanza waited out there for me?

Call your monsters, Daughter. Love them. Embrace your darkest hungers, because your love is the light that will keep the darkness safe from the punishing light of Ra.

He started to fade away into mist, though I could still feel his palm on my cheek. I nestled my face deeper into his caress. The only time my true father had ever touched me. "Will my fire hurt the creatures of darkness?"

His eyes flared with flames, and he chuckled as he dispersed into the darkness. *Mount Vesuvius has always been my domain. The hottest hells of the earth cannot touch our kind. Know true darkness by how it embraces your fire, your blood, or both, and beware the bright light of day.*

"Thank you, Father."

I swallowed the knot in my throat and reached out to stroke my fingers through the velvety dark purple flowing around me. It responded to me, the same way my blood quickened. I wasn't sure how I would use it yet, but I'd learned a very important lesson already.

Every gift I'd been given so far had made a difference in our survival. I would heed his warning and embrace his gifts, until I thoroughly understood how to save us when the time came.

For now, I willed my blood to light Keisha's body with the hottest flames I could imagine. The purple flows tightened around her like an impenetrable net, keeping the beetles from escaping. I watched as my blood and fire crisped Keisha Skye into ash that compacted itself into a small black ball. I crushed her into dust and allowed the tides of darkness to disperse her to the four winds.

"Okay," I whispered, reaching up to wrap my arms around Rik's neck. "I'm finished here."

I was so tired, and there was still so much to do. I rested my eyes, drooped across his chest as he headed for the elevator, but my mind raced.

:*Do we need to post some guards here to keep an eye on Skye Tower?*:

:*Already taken care of, my queen,*: Rik assured me. :*We'll have two Blood present at all times. Daire and Ezra are evaluating all our former sibs to see who might be good candidates to use as additional protection until you're able to make your own blood circle.*:

My heart lurched at the thought of leaving two of my Blood behind. :*What about when we go home to the nest? I can't leave anyone behind. I won't.*:

:*We'll figure something out when the time comes.*:

:*A sib would be your best bet,*: Guillaume said in the bond. :*They'll be yours, and hold the territory in your stead.*:

I'd felt several queens during our procession to meet Keisha. Several of them had followed me and responded to my power, but I didn't know if they'd be strong enough to hold New York City for me. I touched my consiliarius's bond. :*Could you prepare a short list of potential queen sibs who you think would be good candidates to hold the city for me?*:

She couldn't answer me in the bond, since I hadn't tasted her blood, but I sensed her immediate agreement. Knowing Gina, she'd already started compiling the list. She was just that good at her job.

With my eyes closed, I allowed my mind to drift as Rik carried me down the hallway toward the service elevator. If I'd had my eyes open, or if I'd been upright and walking, I probably wouldn't have noticed the faint tug in the eddying violet power.

"Stop," I whispered.

He paused, and I felt his senses stretching outward, looking for anything amiss. Xin's wolf immediately ghosted past us, his ruff rising on a silent snarl.

:*Do you sense anything?*: Rik asked Xin in the bond.

:*Nothing. If there's anyone else down here, their scent is well masked.*:

Shifted into his black dog, Itztli paced ahead of us, sniffing the concrete floor and the currents of air. :*Agreed. No scent, not even like Ra's minion that attacked us in Mexico.*:

But I felt... something. Keeping my eyes closed, I let the dark flows of the basement pass around me. Cool shadows, safe darkness, but sterile. I didn't feel any of the goddesses' touch here. No earth magic or spark of life. Just darkness. My father's domain.

Something tugged ever so faintly on my attention. A small snag, like I was walking through the woods and my scarf caught on an invisible twig. It broke away to nothing as soon as I tried to look for it.

Rik took a few slow steps and paused. "There are halls off to the left and right. Do you feel a direction?"

The faintest tug came from the left, like a tiny spider web

tickling my cheek. I pointed down the hall without opening my eyes. Xin and Itztli crept in that direction, while Rik remained in the main aisle. My alpha wasn't going to take me into an unknown threat.

:These look like prison cells,: Xin said. *:No windows, iron doors, lots of salt.:*

"Salt? Does she have thralls down here? Who would keep thralls?"

Rik shook his head grimly. "Even Keisha wouldn't have kept thralls inside her nest. It has to be something else."

"But what else does salt work against? I wonder if it would have affected Tanza."

:All the cells are empty except one,: Xin said. *:You need to see this, my queen.:*

Rik headed down the corridor. Tlacel and Nevarre joined Itztli's black dog in front of us. Guillaume, Llewellyn, and Mehen guarded our back.

I opened my eyes, but I didn't ask Rik to set me down. "We need to search the tower thoroughly, especially this basement. With Tanza hidden away, and now these cells, I'm nervous about what else Keisha may have hidden down here."

"Agreed," Rik replied. "The last thing we want is for you to drop a blood circle with something nasty inside."

My Blood formed an arc outside a rusted metal door at the end of the hall. Dust lay thick in the air and coated the floor. Other than our footprints, it didn't look like anyone had been down here in years. Yet there was a thick line of salt poured along the doorway, and a heavy lock and chain barred the door.

Guillaume touched the old-fashioned lock. "Silver. Whatever's inside, they took every precaution to be sure it stayed put. I'd bet they blessed the door with holy water too."

Xin and Itztli sat on their haunches, alert but not growling. "Can you sense anything alive inside?"

:Nothing, but that could be the protections,: Xin replied.

I blew out a breath. "Well, I guess we need to open it up and see what Keisha was so scared of. Put me down so I can take a closer look."

For once, Rik didn't obey me. In fact, he tightened his grip on me, tucking me closer against him.

Surprised, I looked up into his face. I didn't need light to sense the heat blazing in his eyes.

"I will, my queen. After you feed."

2

_____

RIK

I would carry my queen every moment of the day and night if she'd let me. I never wanted to set her down. If she was in my arms, all was right in the world. Nothing else mattered. Let the Keishas of the Aima courts try to defeat her. Let the demons drain me dry. My queen would tear down the foundations of the world to reach me. So I could hold her again, like this. Always.

Even more, *I* needed her in my arms. I needed to feel that connection with her as assurance that we were both alive and well. She'd been victorious, and though we'd taken some damage, it wasn't anything we couldn't recover from. It wasn't something *I* couldn't recover from.

I didn't want to remember the way Tanza's blood had burned into me, destroying everything I loved. It hadn't been the pain that hurt so badly. It'd been the doubt. The crippling fear that I would be so broken and damaged that I wouldn't be able to serve as Shara's Blood ever again. Let alone as alpha.

Tanza had tortured my mind as well as my body by taking images from my memory and twisting them. Like when Guillaume had first come to our queen's call. He'd chopped off my head, but only after making me watch him take my place in her bed. My place as her alpha at her back. My place in her heart.

That vision hurt more than the lingering internal damage.

Even though I'd been hurt, I wanted her to come to me first for protection and assistance, pleasure and blood. I needed her to reinforce my position as her alpha.

I thought she would refuse me. I wasn't one hundred percent yet. Something still felt... raw inside me. But she needed to be stronger if something nasty waited on the other side of the cell door.

Her dark eyes gleamed, missing nothing. Her bond shimmered in my mind like pure moonlight, spinning crystals though me. Shining her light on those dark, shadowed places that still hurt.

"Okay," she whispered, reaching up to cup my cheek. "But I'll need your help."

My throat ached. Shara had never liked asking for help, especially when it came to feeding. At one point, she'd almost starved herself as her power started to come in, though her fangs hadn't, simply because she hadn't wanted to ask for assistance.

So for her to ask—for anything—was a priceless gift.

She was fully capable of asking Guillaume for a blade, but

she left the decision to me. She wanted me to be her alpha in all ways, even something as minor as this.

"Nevarre." My voice was rougher than I intended, though her raven Blood came to us without complaint. "Bite me for our queen."

He gave me an agreeable grin and slid close, tucking Shara between us. His long black hair slid over her shoulder like a silken blanket, making her give him a sultry look. "It's been entirely too long since I had you in my bed, Nevarre."

"I agree, my queen." He winked without animosity and leaned in toward my throat, but he paused, waiting for me to give him the okay, even though I'd ordered him to come to our queen's aid.

I'd chosen Nevarre for several reasons. She was right—he could use some more time with her. He'd come to her at the same time as Mehen, whose gigantic personality and ancient power easily overshadowed everyone around him. Then she'd added the twins in Mexico. Nevarre wasn't as grumpy or playful or formidable as the others. He and Xin carried a quiet, deadly power that was easy to overlook.

Nevarre hadn't shifted, so it made it easier and quicker for him to help her. But I'd also chosen him because of his personality. He hadn't complained or ruffled any feathers despite other new Blood joining the fold, and he wasn't going to bitch or complain like Mehen. And Guillaume...

While I trusted him implicitly, the scene Tanza had put into my head was too fresh to ask the headless knight to tear open my throat, even in service to our queen.

I gave Nevarre a nod and he sank his fangs into my

throat, just long enough to make the wound for her. Shara made a low sound of hunger that made my fangs and dick throb with anticipation. Closing my eyes, I sank into her bond as she sealed her mouth over the punctures. My blood slid down her throat. I felt the rush of alpha power flooding her system. The surge of desire that tightened her body. She had a hand fisted in Nevarre's hair, her arm locked around my neck. Nevarre tucked his face against her back, soaking her in even though she wasn't feeding on him.

Guilt twinged. I needed to do a better job of making sure each of her Blood had time to touch and hold her. And with as much as she loved each of us, she needed the time too. They needed to feel her love and revel in her pleasure, the same as her alpha.

She licked the punctures closed and lifted her head. Too soon. I felt her hunger still burning in her veins like a ravaging fever. Turning in my arms, she reached for Nevarre. His eyes flared with hope, another stab of guilt through my heart. She didn't have to ask me to lean down and sink my fangs into him so she could feed.

:I'm sorry, Nevarre. I'll make sure you have more time with her.:

:No apology is needed, alpha. I know all too well how difficult it is to balance each Blood's duty and service for a powerful queen. My need is nothing, as long as hers are met.:

:I need you, too, Nevarre,: she whispered in the bond with a sense of aching need that had us both pressing her harder between us.

She fed from him long enough that I felt his heart thudding

heavily in the bond. Reluctantly, she lifted her head and pressed her lips to his. *:You always taste like magic.:*

:My magic and my blood are yours, my queen.:

I did a quick sweep through her bond to check her health and strength level. She could still stand to feed from at least another couple of us, but she was plenty strong enough to deal with whatever was behind this door. Even if it was another queen as strong as Keisha.

Which was a sobering thought. Before I'd left in search of my own queen, I'd been in awe of how strong Keisha was. She'd held New York City and was the strongest queen in the Americas. Her power had dwarfed my mother's Hyrrokkin queen, though we weren't known for immense power, only our physical strength and size.

Keisha's power was a drop in the bucket compared to Shara's. She was the strongest queen in the Americas now, and very likely rivaled even Marne Ceresa or the Dauphine. The Triune queens, with one seat open.

I couldn't claim any knowledge of the goddesses' plans for my queen, but I'd be a fool to not expect the Triune call. Only Shara would be strong enough to hold that third seat and stand against the other two queens. The scope of those duties…

Already, she wanted nothing to do with the seat, and she didn't even know a fraction of the responsibilities that would come with it. Though we needed the Triune whole and strong. Aima were losing our courts and queens faster than new queens could possibly be born, even now that some of the ancient lines had been rejuvenated with godly sires. The Triune needed her, whether or not Marne or the Dauphine would admit it.

"I'm ready, thanks to you two."

I set her down in front of the door. She stretched out her right hand and touched the silver lock. "Does silver affect us in any way?"

"The legends are always somewhat based in fact." Guillaume reached over his shoulder and pulled a foot-long heavy blade out of a spine sheath beneath his shirt. "Even the rock troll would have a difficult time breaking free of silver chains this thick. Allow me to break the chains and lock for you, my queen."

With a nod, she stepped back against me. I slipped my arm around her waist and she closed her hand over mine on her stomach. Her hand was so small in mine, and her head barely reached my sternum. But it suddenly dawned on me....

She was protecting me. Offering me her strength, her touch, her love a shield, as the knight stepped closer to us. The knight who'd killed me over and over in my head while Tanza tortured me.

I clenched my jaw so hard I almost broke a tooth. My queen. Protecting me. It was all I could do not to sweep her back up in my arms. Or better yet, carry her to the nearest bed and bury my face between her thighs.

Guillaume slipped the tip of the heavy blade into a link and carefully pried the chain open. The lock fell with a clatter to the floor and he stepped back, lifting his gaze to mine. The consummate gentleman and honored Templar knight held my gaze a moment, and then inclined his head. To me. Not to her.

Our bonds were all strong enough that I'm sure Guillaume had no difficulty picking up the shuddering memories implanted in my head. Memories that had not happened, would never happen, but hurt just the same. The man had been tortured too, physically in prison, and then mentally and emotionally by his first queen. He knew firsthand the toll it took on a man. Especially a man used to being the strong protector.

He didn't say anything. He didn't have to. And I respected him all the more for that small gesture of respect and honor.

Resisting the urge to push my queen behind me to fully protect her, I planted my palm on the heavy door and shoved it open. The hinges groaned with disuse. Guillaume slipped inside, followed by Xin and Itztli, both still shifted, their mighty noses working overtime. Through our bonds, their senses flooded me with rich colors and textures of smell. Thick, ancient dust. Coppery rust. A hint of decay. No, not a rotten scent. Extremely old, wasted away, desiccated…

"A mummy," Shara whispered. "But who is it? If they're dead, why all the protections?"

She stepped forward and I glided with her, keeping contact with her body though I didn't hinder her steps or try to keep her back. We entered a small cell with no windows. The air was thick and heavy. One of the Blood flipped a switch, and the hallway flooded with sudden light, spilling into the cell and illuminating a table in the center of the room.

Nevarre hovered at the door, protecting our back, along with Mehen and Llewellyn.

The table looked like an exam table from a doctor's office. On top, a body laid tightly wrapped in yellowed rags, very much like a television mummy. More silver chains bound the body tightly to the table, and a heavy crucifix lay on top of its chest with a wreath of garlic.

"Silver, salt, garlic, holy objects," Guillaume whispered. "It's like they threw everything they could think of into the ward."

She held her hand out over the body and drew her hand down its length without actually touching it. Her eyes fluttered shut and her head tipped, as if she listened to something only she could hear. "The prison isn't the silver chains or even death. His prison is complete and utter darkness." Her eyes opened, glinting like Guillaume's blade. Hard, cold steel. "He's one of Ra's followers."

Guillaume didn't move, exactly, but the blade in his hand seemed bigger, longer, ready to cut the mummy apart in one mighty blow. "Egyptian?"

"No. He doesn't..." She blew out a disgusted sigh. "He doesn't feel like Isis. When I think of Her, I see sands and smell the desert wind. I see Her pyramid and the moon hanging above. Or I feel Her hair blowing in my face and smell jasmine."

"What do you sense from him?" I asked.

Her mouth tightened into a flat, hard line. "Sunlight and blood."

Itztli rumbled a growl. His ruff spiked around his neck and started down his spine. :*Huitzilopochtli.*:

The Aztec sun god of Tenochtitlan.

"Fuck," all eight of us said in unison.

SHARA

I backed away from the mummified body, my mind racing. He did feel ancient and... deep. That was the only word I could think of. His force of personality and will was as old as the bedrock, like Tepeyollotl and gods who were worshipped centuries ago.

"Why the fuck would Keisha Skye have the Aztec sun god imprisoned in her basement?"

"Vega might know," Rik said. "As Skye's alpha, she's the most likely to know what was going on down here. Though she didn't seem to know about Tanza, so who knows."

For a moment, I felt another twinge of sympathy for the dead queen. I couldn't imagine having a secret as massive as a daughter, whom I'd told everyone decades ago had died, hidden in the basement...

While my alpha knew nothing about it.

I couldn't imagine keeping a secret like that from Rik. Even if I wanted to, and I didn't, I didn't think it would be possible. Our bonds were too deep. We'd shared too much blood to keep that kind of secret. That bond had allowed me to save him when he'd sacrificed himself to protect me.

For all of Keisha's power and her many sibs living in this tower, she must have been very alone. In the end, she'd had no one but Tanza.

"Will you resurrect him?" Rik asked.

He didn't ask if I *could*—but if I *would*.

My power was great enough that I could resurrect a long-lost god. That was a stomach-turning realization. The immense responsibility weighed like a crushing boulder on my heart. If I made a mistake, it wouldn't hurt only me, but my nine Blood. No, my *ten* Blood. Llewellyn might have been my mother's alpha, but he'd taken my blood. He was mine now, whether I wanted him or not.

What if I resurrected this mummy, only to discover that was exactly Ra's plan all along?

"My queen," Tlacel said, drawing my attention to him. "I would recommend against resurrecting Huitzilopochtli unless your need is great. What I saw…"

A shudder rocked his shoulders at the memory of what we'd seen on the other side of the portal. I'd mostly been concentrating on Xochitl so I could grab her and pull her back to our world, but I remembered people waiting below us. They'd looked strange, and it made me remember the bits I'd picked up from his brother's bond. Itztli had said there had been a Blood descended from the Flayed God who liked to strip people's skin off whole and give it to his queen to wear.

Those "people" waiting to catch us as we fell out of the sky had looked more like empty skins rather than whole bodies. Rays of golden light had glowed where their eyes and mouths should have been.

"It was nothing for hundreds of sacrifices to be made to him during a single festival," Tlacel continued. "He was the patron god of Tenochtitlan, war, and the sun. The steps of the Templo Mayor dripped red with blood on his holy days. And that was before Ra corrupted him."

"This is too risky to rush into a decision," I finally said. Absently, I touched the glistening red snake embedded in my skin. Its head lay over my right breast and the rest of its body curled around my neck. "When I saw Coatlicue on Snake Mountain, She asked me to kill Ra so She could be reunited with her son. Huitzilopochtli will be key to our showdown with Ra, but I don't know how yet. If I bring him back too soon..." I shook my head. "I know where he is. I wish we knew why or how Keisha Skye kept him locked in her basement. Was he a gift from Ra? Or was she imprisoning him to spite Ra?"

Guillaume grunted sourly. "The only way to know for sure is to wake up the bastard and ask him."

I turned to Llewellyn. He'd been imprisoned by Keisha too. His eyes had been gouged out, his head covered in a leather hood, and his body bound in chains so heavy that he could barely walk. "Do you know anything about other prisoners Keisha might have?"

He gazed back at me steadily with dark eyes that glittered occasionally, as if a spark flew past a dark window. I'd healed his eyes and restored his power, but I really knew very little about him, other than he'd been my mother's alpha.

Oh, and the fact that he'd willingly allowed himself to be imprisoned and tortured by her enemy for twenty years so that he'd be in place when I needed him. That told me a great deal about his loyalty and honor.

"Unfortunately, no, my queen. I was kept away from this level and knew nothing about the child or this cell. Though I know a great deal about what went on above stairs."

I nodded and turned to leave the cell. I wasn't sure how I felt about him yet. He'd been in the tapestry that I used to check whether an Aima was meant to be my Blood or not. I didn't doubt my decision to give him my blood, and I certainly never would have left him trapped and crippled by Skye's people. But was he really supposed to be *my* Blood? Or would he always be my mother's? Did it matter? "We should sit down tomorrow and go over everything you can think of."

"It will be my pleasure, my queen."

I waited until all my Blood filed out and turned my attention to the door. "Do you think we need to set a guard? Or find a way to put these chains back in place?"

Something rustled up above us. Guillaume's blade glinted. Rik tightened his grip on me, ready to shove me behind him or sweep me up into his arms. Xin and Itztli both crouched with vicious snarls.

Little eyes flashed in the vent near the ceiling. It was askew enough that a small rodent pushed through and scurried down the wall.

Mehen growled. "I fucking hate rats. I ate way too many while I was imprisoned. They taste like shit. Literally."

An idea sparked as I watched the rat come closer. It ran along a faint ledge in the stonework and then sat, facing me, as if awaiting its orders.

"Are rats considered creatures of the dark?"

"Sure," Mehen replied. "That's why they could cross over to my prison lair. Bats, crows, snakes, spiders. Anything humans are normally frightened of, and for good reason."

Maybe that was why the crow had wanted a strand of my hair to line her nest. I'd assumed she was friendly because of Nevarre's raven, but maybe she'd responded to my father's power instead. "Anyone speak rat?"

"Fuck, no. I ate them. I didn't talk to them. Well, I talked, but they never replied back." Mehen grimaced, shaking his head. "I got a little crazy toward the end. I would have talked to anything or anyone just to not hear the intolerable silence any longer."

My grouchy dragon needed lots of affection and companion-ship after his long imprisonment. His pain wouldn't be wiped away in a matter of days or weeks, no matter how much I loved him.

His eyes flared and he swallowed hard. He'd heard my thoughts, though I hadn't meant to broadcast so loudly to him, or any of the Blood, not deliberately. Another side effect of our deep bonds, and one that I fully embraced, even if it accidentally exposed my deepest, most secret thoughts. Mehen didn't say another word, but he stepped closer and put his palm on the small of my back.

I turned my attention back to the rat. "Do you understand me?"

It squeaked and nodded, whiskers working with excitement. She. I was sure of it. Even with the hallway light on, I could feel the flows of dark power around me. Those streamers carried a sense of what they flowed past, everything from a mummy locked in this cell to a rat eager to serve a queen who under-stood and would value her services.

"Can you watch this cell and alert me if anyone tries to enter or leave the room?"

She nodded and squeaked again, a complicated response in rat speak that I couldn't follow. I listened to the dark power, trying to gain a sense of what she said, but all it told me was her intent. She wanted to serve me. Her excitement flavored the power like a punch of spice despite her diminutive size. She looked at me, her nose twitching, and I felt a sense of waiting from her. Hope. Expectation.

Of course. She wanted some kind of payment, or at least an exchange. The raven had wanted a strand of my hair. I wasn't sure what offering the rat would want, but I figured my blood was the universal currency. She would gain power from my blood, and it would give her a bond to me. Though I couldn't see myself tasting her blood so I could understand what she was saying.

I held my index finger out to her. She shivered, her whiskers working rapidly. Her eyes closed, and I was afraid I'd made a mistake. Perhaps I'd insulted her with an offer of blood. Rats weren't vampiric in nature.

But then she grasped my finger in her little paws and rubbed her face against the tip of my finger. Relieved I hadn't insulted her, I stroked the top of her head with my finger.

She turned her head slightly and bit the tip of my finger. She had sharp little teeth that had no problems puncturing my skin. She lapped delicately at the wound and then released me. I stroked my fingers down her back, enjoying the softness of her fur. "Thank you for helping me."

She squeaked and scurried back up to the vent, taking up position in the darkness there.

As we walked back down the hallway toward the elevator, Mehen snagged my hand and scowled at my injured finger. It was only a little bite and I didn't think we could carry infections, at least not like humans.

He finally grunted. "I almost regret eating so many of her kind." Then he swiped his tongue over the wound and took the tip of my finger into his mouth so he could suck. Thoroughly.

I didn't try to hold back the low moan of approval that made his eyes glint like faceted emeralds.

"I had to make sure the wound was clean."

"Yeah, sure," Rik growled without any real heat. "I think you were just thirsting for some rat spit."

For once, Mehen actually laughed. "I'd drink rat piss if my queen's blood was mixed into it."

I shuddered at the thought, but the rest of my Blood said, "Agreed."

3

SHARA

When the elevator doors opened, Gina stood waiting for me with a no-nonsense look that told me we wouldn't be leaving Skye Tower for the evening anytime soon.

"We have a situation."

Sighing, I nodded but didn't ask Rik to put me down. If I had to do some queen-level shit, I was going to conserve my energy as much as possible.

"Rosalind Valois has reached out to me and indicated that she will take over House Skye since she was Keisha's sib."

"Like hell she will."

"She could take the issue to the Triune, though I think that was a bluff on her part. Her sib relationship with Keisha was weakly defined, to my understanding, at least. They both put forward the claim that the other queen was subordinate, but naturally, that's impossible in a true sib relationship."

My lips quirked as a thought came to me. "Tell her if she'd like to push the sib relationship, she's welcome to come to House Isador and accept me as her queen. I'd be thrilled to make her my sib in Keisha's place, since she's no longer with us."

Gina laughed. "Now that will be a pleasure to tell her. We do want to be sure and put forward a strong, united front. That means you need a fairly strong sib established here as quickly as possible to hold the territory for you."

"Do you have a few candidates?"

She nodded. "I've interviewed all the queen sibs that remained after Keisha's demise. Most are fairly weak as far as I can tell, though you'll be a much better judge of their strength. There are a few that have the power and stature that I'd like you to meet and evaluate yourself."

"Will I be able to tell how strong they are? Even before I take their blood?"

Gina nodded. "It takes a little experience, but for me, it's like a weight in the air. A weak queen is like a grain of sand. Annoying, and it might sting a little if the wind blows hard enough, but ultimately, not dangerous. Others are more like pebbles or slightly larger stones. Truly strong queens can make it difficult to breathe if they wish. It's like they clog the air with their power, making it unbreathable for mortals."

"I don't do that, do I?"

She smiled and patted my arm. "Not deliberately."

Guillaume grunted beneath his breath. "You're strong

enough to make the air weigh like a solid wall of concrete and granite if you wished."

Another facet of my power of which I'd been completely oblivious. "When I'm making it hard for you to breathe, I want you to tell me. That way I can be more conscious of what I'm doing and broadcasting. I don't want other queens to know how strong I am, unless it's deliberate."

Gina inclined her head. "Of course, my queen. That's a smart strategy."

"Should I select a sib before we leave for the night?"

She nodded apologetically. "That would be best, if you can manage it. That way she can be hard at work for you while you rest. Plus, taking a formal sib will give you even more power to draw from, so you can spare your own reserves more."

I grimaced, but nodded. "I was thinking fondly of bed and Blood but I suppose I can wait a bit longer. I wish I had some clean clothes that weren't quite so ostentatious. This dress served its purpose, but the lace is scratchy as hell."

"Winston is waiting in a private room with some clothes you can choose from."

"Thank the goddess. Bless you both."

Stationed in a small room off the formal presentation hall, Winston had brought me several less-formal dresses, a couple of pant suits, and yes, even jeans to choose from. Of course, I chose the latter along with a soft, fluffy sweater. The hell with formalities. If I had to sit through sib interviews, then by goddess, I'd be comfortable. But maybe I wouldn't have to spend much time on this...

I tugged on Llewellyn's bond and he immediately stepped inside with me, Rik, and Nevarre. "My queen."

The scent of his blood made my fangs throb and descend. I hadn't intended to ask him to feed me, but now that I smelled his blood, that was all I could think about. He held out his bleeding wrist, a tidy cut, rather than punctures or tears, telling me it was likely Guillaume's handiwork.

"Are you sure?"

Llewellyn's eyes flared and the sparks tumbling through his dark eyes quickened like a meteor shower. "Forgive me, my queen, if you doubted my determination to serve you in any way you wish. I would have gladly fed you earlier once I was freed, but you had other more pressing needs to address."

"It's just... Um..."

He looked to Rik, his brow furrowed. "Is there a problem, alpha?"

Rik's lips quirked. "Our queen revels in her Blood in *all* ways."

Llewellyn nodded, his brow still creased. "If I understand, that's far from a problem. I'm eager to serve again. The promise of an Isador queen's return was the only thing that kept me from embracing the darkness and turning thrall so I could slaughter at will."

"You were her mother's Blood. Even more, you were her alpha."

"Ah." Llewellyn met my gaze. "What would you like to know about her, my queen?"

A thousand questions fluttered in my mind. I wanted to know everything about my mother. How long had she tried to have me? When had she first decided to set her plan in motion? When had she gone to my father? But the most important question at the moment... "If you were hers... I don't know how I'd feel if you were mine, too."

His eyes widened again, and he looked back to Rik for help. "But I'm already yours, my queen. I've had your blood."

"She means in bed."

"You don't want to fuck me because I fucked your mother?"

Now it was my turn to blink as he slowly came toward me, his eyes spinning like endless falling stars.

"What if I told you I fucked your aunt too? But I've never fucked anyone else, because I can only fuck Isador queens. It's encoded in the blood that pumps in my veins. I've never lain with any woman who wasn't an Isador queen, and I won't. Ever. I can't."

He stopped in front of me, too close to be polite, but not touching me.

"Keisha and her Blood wanted to use me. They tried everything they could think of to arouse me, but gryphons mate for life, and I'm mated to House Isador. Keisha had to settle for having her males fuck me a few times, but they quickly tired of such sport when they couldn't arouse even my fear, let alone my desire."

He lifted his bleeding wrist, but only to tuck a strand of my hair back from my cheek. "Male gryphons have always been rare. We're bred to serve any of the females in the family. I understand if that offends you, my queen. I will still gladly serve in any way you wish, though I will regret never touching an Isador queen again."

My brain was still floundering at the thought of him fucking Mom—the woman who'd raised me—as well as the woman who'd birthed me, but I couldn't deny the appeal of his blood. My hunger raged, all too eager to taste him. Even if he'd gone to my mother and aunt too. I cupped his wrist and drew the wound to my mouth. He watched me with those falling star eyes as I tasted his blood.

The rush of feathers and wings swept through me. He smelled more like Daire than Nevarre. Cat. Or, rather, lion, in this case. He bent down, folding himself around me despite his towering height. He didn't have Rik's bulk, but topped him by several inches. I'd never met anyone so tall. His blood tasted like fiery sparks, his rage a blazing fire that would never be banked. He would have gleefully torn apart every single Skye sib, tossing bloody chunks out the high-rise windows until the streets of New York City were littered with the dead.

My fangs ached, and I had to concentrate on not sinking them deeply into his wrist. There was no need to bite him, other than my hunger's desire to claim him as mine. Make him remember the feel of Isador fangs.

:*She could make me come just thinking about her fangs,*: he whispered in my mind. :*I can only hope and pray that the Great One saw fit to pass that gift on to you as well, my queen.*:

In answer, I sank my fangs into him. He shuddered against me, and in our new bond, his gryphon shrieked. Pleasure surged through him, sweeping me along like a tiny stick in a ravaging flood. He hadn't come in well over twenty years. Resisting that soaring release was impossible. I clung to him as we both shuddered, and I drank from him through every spasm.

Panting, he clutched me against his chest and kept his wrist pressed to my mouth much longer than I probably should have fed. He'd been tortured and denied for decades. He'd probably need me to feed him more often over the next few weeks, especially if I kept him drained like this.

But I couldn't help but feel like each swallow of his blood brought me closer to my mother. I could almost taste her in his blood. Beneath the gryphon wings and talons and his raging fury, I tasted…

Moonlight. The quiet dapple of silver on sands. Perfect diamonds and crystals lying beneath a full moon.

:I will always carry your mother in my heart and soul.:

Tears burned my eyes. :Did her geas not affect you? You seem to remember more than anyone else.:

:I cannot utter her name, but I carry too much of her blood to be denied my memories of her.:

Reluctantly, I licked my fang marks and the thin cut on his wrist, making sure to clean up every drop. I looked up into his face and gasped. His once dark eyes were completely red-gold. The falling stars had taken over completely.

"This gryphon swears undying loyalty to you, my queen."

"Shara," I said softly, holding his gaze. I didn't want to just be the next Isador queen he served. I wanted him to know me. Want me. Need me. Only me.

"What did you wish to ask me?" He said aloud, his voice a soft rumble. "Shara?"

"I need to establish a sib to hold New York City for me. What do you know about the queen sibs Keisha claimed? Is there anyone I should avoid, or anyone you know is strong enough to hold my territory in my stead?"

"There are a few strong enough to make decent sibs for Isador, but only one or two that I would guess worthy to serve you. Most of them were all too eager to fall in with Skye and embraced everything that Keisha commanded them to do."

"Exactly. I don't want to claim someone like that for us."

"Then avoid Virginia and Alessandra. They both have strength, but I can attest to their willingness to abuse or take advantage of people they deem lesser than themselves. They both voluntarily watched as Keisha tortured Conall, her last alpha. Carys isn't as strong as either of them, but she has a quiet strength that I think will appeal to you. She never watched the torture, unless Keisha ordered all her House to attend."

"Thank you. That's exactly the kind of information that I hoped you'd be able to share."

His tone sharpened, vibrating with bloodthirsty intent. "Have you decided what to do with Vega and the rest of the Furies?"

"Did they participate in the torture?"

"Mine, or the alphas?"

"Either."

"Usually the alphas, but they enjoyed making men suffer in general, so I wasn't immune from their efforts. Though I believe my vengeance has already been delivered in part, thanks to your poisonous Blood. I heard that five of them perished in the elevator, and Ashlee was one of the worst offenders."

This was the part I'd been dreading. My brain wanted to run

away and concentrate on something else. I had so many crucial things to do, like choosing a sib and making sure the tower was secure. All valid and necessary tasks.

But first, I had to face the most unpleasant task of deciding whether several people should live or die. I didn't want to be responsible for their punishment, but they were my responsibility now.

"You don't have to make the decision tonight," Gina said, touching my arm lightly. "Rest first. They'll hold until tomorrow."

"Will they, though? Or will they turn thrall and add human deaths to their list of sins?"

"If they turn, we'll kill them immediately." Llewellyn's head cocked slightly, very bird-like, as if he'd spotted his fleeing prey miles away with his razor-sharp vision. "Then you don't have to decide."

I blew out a sigh. "That's the coward's way out."

His eyes widened and he bent over my hand, pressing my knuckles to his forehead. Surprised, I didn't know what to say.

"Forgive me, my queen." Moisture dripped onto the back of my hand. "You suddenly sounded very much like your mother."

Good. That confirmed that I needed to make a decision, rather than wait and see what would happen. "Gina, what Triune laws apply in this situation?"

"As the ruling queen, it's within your rights to exterminate every sib and Blood in this House, for any offense of which you deem them guilty. You could blot Skye from the earth completely and no one would bat an eye, except possibly

Rosalind, for fear that you might come after her next because of her former ties to Keisha."

"Everyone?" I asked, my voice shaking. I'd been worried about dealing with Keisha's Furies, but it hadn't occurred to me that everyone might be scared to death. Literally.

When I'd gone to make Mayte my sib, her people had been nervous and even angry at first, because they feared I'd take everything away from them. Even if Keisha had been victorious and claimed Zaniyah as her siblings, she wouldn't have killed them all. She'd have taken Xochitl from Mayte. She might have killed Mayte's Blood in the skirmish. She might have forced Mayte to leave her nest and come here to Skye Tower. But I didn't think she would have killed everyone left behind.

:*Desideria did so, and quite often.*: Guillaume's bond rang like drawn steel. :*Once the queen falls, the nest is yours to do with as you please.*:

"No wonder so many people fled," I whispered aloud, shaking my head. "I thought they were merely scared of what I'd ask of them before letting them join House Isador."

"Zaniyah was different," Gina said. "You didn't go in with the intent of killing Mayte, but of taking her as your sib. You valued her House for their numbers and the strength they provided you. For all House Skye knows, you might want retribution for almost losing Alrik. Or for Skye's audacity in claiming your Blood as hers and dragging you here to address her formal claim. Or for her Blood insulting you in the elevator and feeding on your Blood. Or perhaps your mother slighted in some way by Keisha. The rumors are probably running through the floors like wildfire. That's why picking a sib tonight and declaring your intent to build upon this House, rather than destroy it, will help settle the peace quicker."

I took a deep breath and looked inward a moment, scanning through my body. I was weary, definitely, both of politics and danger. But I wasn't in danger of tapping my reserves too deeply yet, not after three of my Blood had fed me.

I refused to think about how much of Keisha's blood I'd taken, along with her life.

A couple of hours, tops, and I should be able to retire to my mother's house and leave Skye Tower to fortify itself.

"Isador Tower," Rik rumbled beside me.

I nodded, quirking my lips. "Add that to our list of a million things to do. We need to pull down any reference to Skye Tower on my building."

Gina smiled. "Already on the list, my queen, though the list is about *two* million long already. Which leads me to the other thing I'd like to discuss with you, if you have the time."

Llewellyn drew my gaze to him with his lips on the back of my hand again. This time, he swirled his tongue over my knuckles and flashed those smoldering falling star eyes up at me. "By your leave, my queen, I'll go fetch Carys so you may meet her."

I turned my fingers in his, so I could trail my fingertips over his cheek as he straightened to his impressive height. "Thank you, my Blood. I'd like a private discussion with her first, and then we'll arrange the formal sib ceremony. Though I don't want to use Keisha's throne room. Is there another place in the building that's big enough for everyone to hear me address them?"

"The ballroom. I'll have them make it ready for you."

I nodded, and he backed away, inclined his head once more, and then whirled smartly on his heel to exit the room.

"Should I leave?" Nevarre asked, already hovering at the door.

"No. Stay. What else did you wish to discuss, Gina?"

"I think Madeline would be an excellent addition to your team as second consiliarius."

A surge of emotion tore through me at the thought of losing, or replacing, Gina in any way. I depended on her. She'd been the one to help me after my first two Blood found me. She was my connection to everything that I'd unknowingly lost my entire life.

Then I realized she'd said *second* consiliarius. She wasn't leaving me.

"Of course, I'm not leaving you," she retorted smartly, though her eyes were teary and she lightly touched my arm again. My reaction must have been strong enough that she had felt my emotions in her bond. "We can certainly look elsewhere for assistance, but we will need to hire quite a few staff members to organize the Skye legacy and meld it with yours. It's not as immense, but the holdings are in crucial cities, like this tower, and are fixtures of society in a way that Isador holdings are not. It would be easier to bring Madeline, and her full staff, into yours, and then she and I can work together as you see fit."

"That makes a lot of sense," I replied slowly. "I'm just not sure if I can trust her. Mayte trusted Bianca and look what happened."

The former Zaniyah consiliarius had betrayed her House to Ra, and their heir, Xochitl, a precious little girl, had nearly paid the price of that treachery.

"And you with her." Rik pulled me back against him. "I will never trust anyone with your safety who isn't Blood."

Gina's face blanked into a smooth, perfect mask. Try as she may, she would never be my Blood.

I took her hand and stepped closer to her so I could hug her with my other arm. Naturally Rik moved with me, though he didn't touch her. Only me. "I trust you implicitly, Gina. Blood or not. I trust Winston implicitly. You're my family."

Nevarre didn't say anything, but I felt him still hovering at the door. Alone.

:Come to me, my raven.:

In a heartbeat, he was at my side, carefully sliding his arm around my waist without touching the other woman.

"You're all my family."

Rik pressed his lips to my hair, lightly brushing his mouth back and forth. "You're our everything, my queen. You're *my* everything. And while I know you love Gina and Winston as family, I say as your alpha, that I will never trust anyone not Blood with your safety. That doesn't mean that I don't trust them. Not at all. I believe they're as loyal as mostly-humans with a bit of Aima blood can be. But they aren't Blood and never will be. They can be compromised, just as Bianca was compromised."

"Are you saying a Blood cannot be compromised?"

"Never," he replied. "With even a shallow Blood bond, you would know their heart and minds. You could use your power to drag out any secrets, no matter how deeply they try to bury them. If any other queen or god planted a spell, geas, or other trap inside them, you would sense it. Your blood alone would attack it. The more blood you share, the deeper the bond, and you're a queen who gladly feeds us. No one would be able to hide from you."

His words triggered something inside me. Like a tiny seed that was barely a speck, the idea sprouted ever so slightly. My blood was the key to my power.

And the key to who I could trust.

Without effort, Gina's mind was accessible to me, like a box that had suddenly popped open. My blood unlocked her like a key, no matter how mighty the chains she might have tried to use to keep me out. She hadn't tried, not at all, but everyone had secrets. She wasn't the exception, though I felt her intentions. She hadn't kept the secret out of a malicious desire to harm me at any time. Rather, out of shame, she'd hidden this item from her past so deeply inside herself that even she had almost forgotten it.

Almost. But not quite.

There was a reason she only ever talked about Grandma Paula, and never her mother. Janae Talbott had betrayed House Isador. She'd paid for that crime with her life under my mother's rule as queen. Her execution had been done quietly out of respect to the long line of Talbotts who'd served my family without even a hint of betrayal or impropriety. No one outside Esetta's immediate circle of Blood and the Talbotts even knew.

Paula had continued to serve as consiliarius and brought

Gina into the family business sooner than planned to compensate for Janae's absence.

I wondered what Janae had done to earn her death. The answer was there in Gina's head, a glimmer of something buried, but slightly visible. With a bit of effort, I could draw that information out.

But out of respect for all she'd done for me, I left that secret buried. I didn't need to know.

My touch in her mind had been so light that she didn't even know I'd seen that glimpse of the dark secret that haunted her past. It didn't make me think any less of her. I still trusted her without question. In her whole life, that was the only thing she had closed off from me, and it'd only taken a few swallows of my blood to open her mind so much that I'd gleaned that information without even trying.

"Would Madeline agree to take my blood as you did?"

Gina's eyes widened. "I'll ask her, of course, if that's your wish. I don't know why she wouldn't. It's a great honor."

"I wouldn't do it to honor her, though it's alright with me if that's what she assumes. I'd do it so she couldn't ever betray me."

"I'll ask her." Gina pulled away from me and smiled, but I was sure a hint of pink darkened her cheeks and she couldn't quite meet my gaze. "I also prepared briefs on each of the three queens Llewellyn mentioned. They're in the folder." She nodded her head at the desk near the window. "I wasn't able to find out much on such short notice, but at least you'll have access to their lineage. I agree with him that they're your best options from the queens I interviewed."

"Thank you, Gina. Seriously, I don't know what I would do without you."

She laughed, more like herself, and breezed to the door. "You'd manage. You'd have a thousand candidates waiting outside your door, begging for the chance to serve Isador."

"No one will ever replace you." I kept my voice light and teasing, though each word echoed with certainty.

Turning at the door, she gave me a beautiful smile that lit up her entire face. "It's been my greatest honor to serve you, Your Majesty, and with the Great One's blessing, I hope to serve a very long time."

4

I sat in my favorite place—between Rik's thighs with his arms around me—waiting to meet this new queen. The room I'd changed in was quiet and large enough for all my Blood, so I decided to meet her here. Nevarre had fetched the large chair I'd used earlier, and its mate sat across from me, a safe distance away, but close enough for easy conversation. Once I met Carys, I could hopefully make a quick presentation to formalize our agreement and go home.

I wasn't scared or nervous, not like when I had to meet Mayte for the first time. I'd faced Marne Ceresa, one of the most powerful Triune queens, in the mirror. I'd survived Keisha's attack when we'd first arrived. I'd met powerful, ancient goddesses face to face. I didn't think I'd ever be nervous meeting an Aima queen again.

Gina's file on each of the three queen candidates was sparse, but combined with Llewellyn's assessment, I only cared to meet Carys Tylluan. She was descended from Blodeuwedd, the Welsh goddess of spring. House Tylluan's claim to fame was a legendary sunken kingdom where their nest had once been. It had disappeared several hundred years ago, and they'd joined House Llys for another couple of hundred years, only to eventually be absorbed by House Skye.

At some point, Keisha Skye visited their nest and had chosen Carys to come live permanently in New York City. Gina didn't note a reason, but I guessed it was because of Carys's strength. Keisha had been concentrating her power base as much as possible.

:She's here with Llewellyn,: Guillaume said in our bond. He stood guard at the door with Itztli, Tlacel, and Nevarre. Rik had asked Xin to remain invisible and close to me, just in case we had any issues with this unknown queen. Mehen stood on my other side with his fierce glare ready. *:Daire and Ezra have joined them. She has no Blood of her own present.:*

:Thank you, G. Send them in.:

The door opened. Daire and Ezra came in first, followed by Carys and Llewellyn. Guillaume and Nevarre followed them, while the twins held the door. My warcat immediately came in close for a kiss and he didn't hesitate to drop down on the floor beside me. I combed my fingers through his hair. My eyelashes fluttered a moment, soaking in the deep rumble of his purr.

"Humph." Ezra stomped closer and glared at Daire. "I suck it up and play bullshit politics all day, but he gets the cuddles and kisses."

Daire snorted. "If you went down on your knees and asked for a kiss, I'm sure you'd receive one too."

Grumbling beneath his breath, Ezra dropped down on my other side and shoved his face close to mine. It made me laugh, because for all his complaining and growling, he didn't even touch me without permission. I reached out and grabbed a handful of his beard in one hand and his shaggy hair in the other and pulled him in for a kiss.

He thrust his tongue into my mouth and slanted his head so he could stroke his tongue over the roof of my mouth. For all his gruffness, he was a consummate kisser. His tongue found the small holes where my fangs hid. Shivering, I started to pull back, afraid I'd puncture his tongue accidentally, but he moved closer, keeping his tongue pressed to that sensitive hole.

:Your fangs won't come down as long as I'm pressing on them,: he said in my mind. *:I'm surprised Rik hasn't done this for you yet.:*

His tongue worked the roof of my mouth as thoroughly as he would lick my pussy. Surely those little holes, just big enough for my fangs, couldn't be as sensitive as my clit, but with his tongue gliding and probing firmly, I was about to come.

Panting, I jerked my head back. My fangs shot down so hard and fast that I groaned. They ached, longer and more sensitive than ever. I pulled his head to the side and buried them in his throat.

He bellowed with release and leaned harder into me, his rough hands cradling my head like I'd break into a thousand pieces. His scent stirred my hunger even more. Not just for his blood, but for his big burly body. He was such a grizzly bear on the outside, and the sweetest, gooey marshmallow on the inside. And that fucking hook...

Groaning roughly, he stroked my cheek with his thumb. "Anytime, sweetheart."

Reluctantly, I pulled my fangs out of him, delighting in the way he shuddered and groaned again. "Later. I have business to complete first."

He kissed the tip of my nose and then shifted down to his butt to sit against my knees, turning to face the newcomer. *:I'll hold you to that promise.:*

Once upon a time, I might have been embarrassed by the fact that I'd just made one of my Blood come in public, and I'd been damned close to release myself. Even now, it felt like I had two throbbing clits in my mouth, aching for more of his tongue. If I had Daire busy between my thighs, and Ezra torturing my fangs...

"Fuuuuuck," Ezra muttered and reached down to adjust himself, already hard again.

I pushed that image aside and focused on Carys Tylluan.

She looked nothing like what I'd imagined after reading Gina's notes. Granted, I had limited exposure to other queens, but everyone I'd met so far had projected elegance and regal beauty. They'd looked young, perhaps in their thirties at most, even though they were several hundred years old.

Yet here Carys stood before me, dressed in a dowdy men's tweed jacket, baggy trousers, and muddy boots. A giant equally-scruffy gray owl sat on her shoulder. She was shorter than me and quite stocky. Her hair was cut in a short, no-nonsense pixie. She looked at least forty years old, with fine lines around her eyes and mouth that spoke of experience and laughter and yes, frowns.

This woman didn't take shit from anybody.

So how had she found herself sworn as sibling to House Skye?

Intrigued, I held out my hand to her. "Thank you for meeting with me, Carys."

Her eyes narrowed, but she took my hand and bowed like Guillaume or Llewellyn to kiss my hand, though she didn't lick my knuckles. The owl flapped its wings and dug in heavy claws to stay in position. Now that Carys was close, I could see deep rips in her jacket from the owl's talons. And yeah, some white streaks down her shoulder and back that had to be bird crap. "Your Majesty. How can I be of assistance to House Isador?"

Gina stepped forward. "Her Majesty is offering to make you a sibling to House Isador."

Carys glanced at the two Blood on the floor beside me and my alpha at my back. "You're strong, I'll give you that. You call good Blood. Interesting Blood. But you're inexperienced and too fucking young to play with the Triune."

My Blood tensed against my knees and Rik felt like solid granite against my back, though none of them said a word. I wasn't going to argue with her. I was inexperienced. I certainly wanted nothing to do with the Triune. "I've had a taste of Triune politics and I want no part of it."

She scoffed. "Keisha Skye was not Triune."

"I'm not speaking of her."

When I didn't elaborate, Carys arched a brow at me. "Indeed. Then I'm interested in that tale."

Even Daire bristled. *:She isn't showing you respect at all.:*

I stroked my fingers through his hair, unconcerned. *:I don't care about politics. I like her.:*

Mehen grunted sourly. *:Great. The last thing we need is a grumpy sib.:*

Ezra snorted softly. *:Irony's a bitch, ain't it, dragon?:*

"I'm assuming you know about Marne Ceresa's favorite way of communicating with other queens."

"She sent you a bloody mirror? I'll be damned." Whistling softly beneath her breath, Carys shook her head. "Maybe you can play with the big dogs after all, girl. There's an empty seat on the Triune. That's why Keisha came after me."

I tried not to bristle at *girl*, though my welcoming attitude definitely cooled. "What does the Triune seat have to do with House Tylluan?"

"Absolutely nothing. She didn't come after my house. She came after *me*." Her tone sharpened. Evidently, she liked repeating herself about as much as I enjoyed being called girl. "I have a unique gift that makes me very valuable for a powerful queen with an eye on the Triune. Hell, any strategy, but especially the greatest game of all. We tried to keep it quiet, but some moron blabbed and here came Keisha Skye, demanding we solidify an ancient sibling agreement that no one had cared about for centuries."

Intrigued, I tried to think what unique power she might possess. She didn't feel that strong to me, though I didn't have much experience on which to base such a judgement. Gina said a queen's strength was like a weight in the air, but I sensed nothing.

Carys laughed, shaking her head. "You can't feel me, right? I don't feel like I have any power at all, and compared to you, I don't. But I do have one specific power that can make me extremely valuable to the right person."

If she wasn't strong with power, then she might not be the best sib to hold New York City. I touched Gina's bond. *:I think we need another candidate to hold the city.:*

Gina nodded slightly in agreement and headed for the door.

I studied Carys a moment, weighing my alternatives. I decided to lay my cards on the table. "I'd intended to ask you to hold New York City in my stead."

She recoiled like I'd slapped her in the face and called her a filthy name. "Goddess preserve me, no. Please. I'd rather be burned at the stake or drawn and quartered than ever run a nest this size. I know my limitations. I'd be horrible at running a nest. Absolutely horrible. Any nest, but especially in a city this large."

The owl on her shoulder chirped and rustled its feathers, puffing itself up like it was angry. Or excited. I couldn't tell which.

Absently, Carys reached up and stroked the owl's head. It nestled against her neck and started making a whirring sound somewhere between a purr and a dove's coo. "There, there, Winnie. She doesn't know. She didn't mean it."

I leaned back against Rik and waited for her to settle herself and the owl, so she could explain what the hell was going on. Rik stroked me, one hand on my arm, the other sliding beneath my arm and up my sweater so he could palm my stomach, spreading his fingers to cover as much of my skin as possible.

Hunger stirred again, even though I'd just had a taste of Ezra. A taste wasn't enough, especially after all the shit I'd already done today. I just wanted to go home. Home home, my manor. My nest. I ached for it almost as badly as I ached for Rik to bury himself deep inside me, both fangs and dick.

An idea sprouted. :*Remember how we rode your motorcycles to Kansas City that first time? Do you think we could ride back to Eureka Springs?*:

:*If you'd like:* Rik nuzzled my throat. :*Though I'd rather have you safely in a car.*:

Daire laughed in our bonds. :*Better yet, a tank.*:

:*No tanks. I want to feel the wind in my face. Surely with all of us together, we'll be strong enough to make such a short trip.*:

Carys focused on my face, though she was still pale, as if she'd seen a ghost.

Rik gripped my throat in his teeth a moment, making me moan softly, even though he didn't puncture my skin. :*What about Ra?*:

My face hardened. :*I have to face him eventually.*:

"Oh. Oh, my." Carys stepped closer, drawing a rumbling growl from Ezra and Daire. She jerked to a halt, but then dropped to her knees in front of me. "I'll swear to House Isador."

I leaned forward, searching her eyes, watching for anything suspicious. "Why now?"

"Whatever you're planning, I need to be a part of it. You need me."

"How do you know?"

She lifted her hand up to the owl and stroked its head again. "Winnifred tells me things."

"Your power is speaking to your owl?"

Carys snorted and the owl chirped again with a decidedly disgusted tone. "Not at all. She can speak to whomever she chooses. However, she will only speak to people she trusts. Winnie is Blodeuwedd's avatar and my very good friend."

I looked at the owl and inclined by head. "I'm very pleased to meet you, Winnifred."

The owl picked up its tail and pooped another stringy white glob on Carys's shoulder.

Carys didn't seem to mind and scratched the bird's chest. "Oh, she likes you."

Daire snickered. *:I didn't know that bird crap indicated friendship. Why haven't you crapped on anyone, Nevarre?:*

:I'm saving that signal of friendship for our challenge on the green,: Nevarre replied.

Gina stepped inside, drawing my attention. "Your Majesty, the other candidates are ready for you. How would you like to proceed?"

Carys scrambled to her feet, the owl flapping her wings and digging in so hard that I winced, though the other queen didn't seem to mind. "Excellent. Let me show you how my power works, Your Majesty, before we make things official."

"How many, Gina?"

"There are five queens that seem strong enough to make decent sibs, though there are twelve all together still remaining."

I looked at Carys again, trying to sense her power and

strength, but I still had no idea what she had to offer. "I only want to do this once, so let's get all the queens in one place."

"Even Virginia and Alessandra?" Llewellyn asked, his voice carefully even and without censure.

"Yes." My mouth twisted and my stomach tightened with dread. "And the former Furies. I'll get all the unpleasantness dealt with at once."

As I stood, Guillaume came closer and went down on one knee before me. "Your Majesty, your sword waits only for your orders."

Llewelyn and Mehen both joined him on either side. I wasn't surprised by them. But then Daire and Ezra both pushed away from my knees and joined them. And Nevarre.

Xin still waited behind me, guarding my alpha's back, who guarded me. :*I eagerly await for your orders, my queen.*:

"And I," Itztli called from the door, unwilling to leave his post.

Tlacel added, "My brother and I are ready, my queen."

Rik took my hand and lifted my fingers to his lips, drawing my gaze. :*If you wish me to give the specific orders, I will do so gladly as your alpha. I will see your will done in all things, especially the unpleasant ones.*:

I cupped his cheek, soaking in each of my Blood's calm, unquestioning loyalty. They would do anything for me. Even something as distasteful as execution.

"It's not distasteful," Guillaume said aloud.

I turned, searching his face. "You told me Desideria used you to exterminate entire nests before. I won't be that kind of queen."

"You could never be that kind of queen," he retorted, shaking his head emphatically. "A queen must protect the nest and her House. Sometimes that involves punishment. Sometimes that involves death. As your Blood, it's our honor and privilege to assist you in any way possible. Use your weapons, my queen, because we revel in your every wish and command. There's a reason that your goddess gave you the last Templar knight. There's a reason She gave you the king of the depths. A silent assassin. A deadly shadow. We're killers. We're here to protect you, and we're here to enact your law. My sword is yours to command."

"I thirst for retribution," Llewelyn said.

"I didn't kill nearly enough of these assholes yet," Mehen growled, his voice deepening with a hint of Leviathan's roar. "They would have seen you hurt. They would have seen Rik tortured to death for that demon child's amusement. Let me roast them in hellfire and toss their charred bones into the streets of this fucking city as your warning that there's a new queen in town."

My eyes burned, and I swallowed a giant lump in my throat. "My Blood. How I love you all."

They pressed closer, each of them touching me. My twins stayed at their post, but in our bond, I felt Itztli's black dog press a cold nose to my palm, and Tlacel's feathered tail curled around my back like a shawl. Closing my eyes, I soaked them in a moment. Drawing on their courage and strength.

When I opened my eyes, I gave them a fierce, hard smile. "Let's go finish this, so we can go home."

5

SHARA

With my arm tucked around Rik's bulging biceps, I paused outside an ornate door. My stomach ached with cramps. I was barefoot, with raw spots on my heels and toes from heels that I wasn't accustomed to wearing and couldn't even remember where I'd left them. At least my clothes were clean. Mostly.

I'd gotten a little of Ezra's blood on my sweater. I might be the queen of House Isador, but I was still learning how to drink blood without dribbling it down my chin.

:I love it when you wear my blood,: Ezra growled in our bond. *:Wear me every day.:*

The rest of my Bloods' bonds vibrated with their instant agreement.

I didn't want to be announced. This was my fucking building

now. I didn't need to shout our house names. Until these former Skye sibs formalized a bond with me, I'd still allow them to leave. Gladly. I didn't want anyone to stay out of fear.

I gave a nod to Llewellyn and he pushed the doors open without a word. My Blood entered the room in pairs, taking up positions as they saw fit to protect me. As Rik and I stepped through the door, Llewellyn fell into step on my opposite side. He didn't reach for my arm, so I looped my arm through his and tugged him closer. I wanted them to know exactly why he was with me. I glanced up—way up—and smiled at him. I still couldn't get over how tall he was.

Which lead to some interesting musings as we walked toward the waiting large easy chair my Blood had moved here for me and Rik. If Llewellyn's dick was as big as he was tall...

He laughed softly in our new bond. :*I don't think you'll be disappointed in that regard, my queen.*:

A small group of queens and their Blood waited on my right as we walked in. I didn't look at them as we passed, but I tried to use my other senses to gauge the power in the room. I still didn't really feel anything, especially nothing like rocks in the air, as Gina had described another queen's power. I did feel a bit of soundless vibration humming through the air. Rik sat down and widened his thighs, drawing me into the cradle of his body, and I lost the sense of anything except the feel of his warmth against my back.

I didn't say anything, but took my time looking over the people gathered before me. Vega and Keisha's other former Blood stood on the other side of the room. They stared at the floor, sweat shimmering on their skin. Even ten feet away, I could smell their fear and anxiety. Good. After everything they'd done, they should be afraid of what I would do.

As Carys walked in, flanked by my twins, a few of the watching queens whispered among themselves. When she came to stand on my left hand side, with Gina on my right, the whispers abruptly silenced.

"Let's get the worst over as quickly as possible," I finally said. "Vega, bring your group to stand before me."

The former alpha flinched but gave a sharp jerk of her head to her comrades. The closer she came to me, the more she slunk. Shoulders and head down, she dropped to her knees a few paces away. The rest of Keisha's Blood followed suit, including the one Blood who'd planned to feed on Daire in the elevator. Though I couldn't remember her name. Was she a friend of his?

:Lissa,: My normally cuddly, purring warcat let out a vicious snarl in our bond. *:Show her no mercy, my queen, especially not on my account. I didn't want her fangs. She would have bitten me anyway and stolen what is only yours.:*

"Do any queens present wish to claim some of these former Blood as their own?"

The other queens shifted nervously, but no one immediately answered. I didn't have to have a blood bond with any of them to know what they were thinking. If they claimed one of Keisha's Blood as their own, would they share in that Blood's fate? I couldn't make any promises in that regard, but it would definitely tell me which queens were willing to overlook past sins. I was willing to forgive much, but not torture.

One of the queens stepped forward, taking on the role of

spokesperson. "Your Majesty, may we ask a few questions first?"

I inclined my head. "Who are you?"

"Alessandra Sito."

She was one of the queens that Llewellyn had warned me about. She said her name proudly, as if her house was important. I had no idea of the significance of her name. I started to reach for Guillaume's bond, hoping my Templar knight would know, but it was Daire's bond that sparked first.

:*She's related to Marne Ceresa and is descended from Demeter, the Greek equivalent of Ceres.*:

:*He speaks correctly,*: Guillaume added. :*Well done, young Blood.*:

Daire blushed and purred contentedly. :*The relationships between the ancient houses has always interested me.*:

She did resemble the perfect golden goddess image that Marne Ceresa displayed so well. From her designer stilettos to the diamonds around her throat and her perfectly coiffed blonde hair, Alessandra looked like she'd walked off a magazine cover for America's rich and famous. Even her nails were impeccably painted and glittered with tiny jewels. "Ask your questions."

She arched a brow at me, as if she didn't like my informality or my briskness. "What are your plans for us? For this nest? Because I can certainly take some of these Blood myself to help guard the tower."

Her arrogance set my teeth on edge. Even if Llewellyn hadn't warned me of her, there was no way in hell I'd ask her to be my sib. "You may take any of these Blood that you wish, but none of them, or you, will be guarding so much as an outhouse, let alone my nest."

Her chin tipped up, her eyes flashing. "You must not know who I am, because I don't understand how you could possibly select anyone else to run a nest of this size. Unless you intend to live here, of course." She let her gaze flick over my jeans and huffed out a derisive laugh. "Which I hardly see as likely, given how you're dressed. The queen of New York City has a high level of elegance and class to live up to. Skye Tower hosts events all year long, from fashion shows to charity galas."

I concentrated on taking a deep, even breath, and another, before saying softly, "Isador Tower. I have no intention of living in New York City, but if I wish to attend any event in this fucking city, I will do so. In whatever attire I wish. Because I am the fucking queen of New York City."

"Long live Shara fucking Isador," Daire's voice rang out.

"Last daughter of the Great One," Mehen retorted. "The only queen to bring Leviathan, king of the depths, to heel."

Guillaume didn't say anything, though he suddenly had his biggest knife in his hand. He casually examined the massive blade's edge with his thumb.

The smell of his blood, even a single drop, made my voice thicken with hunger. "Unless you'd like to challenge me?"

She blinked rapidly, as if suddenly surprised to find the insignificant little mouse she'd picked up suddenly had giant teeth and claws. Had she not seen me handle Keisha Skye? Or was Alessandra so confident in her house name that she thought she'd be immune? "You need a sibling queen to hold the city. Someone well known and strong."

"With elegance and class," I said dryly. "We've been over this."

She drew herself up, her chin rising to a haughty angle. "They say you weren't raised in a nest, so it's understandable that you wouldn't know my house's reputation or what we can accomplish together. Marne Ceresa herself arranged for my alliance with Keisha Skye."

"But you arranged your downfall."

Alessandra recoiled, and her perfect complexion drained of color. "Why? What have I done?"

I stared back at her steadily. "No one in House Isador will stand by quietly while others are tortured. They certainly won't assist or participate."

"She made me," Alessandra whispered, her voice raw. "She made us all."

"That's not true and you know it," Carys retorted. "I never participated. I never even watched, except for the one time she threatened to kill Winnifred if I refused a direct order. What happened in House Skye was sickening and I wanted no part in it."

"A queen sibling stands with her queen. Wouldn't you want that kind of sibling, Your Majesty? Sibs that always do as you order without question? That's the kind of loyalty I offer."

Slowly, I stood. Rik leaned forward, his hands on my waist, but he didn't rise. I didn't need my alpha's strength and impressive size to intimidate. "Actually, no. Not at all. I don't want people following my orders blindly. If I do something as terrible as torture another person, I want someone to stand up and tell me to my face that I'm wrong."

"You don't understand everything Keisha had been through." Alessandra dabbed at her eyes, trying to sell her act of being the hapless, loyal supporter. "She lost a child. It devastated her. You can't possibly understand that kind of pain."

"My mother and father were murdered in front of me, so don't tell me that I don't understand the pain of losing your only family. It's still no excuse for what Keisha did. And there's no excuse for what you did if you ever assisted her in any way."

"I didn't assist in torturing her alphas. Not once."

Llewellyn came forward and dropped to one knee before me, bowing low. "Your Majesty, I beg your forgiveness."

I cupped his cheek and turned his face up so I could see his eyes. "What is it, my Blood?"

"I wasn't entirely truthful before. I neglected to tell you one very important fact, out of selfishness, I admit."

Mind whirling, I tried to keep my face smooth, rather than betraying the thousand questions fluttering through my head. Without hesitation, he'd already torn apart his handler and many of the other Blood who'd participated in his torture. So what reason could he possibly have for hiding something about Alessandra until now?

His eyes flickered with drops of golden fire. "I was tortured by Skye's Blood for years before they gave up trying to get much of a rise out of me. I watched everything, though, because that's my gift. When I see something with my eyes, it becomes a permanent part of my memory. My queen can then access those memories as if they're her own and play them aloud for others as if they're a movie. I wanted you to see and play this particular memory with my eyes."

I nodded, still stroking his cheek. "How do I access this memory?"

"Through the bond. Touch my mind. It's always open to you, my queen."

Still touching his face, I sank into his bond. His gryphon's feathers enfolded me, a deep rumbling whirr rising from his chest. I'd often touched my Blood's memories, but I'd never tried to play them aloud before. I wasn't sure how that would even work. It wasn't like he had a play button inside his head.

His life stretched out before me like a wide, slow-moving river. Deceptively calm and still, inviting me to jump in even though I could feel brutal undercurrents just beneath the surface. I brushed lightly across that smooth surface. Images flickered through my head. Faces I recognized, that squeezed and crumbled my heart into dust.

Esetta. My mother. Her face was perfectly clear in his memory. I paused, drinking in the deep, endless darkness of her eyes.

:*Don't watch that one yet, my queen,*: Llewellyn whispered in our bond. :*Let it be just for you and I, and your alpha, if you wish. But not here.*:

Reluctantly, I let that image sink back into the river flowing through him.

:*This one, my queen.*: He filled my mind with an image of Keisha sitting on her throne. :*Drag it up and out of me so they can all see it.*:

I touched that memory and it rose up out of the river eagerly. I didn't have to tug or wrestle, and I suddenly heard voices echoing above our heads. I opened my eyes and gasped. Llewellyn's head was tipped back, his eyes strained wide. Red-gold rays burned from his eyes, almost too bright for me to look at. I followed them upward to an image reflected on the ceiling. He was the camera, his eyes the lens, tracking two people whispering in the corner. The room was dark. I could feel his intensity radiating in the image. He didn't breathe or move but focused silently on the two women talking.

Their whispers clicked louder, as if he'd turned the volume up. He blinked, and the image sharpened, as if he'd zoomed in. I recognized Alessandra, speaking to another woman I didn't know.

"When does she want us to act?" The other woman asked.

:*Virginia Athos:* Llewellyn whispered in my head. The other queen he'd warned me about.

"Not yet," Alessandra replied. "She sees something lurking deep in the background that Keisha doesn't want anyone to know. She needs us to find out what it is first. But then, House Skye will be mine."

She turned toward Llewelyn and gasped, her eyes flaring with shock. "What are you doing here? Where the fuck is that hood? Your handler?"

"I was told to wait here until she returned," he replied.

Someone approached from behind him. "Fucking nuisance," a woman retorted and jammed something down over his head. Darkness replaced the image on the ceiling.

I glanced down at his face, but he didn't move. He continued staring up at the ceiling with his glowing eyes, so I looked back, waiting for the memory to continue. His past emotions still flickered through me. His gift was extraordinary. I could feel his rage bubbling through him. He hated the hood. He hated the handler. He hated every single person in Skye Tower. He raged silently, eager to kill and feast and kill some more. Yet he had a purpose. He was to wait, and watch, and be ready.

For me.

He was sent to capture every single thing he could with his gift, so I would have the background information I needed when the time came. Keisha must have known about his gift, though, so I wasn't sure how many memories he would have captured if they'd kept him hooded.

I wasn't sure how much time passed. It was long enough that I started to get a crick in my neck from staring up at the ceiling. I heard shuffling and the quiet whisper of clothing. I glanced over at Alessandra. She'd tried to slink away, but Guillaume and the twins had blocked her path.

Voices played from above, drawing my attention back to it, though the image was still black.

Alessandra's voice echoed down from the ceiling. "I'm surprised that you've been willing to keep him around so long, given his dangerous ability to spy on you."

The blackness was replaced with Keisha Skye sitting on her throne. Llewelyn must have been on his knees in front of the dais, looking up at her. The image shook briefly, and I felt a surge of fury roar through him so viciously that he trembled. He hated her. He wanted to kill her. His mouth watered at the thought of tearing her throat out. Yet he said nothing.

"He has his uses," Keisha replied with a shrug. Her lips curled with a hint of smug amusement. "Tormenting him pleases me greatly, though he responds so little nowadays. Besides, his beloved queen is dead. Who would he report to now?"

The woman behind him muttered loudly enough for her queen to hear. "He doesn't even scream anymore."

"Then you don't have any imagination," Alessandra said.

Keisha narrowed a hard look on her. "Do you have any suggestions?"

Alessandra thought a moment, tapping one elegantly tapered fingernail against her chin. "Oh. I know. You could take his eyes."

The handler let out a grunt of disgust. "Her Majesty said no permanent physical damage, or trust me, I would have taken those cursed eyes out a decade ago and saved myself the trouble of this fucking hood."

Llewellyn didn't move, but his fear tasted sour on my tongue. I could feel his heart pounding as if trying to escape his ribcage. He didn't want them to know how much the thought of losing his sight, and especially, his gift, upset him. He had a purpose. He needed his eyes to complete it.

"No..." Keisha replied, drawing the word out on a long sigh.

Llewellyn didn't relax. He watched her intently, blinking again so his camera-focus narrowed in on her face. The glint of cruelty in her eyes.

"*I* won't take his eyes. *You* will. And you, Wasinga, will still use the fucking hood every moment of every fucking day and night."

His camera vision flickered again, zeroing in on Alessandra's face. He watched her swallow, her delicate throat tensing, though her face didn't betray her. She walked toward him, and with each step, his vision clicked and snapped, adjusting to keep his focus on her face. Even as she raised her hands, the jewels on her lacquered nails reflecting the light. Approaching his eyes. Snap. Closer. Tension coiled in him, and in me, as I watched. I couldn't breathe. Fire exploded in my eyeballs and the shrill scream echoed through the room, resounding in my head. His scream. Mine.

Rik's hands held me steady as I swayed. I clamped my mouth shut, and the wailing scream of pain shut off. I panted, clutching Llewellyn's face. Even with Rik's heat and strength at my back, I still wanted to frantically touch my own eyes and make sure they were still there. That she hadn't taken *my* eyes.

Goddess. It was awful. His memory still ached inside me like a nest of inflamed, raw nerves.

"You lied," I rasped out in Alessandra's general direction.

"No, no, Your Majesty," she babbled. "Not exactly. I said I'd never participated in torturing Keisha's alphas. Which is true. I never touched them."

"Shut the fuck up!" I roared, wincing at my own volume. I finally managed to convince my eyes to open. I blinked away tears and winced again at the tenderness in my eyes. They remembered being ripped out by this woman. I still clutched Llewellyn's face so hard that my nails had broken his skin. I dragged his face against my chest and wrapped my arms around his head, holding him over my heart.

Still panting. His pain raw inside me.

I looked at her and I wanted to sprout my own nails and claw her eyes out. Instead, I said one word. Or rather, one name.

"Guillaume."

He moved, so elegantly and quickly that I doubted she felt a thing. Just like in Kansas City, when he'd killed the curious saleslady who'd been tainted by Marne Ceresa, he effortlessly beheaded Alessandra Sito.

The rest of my Blood inched closer to me, shoulders tensing. Hackles rising. Teeth bared.

They wanted blood. They wanted to kill, too.

Three men ran forward, jostling my Blood to get to Alessandra, evidently their queen, but they were too late.

I looked at Vega and she dropped to her belly on the floor and hid her face.

"Must I look through Llewellyn's eyes to see your sins, or will you face what you've done?"

"Kill me, Your Majesty," she whispered, her voice shaking. "I beg you."

The rest of Keisha's Blood mirrored her, falling forward on the cold marble. Alessandra's three Blood joined them silently. Accepting their fate.

I glanced at each one of my Blood except for Rik and gave them each a nod.

My stomach churned. My eyes still ached in my skull. But I watched every moment as my men executed the dead queens' Blood.

6

MEHEN

I enjoyed drinking blood, but it was wonderfully feral to tear apart my queen's enemies and feast on their flesh. I curled around the chair where she sat, my head on my tail, my belly pleasantly stuffed. It'd been a very long time since Leviathan had been so well fed. I hadn't even digested the Skye sibs I'd eaten earlier when I'd finally managed to break through the fucking roof.

The warcat jumped up on top of me to get closer to our queen and I didn't even bother with a growl. Daire stretched out along my heaving side and settled in to lick his muzzle and claws clean. The marble floor was coated in congealing blood, shredded fabric, and a few grisly remains that even I wouldn't bother with.

On his knees, Llewellyn had folded himself up so she could

cradle his head against her breasts. Lucky asshole. Even if some bitch queen had torn out his eyes. Rik had his beefy arms wrapped around her, his giant body swallowing her up. She drooped a little, her face pale, though she'd watched us carry out her orders without flinching. Even if that meant tearing into meat while it was still kicking.

"Call the blood to you," Rik rumbled softly. "Then you won't have to look at it."

"It's not my blood to call."

I'd never heard her voice so... fragile. My slitted eyes locked on her, nostrils flaring. If she needed blood, I'd shift and offer a vein, even if my human belly would hurt for a week.

"It is," Rik insisted gently. "This is your building. These are your sibs, even if you haven't taken them. Their blood will come to your call."

She allowed her head to fall back against his shoulder with a weary sigh. Closing her eyes, she relaxed against him. My scales itched as she called up her magic, the row of barbs down my head and spine rising with interest. Dried blood peeled away from my hide and floated toward her, joining the droplets from the floor and the rest of her Blood. She absorbed it with a small shiver.

If I hadn't been in my dragon form, I'd probably have shit myself. Soaking in that much blood energy was no easy feat. Yet she took it into her reserves like she'd dribbled a little blood on the floor, rather than the slaughtered remains of fifteen people.

Her color improved, and she didn't wilt so heavily against Rik. When she spoke again, her voice rang with confidence. "Virginia, come forward."

A crying woman with a Blood on either side of her approached our queen. Lushly beautiful with full ruby lips and a curvaceous figure, she was gorgeous even with swollen eyes and drippy nose. I'd let G slice and dice my nuts if she wasn't descended from Aphrodite. Once upon a time, I might have taken a great deal of pleasure in fucking such a queen before I ate her.

Now, though, all I wanted was the dark beauty of *my* queen. My Shara. Mine.

Rik gave an alpha jab through the bond that knocked my possessiveness down a notch, though I still nudged my nose closer to Shara's ankle so I could lick the top of her foot.

Virginia knelt gracefully several paces away with a wary eye on me, even though I made no defensive move toward her. My belly was too full to move quickly, but Daire tensed slightly. He'd be ready to pounce on her at the first moment of trouble.

"Forgive me, Your Majesty. I colluded with Alessandra to bring down Keisha Skye for her, and indirectly, for Marne Ceresa. I didn't object when Keisha tortured her alphas. May Aphrodite strike me down this very moment if I lie. I swear that I never participated in any torture, of any persons. Ever. Not here in Skye Tower or elsewhere. I was weak, yes. I was afraid. I did as I was told. But I didn't participate."

"I appreciate your honesty," Shara replied. "I ask that you leave my tower immediately."

Virginia opened and closed her mouth several times before finally saying, "I must leave? I'm grateful for your mercy, Your Majesty, but I have nowhere else to go."

"I don't trust you. I don't know if I can ever trust anyone

who worked with Keisha, but you have a double strike against you, because you allied yourself with Alessandra, too."

She lifted her gaze to the other queens, who'd drawn into a tight group with their Blood on the outside in a ring. We hadn't threatened them. Yet. If Shara ordered their deaths, nothing would keep us from completing her order, let alone a few paltry Blood. I could squash half of them with my tail without even getting up.

"Your Majesty," Carys said, drawing her attention. "May I now demonstrate my gift for you?"

My queen nodded, so Carys stepped closer to the crying woman and closed her eyes a moment. Her mouth moved, as if she was muttering beneath her breath, but even my sensitive ears couldn't pick up what she said.

Carys opened her eyes and nodded sharply. "My gift lies in pure numbers, Your Majesty, and I can now tell you that the probability of Virginia Athos betraying you is one in two, or roughly fifty percent."

The woman gasped, and two bright red dots spread on her cheeks. "How dare you? I would never betray my queen."

"That statement carries a nine in ten probability, Your Majesty, though I believe the question you must ask yourself is who her queen truly is."

"Marne Ceresa," Shara said flatly.

"While nothing is completely certain, my gift agrees with ninety-nine point ninety-nine percent accuracy."

"Take your Blood and go to your queen," Shara ordered.

Virginia gave a dirty look at Carys, tipped her nose up, and stalked toward the exit. One of her Blood looked back over his shoulder with a snarl on his lips.

Rumbling out a vicious growl, Daire crouched on my back.

"Daire," Shara said. "Let them go. I don't care."

He blew out a disgusted sigh and paced around in a circle before flopping back down on my side with a huff.

She looked thoughtfully at Carys. "You see probabilities? That's what made you so valuable to Keisha?"

Carys inclined her head. "Aye, exactly that, Your Majesty. The strategies are yours to devise. I can only tell you how likely your success or failure will be. The numbers appear in my head as you speak."

Shara rubbed her fingers over Llewellyn's scalp in soothing circles. "So if I had refused to accept my mother's Blood as my own..."

Carys paled. "I see zeroes. Everywhere. I'm afraid that would have been certain death, Your Majesty."

"Please, just call me Shara." She settled back more fully against Rik and breathed deeply. With Llewellyn curled against her, she stilled for several long moments. Her bond quieted, her thoughts drifting away as if she'd fallen asleep.

With my full belly and Daire's steady purr, it was all I could do not to drift away to nap with her. Her bond wound through me like a soft whisper, a sweet lullaby. I smelled sand and felt a night breeze on my face.

"You," she said with sudden conviction. I opened my eyes and lifted my head. She pointed at the group of queens, though her eyes were still closed. The remaining Blood shifted restlessly, the queens looking at one another. "No. *You.*"

A woman stepped around and through the waiting queens. "Me?"

Shara opened her eyes and sat up. "Yes. What's your name?"

"Gwenhwyfar Findabair, Your Majesty, though most people call me Gwen."

:Descended from Guinevere, the White Enchantress, Queen of Camelot,: Daire whispered in her bond.

:King Arthur's Guinevere?: Shara asked. *:Like Knights of the Round Table?:*

:The very one.:

The woman came closer, standing alone before our queen. Her long dark-brown hair hung in a thick braid over her shoulder and down to her waist. She was pretty but nothing much to look at. Though maybe I was too full of my queen's enemies—and Shara's blood—to care about any other queen.

"Carys, what do you see as the probability of Gwen's success in holding New York City for me?"

Absently, Carys reached up and scratched under her owl's wing. "As she stands here, now? It's not very likely, Your Majesty."

Shara frowned, her head tilting as if she listened to a voice only she could hear. "Really? Because she's my choice out of this group, at least."

Carys looked at the other queens one by one and nodded. "I agree. She has the highest probability of success out of these queens, at forty percent."

"That low? Do you not have any Blood, Gwen?"

Gwen dropped her gaze to the floor, but not out of shyness. Her shoulders tensed, and she curled her fingers into fists at her sides. "No, Your Majesty. I've not been allowed Blood of my own."

"By Keisha?"

Gwen raised her gaze to my queen's, her green eyes burning with defiance. "Not directly. Keisha accepted my bond from another queen as payment for a debt, with the agreement that I could never call my own Blood."

Intrigued, even Llewellyn lifted his head from our queen's breast, so he could focus on this new queen.

"Who would make such a deal with Keisha Skye?" Shara asked.

Gwen's face hardened. "Elaine Shalott. Our courts agreed that we should become siblings to help quell the bad blood between our families. I never would have agreed if I'd known she'd been dabbling in shadowed magic. Once I willingly gave her my blood, it was too late. She was strong enough to forbid me from ever taking a Blood, which would give me the strength I needed to break free of her hold."

"How long have you been forbidden from calling your Blood?"

"Nearly four hundred years."

Shara's heart ached, pulling us all closer to her so we could offer comfort in some small way. Daire purred louder, dueling with the whirring sound that rolled from Llewellyn's chest. Rik rumbled softly—which for a rock troll, meant that it sounded like boulders tumbling down a cliff. I lifted my head higher and rubbed my cheek on her knee. I would have pushed my head under her arm, but my spiky spines might have poked her.

"I'm sorry. I can't imagine being alone for so long, especially if I knew my Blood were out in the world somewhere, aching for me too, and I wasn't allowed to call them to me."

Gwen swallowed hard and averted her gaze, visibly struggling not to break down. "She did it on purpose, in the hopes that she could find Lance first. So it has been between Camelot and Shalott for over a thousand years. We are doomed to be reborn and repeat the vicious cycle of our ancient pasts over and over."

"What about Arthur?"

"The once and future king has doomed us to repeat this vicious cycle indefinitely." Gwen jerked her head around, her eyes flashing. "Let's just say the stories don't begin to tell the truth and leave it at that, shall we?"

Shara nodded, but I could feel the curiosity burning in her bond. "I would like to hear the truth someday."

Gwen inclined her head. "I'll do as you wish, Your Majesty. I can do no less."

"That wasn't an order, just a request to consider someday, when we know each other better." Shara turned to Carys. "If she calls her Blood, what's the probability that she can hold New York successfully?"

"If she calls any of her knights other than Lance, the odds improve to sixty percent. If she can call Lance…" Carys closed her eyes a moment, her mouth moving slightly. "At least ninety percent success rate, Your Majesty. I won't be able to tell for certain until I feel the bond spark, but the odds are very good."

Shara smiled. "So you need to call Lance. In the meantime, I'm willing to bet on your success. Gwen Findabair, would you do me the honor of becoming my queen sibling with the intent of helping me establish and hold Isador Tower in New York City?"

"You honor me, Your Majesty." Gwen dropped to her knees. Although tears sparkled on her cheeks, she smiled, and even my old bitter dragon heart softened at the way her face lit up with joy. I could suddenly see why the knights of old may have fought for her hand.

The same way we Blood jostled one another to make our queen smile.

Shara stood, Llewellyn and Rik each taking her arms to lift her up and over me so she could get to the other queen. Gwen immediately offered throat, but Shara hesitated with a wry smile twisting her lips. "I should warn you that my bite carries an orgasmic punch. Would you rather my Templar knight use his knife?"

Gwen's eyes widened, her mouth hanging open with surprise. I didn't need a bond to know why.

She was shocked that a queen of Shara's stature was actually giving her a choice. That Shara cared about her preferences, sexual or otherwise.

"Yes, please," Gwen answered hesitantly, as if waiting for the trap to reveal itself.

Shara nodded and Guillaume stepped closer with his smallest blade ready in his hand. "My lady," he inclined his head to Gwen, but then went down on one knee for Shara. "My queen. Thank you for allowing me to be of service."

Gwen offered her wrist, and he made a small, neat cut in her skin.

If I hadn't been the dragon, goosebumps would have sprung

up on my flesh. Instead, the spiny ridges flared all the way down to my tail. Not from the scent of this queen's blood.

But because I felt my queen's hunger.

I knew that thirst. I'd suffered centuries, unable to feed. Unable to quench the terrible thirst.

Shara had ten Blood at her disposal and still burned for more. Despite the throbbing of her fangs, she gently took the other woman's hand in hers and lifted her wrist to her mouth.

Gwen's blood filled my queen with ancient strength. This queen didn't currently have much power, but her potential was considerable, even without tasting Shara's blood. Honeyed mead filled Shara's senses, along with the clamor of war and the brutal clash of swords. Guinevere had always been at the heart of war. Through the centuries, she'd been blamed for Camelot's downfall. Her infidelity with her husband's knight had led to King Arthur's downfall, so the stories went.

I tasted secrets in Shara's new bond. Dark secrets and old hurts. And yes, far in distant lands, the faint tug on her heart, as if fragile strings stretched almost too far, almost too thin, but held against the world.

Gwen laughed softly, even though her tears fell harder. "He lives. He's still free and he's coming."

"Very nearly one-hundred percent likelihood of success," Carys whispered hoarsely. "If he's at her side, New York City will always be yours, Your Majesty."

"He will," Gwen swore. "Nothing will keep him from me."

Shara lifted her head and licked her lips, her eyes blazing with hunger. She held her wrist to Guillaume, even as she turned to Carys and motioned her closer. Guillaume made the same neat cut on our queen's wrist for Gwen, and then turned to cut Carys so our queen could formalize that bond as well.

Carys went down on her knees and offered her bleeding wrist, but Shara didn't reach for her. Instead, she stared at the owl.

Her bonds surged with fresh strength, but she didn't use any of that new power base to compel or force the giant bird.

"What do you think, Winnifred?" Carys asked, stroking her fingers over the owl's head. She tipped her head a moment, and then she beamed up at Shara. "She says you truly are the Great One's daughter. We eagerly serve House Isador."

Guillaume snapped to attention and the rest of the Blood still in human shape joined him in saluting our queen with a fist over their hearts. "Long live Shara fucking Isador!"

7

SHARA

Two new bonds gleamed in my head. My two new sibling queens, Gwen and Carys, both on their knees, looked up at me with equal doses of awe and terror as they tasted the power burning in my blood and felt the surge in their own gifts.

Isis' blood flowed through me to them, stirring their magic to new heights. Both already felt stronger in my head. Gwen managed to take quite a bit of my blood, much more than Mayte had been able to take the first time. I could feel my power resonating in Gwen like a deep echo. She had plenty of depth to her power, and the social skills that would be beneficial here.

Carys only took a few swallows and slouched back on her heels, her eyes fuzzy, as if she'd downed a pint or two at the pub rather than a little of my blood.

"Oh, my." She giggled, and the owl stepped closer to her neck and nestled up against her cheek. "That is... Wow. Yeah. Shara fucking Isador indeed."

Amused, I gave a nod to Guillaume, and he helped both women to their feet, though Carys needed a steadying hand.

"Your Majesty, what are your orders?" Gwen asked.

"I want the former Skye sibs sorted and formally sworn to Isador if they're going to stay. If they want to leave, that's fine."

Virginia stuck her head in the door. I thought she'd left already, but maybe she really didn't have anywhere else to go. "What about our share of the Skye legacy?"

I looked over at the two consiliari. Madeline scanned through a file on her tablet and whispered to Gina, who nodded and then spoke aloud. "Your Majesty, Madeline has already prepared a final tally for each queen's share of the Skye legacy, according to the agreements between Keisha and each queen at the time of their sibling agreement."

I didn't really care about the numbers. Gina knew that. So she must have a reason for discussing it. "I see. Madeline, what were the details of Virginia Athos's agreement with House Skye?"

"Virginia was to receive a set amount of one hundred thousand dollars each year she remained in House Skye, for a grand total of ten million, three hundred and thirty-three thousand dollars, rounded to the nearest dollar and prorated to include today." Madeline looked up at me, making sure she had my attention. "But all funds were forfeited at Keisha Skye's death."

"What? No!" Virginia strode back toward us, though a low

snarl from Itztli kept her from coming within twenty paces of me. "That can't be."

Madeline's mouth quirked, her eyes gleaming as she tapped on the tablet and then proceeded to read. "'Upon Keisha Skye's death, all sibling agreements will pass seamlessly to her designated heir. If no heir has been declared in writing and legitimately recognized by the Triune, then this sibling agreement will be nullified, and all funds will revert to House Skye's legacy account.'"

Damn, she really was relishing this, especially the accounting and contract aspect. Even Gina grinned as the other consiliarius revealed the intricacies she'd deliberately written into the agreement to protect her house's interest at the time.

"As this court knows full well, Keisha Skye did not have an heir after her daughter's death. She refused to name any other heir until she was able to have another child."

I wondered if Keisha had planned to name Tanza as her heir again, if she could ever be cured from the darkness living inside her, or if Keisha had some other contingency built into her legacy. It would be interesting to discuss with Madeline in private, but I didn't care for these other queens to know the details.

Virginia made a soft sound of dismay. "Then I'm truly damned. No house will take me in if I can't offer a price."

I looked at Gwen. "Do you wish to accept Virginia as our sibling?"

She didn't mask her disgust. "Not unless you order it, Your Majesty."

I turned to Madeline. "Give her the sum Keisha promised to

her. Give any of the queens who wish to leave their share of the legacy. I don't want it, and I don't want them if they wish to leave."

Madeline's eyes widened but she nodded. "At once, Your Majesty."

I looked over at the waiting queens. "Gwen will meet with you one by one and decide whether you're welcome to stay, or if she wishes you to leave. You may leave if you wish. Either way, you'll be paid your share of the Skye legacy. I want this resolved as quickly as possible."

I met Gina's gaze and before I could ask if she'd talked with Madeline about my offer for her to stay on as my second consiliarius, she nodded imperceptibly. "If there are any new amendments to the sibling agreements, I'll discuss them with my consiliari tomorrow."

Gwen stared at me, her eyes wide, though she didn't dare question me in front of the others. I read her shock in the bond. She hadn't really expected much freedom and power to make decisions on behalf of my house.

But the Great One's approval bubbled up inside me every time I looked at my new sibling. Gwen Findabair was Isis' choice to rule New York City.

:I trust you to decide who to keep and who should leave. You know them personally. If you have any reason to doubt or question their intent, send them packing. I don't want anyone here that doesn't want to be with us.:

She twitched slightly at my touch in her mind, and then replied hesitantly, as if shocked that I would allow such liberties. *:As you wish, Your Majesty.:*

She inclined her head and said aloud, "We'll go through the complete registry and write new sibling agreements for each queen and house."

"Call me Shara, please. All of you. Gina, let's schedule a meeting for us first thing tomorrow to discuss contracts and Gwen's choices so far."

Gina smiled. "Of course. Let's shoot for one tomorrow afternoon, but if we need to move it to two, I'll keep our calendars open."

Madeline had a polite, blank look on her face that didn't disguise her confusion, Carys was still higher than a kite, and Gwen had a puzzled look on her face as she said hesitantly, "I thought you said first thing tomorrow? So shouldn't we meet in the morning?"

I laughed out loud as I tucked my arm around Rik's. "On a good day, I'm a late riser, and after the day this has been, I'll probably want to sleep for a week. So even getting here by tomorrow afternoon will be a feat. Madeline, we'll formalize a consiliarius agreement first, and then Gwen and Carys can join us for the sibling discussion."

Gina nodded, already moving away with the determined stride of a general going to war. "Get some sleep, Shara. We've got things well in hand here."

Just the thought of finally slipping away in the warmth and safety of my bed made my knees sag. Rik scooped me up and headed for the door. Closing my eyes, I rested against him, soaking in his heat.

A muffled oomph made me open my eyes and I rose up to look back over Rik's shoulder. Guillaume blocked Carys from following after me. "Her Majesty has no need of you at this time."

"But... but... I need to be with her. At all times. I've seen the probabilities." Carys raised her voice enough the owl flapped her wings restlessly. "Please, Shara, I must come with you. You may need my gift at a moment's notice."

I liked the woman well enough, but it still seemed weird to have people living with me.

Daire snorted in our bond. *:We live with you and that's not weird.:*

:But you're my Blood. You're mine. I want you with me always.:

:She's yours too.:

I glanced back at her, waiting to see if I felt any physical attraction for her. I'd been surprised about how much I'd enjoyed having Mayte in my bed, but I didn't feel any desire when I looked at Carys. I loved her candor and wit, but I didn't see myself sleeping with her. Let alone fucking her.

Her eyes went round, her lips pursing with surprise. Evidently, she'd picked up on my thoughts through our new bond. *:I have no such aspirations, Your Majesty, not for you, or any person, to be honest. Winnifred is my only companion.:*

Daire rubbed against Rik's legs and flicked his tail up to brush over my fingers. *:She's still yours, and you don't have to fuck every sibling you take. Think of her as a sister, or the crazy spinster aunt with a thousand cats.:*

The owl squawked and Carys patted her head soothingly. "No cats. I promise. May this crazy spinster aunt accompany you, Your Majesty? I would rather be close, so that I'm at your beck and call at a moment's notice."

Nuzzling back into Rik's embrace, I sighed. "She can come with us, G. But will someone let Winston know, so he can call ahead and have Magnum prepare a room for her?"

"Already done, Your Majesty," Winston said as Rik carried me down the hallway. "The car is waiting downstairs, and Magnum assured me a suite will be ready for your new sibling as well."

I yawned and almost cracked my jaw. "Out of curiosity, how many bedrooms does my mother's house have?"

"Ten, though several of the rooms are configured to accommodate many more people. I'm sure you could find a bed for at least thirty people."

"So many? Did she ever use them for siblings, or were they for her Blood?"

"You're very like your mother in that regard, Your Majesty. They—"

A crash had us all whirling around. Rik crushed me to his chest. Daire and Itztli both crouched, hackles rising.

Only to see my dragon glaring with disgust as he tried to slide down the hallway without damaging anything else.

Daire made a coughing rattle that was evidently the warcat's laughter. :*Yo, dickhead, I don't think the engineers designed this building for dragons. Why the fuck don't you shift before you bring the roof down on our heads?*:

:*I can't shift, asswipe, until I've digested some of the Skye sibs. My belly already hurts. It'll probably explode if I try to shift to human form.*:

I tried to imagine proud, arrogant Mehen strutting down the hall with a massive food-baby stomach, and I burst into laughter. It was a macabre thing to laugh about—because those were *people* in his belly—but it was still funny as hell. My eyes started to water, which only made me laugh harder. If I'd been standing up, I probably would have sunk to the floor as tension flowed out of me.

It'd been such a dangerous, nerve-wracking trip. I'd almost lost Rik. We all could have died. A little laughter was the perfect medicine. Even if Mehen destroyed the whole building.

"He already tore a hole in the roof," Guillaume reminded me, sending me into another peal of laughter.

"I hate this fucking building anyway," I gasped out. "Tear it all down. I don't give a fuck one way or the other."

Chuckling, Llewellyn raised a hand, waiting for my amusement to quiet. "There's no need to destroy the whole building. As you saw earlier, the gryphon is also a large winged beast with a bloodthirsty appetite, though not as immense as our dragon friend. There's an easy path back to the roof that he demolished here, and I can show him where the roof access is at the Isador house. The entire top floor is open and spacious for exactly this reason."

:But I don't want to be separated from you, even by so much as a single story of your house,: Mehen growled in my head.

"Then you shouldn't have eaten so much," Rik said, making me giggle again.

Mehen glared at him, which only made me laugh harder.

Llewellyn stepped closer and leaned down to lightly press his forehead to mine. "By your leave, Your Majesty, I'll accompany the dragon and stay with him at least until he can shift."

I cupped Llewellyn's cheek. "No." His eyes widened, but he didn't object. None of them would refuse an order from me.

Though I didn't keep him in suspense long. "Go with him now and show him the roof access. But someone else can stay with him tonight. I want you to come to me as soon as you're both safely back. I need to be sure you're healed and well-fed, along with Ezra and Rik."

"Then you're going to need to feed deeply yourself," Rik said, his tone as close to an order as he dared get with his queen.

My fangs ached with anticipation.

"I'll babysit the dragon on first watch." Guillaume said, not even flinching when the dragon snapped his jaws a hair's breadth away from his ear. "Then when someone's recovered enough to walk, come relieve me."

Llewellyn's eyes started to swirl with flecks again. "You feed so deeply that your Blood can't walk afterward?"

Daire started purring. Loudly. :*Among other things. Our queen's hungers are ravenous.*:

My cheeks heated, and I shrugged sheepishly. "I'll try to take it easy on you."

Llewellyn threw his head back and roared with laughter. Now it was my turn to glare a bit, though I was more embarrassed than angry. This man could have been my father, if my mother had been able to conceive with her alpha. I still couldn't quite get my mind wrapped around that aspect of our relationship and all that entailed. I might chicken out in the end and not take him to my bed.

His laughter stilled immediately, and he met my gaze, his eyes burning almost completely red gold. "You misunderstand me, my queen. I beg you to take me, anyway you wish, and the last thing on my mind is worry that you might use me too hard or take me too far. That would be impossible. I laugh only because I am so happy and blessed to have such a queen. After so many years in House Skye, I thought I'd never be able to laugh again. Let alone love."

I softened the glare, and now the moisture in my eyes was for an entirely different reason than uncontrollable laughter. "Then let's make sure you laugh and love as much as possible."

"Long live our queen," my Blood said in unison.

8

LLEWELLYN

My queen's hunger burned, spurring my steps quicker to her side. I left the dragon curled in a miserable ball in the attic, thoroughly pissed that he'd be missing out on what came next. I couldn't blame him.

I'd be pissed at myself too if I had cause to miss a single moment of feeding my queen's hungers, whatever they were.

A sudden wash of guilt drowned my joy at being able to serve again. I paused outside her room in the hallway and pressed my head to the ornate door. I'd passed through these doors many times, drawn by my queen's desire.

My former queen. My new queen's mother.

I loved her. I would have sacrificed my life for hers in a heartbeat if that would have given her the child she yearned for so desperately. Any alpha would have fucked himself into a coma to please his queen and give her a child.

But it would have been a useless death, because my queen had never bred in all the centuries I served her. Had she looked through the future and seen me here, aching to fuck her daughter? Even as I made love to her? Had she seen the years of torture I'd endured, gladly, just to stand outside an Isador queen's door again?

Even if it wasn't hers?

Forgive me, my love.

:There's nothing to forgive, Lew.: Her voice whispered through me like a faint ghost, so soft and distant that it would have been easy to dismiss her touch as my imagination.

But only my former queen had ever called me Lew. I might not be able to say her name, but I knew her touch. Her memory burned like a brand inside me. She'd etched herself into every bone and sinew in my body with her blood and her love.

And if I was extremely lucky, her daughter would claim me exactly the same way.

I waited a moment, making sure Shara felt my presence at the door. She didn't order me inside, but I felt her tug on my bond like a crackling fire on a cold winter night. I entered the room and quietly shut the door behind me.

The heavy-set man who smelled like bear gave me a slight nod. I had a feeling that was as close to a friendly welcome as the man would ever get. The twins stood on the opposite side of the door. They barely even looked at me. Not that I cared. The one with a black sun tattooed on his cheek smelled like pain and death, and his brother smelled like jungle. I couldn't see the wolf, but I smelled a hint of him wafting through the room. It was a special Blood who could hide in plain sight like that, even from former alphas. I had a feeling even Rik wouldn't be able to see Xin, unless he used our queen's bond. I had no doubt at all that she knew and saw everything.

The queen always did.

The Blood with long, black hair and kilt smelled... strange. Not quite right. I couldn't put my finger on what was wrong, but there was a secret there, too.

It was no surprise that her alpha and his purring companion were closest to her. The feline Blood was helping her undress, though Rik hovered close. Damn, he was one big fucker. I was taller, but I'd never seen a man built like our alpha. He put weightlifters on steroids to shame.

Combined with the Templar knight and Leviathan, king of the depths, our queen had quite an unusual array of Blood. No surprise, given that her father was Typhon, the god of monsters. Even her mother had always had a taste for the unique and strange.

A flash of something sharp in the bond drew my attention to Shara. A tear trickled down her cheek.

A fucking tear. Goddess. I felt the track of that salty drop like a knife sinking into my belly and scrambling my intestines. Her emotion became mine times a hundredfold. Blood needed to know when their queen hurt, so they could protect all the better. But this hurt...

Goddess, I didn't know if I could bear it. That was one reason my former queen had released all our bonds before she went to Typhon. Before she conceived, delivered her daughter in blood and pain, and ultimately, died. Because suffering that kind of pain through a Blood bond...

The twin who smelled of pain exhaled, and a fine tremor shook his body. The bear fell down on his knees beside the bed and buried his face against the bedding. His shoulders shook. Rik scooped her up in his arms, tendons and muscles standing out in stark relief, and the cat purred frantically, as if that sound alone could help ease her pain.

"Shhh, my queen," Rik whispered, his voice raw. He climbed into bed with her and held her on his chest, with Daire pressed against them both. "We're all alive. You did it."

Her bond tore open and released a flood of agony that buckled my knees. She'd contained her fear while dealing with the Skye sibs, but now, in the privacy of her bedroom, she wept.

She cried at the suffering Rik had gone through in the demon's circle. The realization that he'd done it to spare her, to spare us all, shredded her heart to ribbons. The thought of losing him undid her. I understood that fear to an extent, but this seemed to go so much deeper than what had happened with Keisha Skye. Her fear mounted, her pain a suffocating weight that crushed my ribcage. I dropped forward on my hands and knees, trying to breathe through the agony. We all did. Her Blood were all down, brought to our knees because of her pain.

"You're alive and well," Rik whispered, each word vibrating with strain as he fought not to hurt her more by revealing how much her pain wounded us. "That's all that matters. If we die..."

"No," she retorted, jerking her head up to glare at him. "No one can die. I can't bear it. I can't. Please, goddess. Please, spare me."

He cupped her cheek and smoothed her tears away with his thumbs. "You can, and you will, because you're Shara fucking Isador."

Bewildered, I didn't try to search her bond for answers, not while she was so volatile. Her emotions sliced through the bonds, stabbing and tearing through me. I'd only had her blood once. I didn't know how Rik and the others could even function with such blinding pain.

:My house's goddess made a bargain with her,: the twin whispered in my head. *:She can kill Ra, but it will cost her a life. One of us will die.:*

I closed my eyes and hung my head, letting despair overwhelm me for a moment. Of course. Her mother had seen what needed to be done from the beginning and had birthed Shara for this purpose. The mighty sun god would not die easily. Better that one of us died and allowed our queen to pick up the pieces afterwards and live happily the rest of her days, free of Ra's dominion.

It would be me. That had to be why her mother spared me. So I could pay this price for her daughter.

:I will, gladly,: I whispered in my head, hoping my former queen would hear my acceptance. *:I will love her as I did you, as long as I can. But then I will join you in the afterlife.:*

:It's not my choice to make.: My former queen whispered in my head, so faint as if thousands of years separated us. I strained toward her, trying to reach her one last time. *:It's not her choice. Only the goddess knows who will be called upon to die.:*

I panted with effort, but as soon as I reached for where I thought she waited, the faint sense of her dissipated like fog. She was gone. Only a hint of her spirit remained, attached to her daughter, the last queen of Isador. The child she'd died to have.

The harsh flood of pain flowing through Shara's bonds eased, allowing me to rock back on my heels. She still cried, but not as desperately, as if everything she loved in this world had crumbled away. "I need to bleed."

"And you need to feed." Rik's voice rumbled to a bass register that rattled the floorboards. "Deeply. As deeply as you can hold."

She sighed, relaxing into his arms. "I don't want to deplete any of you too much."

"Impossible."

She held her wrist out toward the bear, who still had his face pressed to the mattress. "Ezra, let me check your health. I want to be sure we got all of Tanza's taint out of you."

He fisted his hands in the bedding and refused to lift his face. "I fucking failed you, my queen. It was my fault that Rik was trapped. Don't waste a single fucking drop of your blood on healing me. Drain me dry. Use me to heal everyone else."

"Don't be ridiculous," she snapped with enough force that the bear flinched and lifted his face to hers. "You would cause me that much pain, just to soothe your own pride?"

Ezra lurched up enough to press his shaggy head against her stomach. "You would hurt if I died?"

She shuddered, clutching his head as desperately as he clamped his arms around her waist. "Without question. If any of you are called by the goddess..." Her voice broke and she squeezed him harder. "I would rather we all die than lose a single one of you."

Rik leaned back and stretched out beneath her with a welcoming bump of his hips. "Let's worry about taking care of you here and now, and leave tomorrow to the goddesses."

Exhaling slowly, she allowed all the tension and stress to flow out of her. She even managed a small, secretive smile. The kind of smile that made every dick in the room go rock hard.

She slid backwards and lifted her hips to take Rik inside of her. Her head fell back, her hair teasing over the man's thighs.

Need throbbed through me so viciously that I couldn't completely smother the groan. I wanted her hair kissing my thighs. Her skin burning against mine. Her fangs. Her nails. Her blood.

"Yes, Llewellyn. Join us. I need to feed you most of all."

SHARA

I held Rik inside me, squeezing my inner muscles so tightly that he grunted softly. If only I could hold him so tightly in my arms and my magic and keep him safe. Keep them all safe.

Pressing my left wrist to Ezra's mouth, I invited him to feed. His beard was damp with tears and his bond still weighed heavily in my mind. He blamed himself for what Rik had endured for us, but I couldn't see how the showdown would have ended any other way. At some point, Keisha would have presented the same offer to me. Save her daughter to save my Blood, and Rik would have made the exact same choice.

:Without question.:

He didn't move inside me but stroked his big palms over my thighs and hips, his fingers tracing my skin as if I was the most priceless object in the world.

Ezra sank his fangs into my skin ever so gently and I shuddered, unable to sit still with Rik's cock so deeply inside me.

Llewellyn came closer on my right and knelt on the bed beside us. He made no move to touch me, but his eyes blazed with a maelstrom of red and gold flames. I offered my wrist to him, but he hesitated. "You're weakened too, my queen. I don't know that feeding two of us at the same time is a good idea. My thirst..." He licked his lips and dropped his gaze to my body. I could almost feel those flames in his eyes licking my skin. "I don't know that I'll be able to control it. Not after so long."

"I'll drink as I need to, but I feel fine right now. In fact—" I met Rik's gaze and his eyebrows arched with interest. "I'd like to feed you all at the same time, or at least as many as possible. We've never done that before."

I didn't have to turn my head to note that all of my Blood now stood around the bed. Granted, it was big enough they couldn't actually touch me, but close enough to respond between one heartbeat and the next.

"Before you get too distracted, I suggest you do whatever healing you think necessary first," Rik said. "At the first sign of any weakness in you, I'll offer my throat. When I fall, I expect the rest of you to feed her deeply and long until she's done with you, or you pass out."

"Understood, alpha," they replied in unison.

Closing my eyes, I concentrated on Ezra first. My blood

flowed down his throat slowly. He hadn't bitten me deeply and he lapped at the small, tidy punctures. I sank deeper into him, tracing the pathways of blood vessels through his body. Shivering, he whispered gruffly, "Fucking tickles."

Daire snorted and practically crawled into my lap, which put him closer to Rik and Ezra too. "You can feed on me first, if you like, Shara. That way you can enjoy Rik longer."

Throughout Ezra's body, I sensed only my power. I glowed inside him like an opalescent moon, casting swirls of soft pearly light throughout his body. Nothing dark lingered. I opened my eyes and smiled at him. "I don't sense anything inside you that shouldn't be there. If you suspect anything at all, please let me know and I'll check again. But I think I burned all of Tanza out of you successfully."

Lifting his mouth, he grimaced. "I will, at once. I've never tasted anything as nasty as her blood before."

He still felt... stretched, somehow. Tender. Like he wasn't completely whole yet. I pressed my wrist back to his mouth, ignoring his muttered protests. "You need more. Bite me deeper if you need to. You know I like your fangs in me almost as much as I love your dick."

He seized my wrist in his teeth and gripped me firmly. Holding my gaze, he called his fangs down. I don't know how he did it, but they slid effortlessly back into the same holes ever so slowly and controlled. Nothing like my messy bites.

I could feel his two fangs inside me. Anchoring me to him, as thoroughly as Rik's cock connected me to him.

Daire nuzzled my breasts, his manner slow and lazy. He licked my areola and playfully pressed tender kisses to my skin, making my nipples pucker and ache. I turned to Llewelyn, my eyes heavy with lust. I decided to get the worst over with and deliberately pictured him with my mother. I had to know if it would bother me, before I took him too far.

I could imagine his long, lanky body moving over her. But I didn't know what my mother looked like. Not really.

:*She looked like you,*: he replied softly. :*You could almost be her twin.*:

It was easier to picture him making love to Mom. At least I knew what she looked like, though years had softened my memories. It was strange thinking of her with anyone but Dad, the man who'd helped her raise me. The part of me that had been her daughter throughout my childhood, and knew nothing of this Aima life, couldn't begin to think of how many lovers she must have had. Her Blood, plus Dad, plus Llewellyn. Even Greyson had once been her lover, though he'd turned thrall after she'd abandoned her nest and eventually killed her.

I waited for revulsion or regret to make me flinch away from this man, but I still wanted him, even if he'd fucked my mother a hundred times. A thousand. I wanted to soothe the torture from his body and quench his burning thirst. I wanted to taste his blood again and again, knowing that my mother was a part of him.

And now, she could be a part of me too, beyond the blood and power she'd invested in me before her death.

I wanted to bring him to climax inside of me and feel that connection to his past. To *my* past, my family, and my right as an Isador queen.

I offered my wrist to him again, and this time, he didn't

hesitate. He jammed his fangs into me hard enough my breath caught on a groan. My hips moved, making me groan again as Rik inched up deeper inside me. My lust rose to a fevered pitch. My fangs throbbed, sliding down fast and hard.

I sank them into the closest man I could find. Of course, it was Daire. He offered his throat so enticingly, the vulnerable curve of his shoulder as alluring and sexual as his genitals.

He jerked with climax, his spurts hot on my belly. His purr rumbled louder, and he sank against me, completely surrendering to me.

Goddess, I loved him. I loved the way he gave himself over to me completely without hesitation. He nestled deeper against me, sucking on my breast. I felt the sharp prick of his fangs and I arched my back, pushing my flesh more fully into his mouth.

Taking the hint, he sank his fangs into the soft curve of my breast, my nipple in his mouth.

Llewellyn kept his fangs in me, even though that slowed the flow of blood into his mouth. His hunger raged out of control, and I think deep down, he feared it. He was afraid that the taste of Isador blood would sweep him away into a wildfire of thirst that would endanger me.

Even though that was exactly what I wanted.

To compensate for what he took from me, he pressed his wrist to my mouth. I'd tasted him earlier, and he'd been tortured and starved for twenty years. I didn't dare drain him too much, not when I still needed to restore him. As soon as I felt his pulse fluttering like a frantic moth against my lips, I released him.

Behind me, a whisper-soft touch alerted me to the twins as

they came up on either side of me. I rocked Rik deeper inside me, grinding my pelvis harder against him. My clit throbbed, so hot and swollen it felt like it'd tripled in size. "Yes."

Itztli sank his fangs into the left side of my throat, while Tlacel took my right. They, too, held their fangs inside me. Connecting me to them. Throbbing inside me.

I drank Daire down until his purr changed from a deep rumble to a sleepy buzz. I pulled back and Nevarre immediately lifted him aside, so he could slide up against me and take his place.

My mouth watered. I wanted more Celtic magic and black feathers, even though I'd tasted him earlier tonight. But first, I pulled Ezra up to me and sank my fangs in his throat. His grizzly rumbled a greeting, inviting me to walk through a snowy forest to his favorite mountain cabin high in the trees. I left him there, snoring in front of a cheery fire.

Then I fisted my hand in the sleek fall of Nevarre's hair and tugged his head back, making him expose his throat to me. He groaned deeply, his cock jutting up desperately. I sank my fangs into the beckoning arc of his throat, and his immediate release flooding my senses with his pleasure. His blood swept into me like his dark raven, a hot rush of magic and feathers and thick, heavy shadows.

All too quickly, I felt his raven spiraling downward, wings heavy and tired. I licked my marks on his throat and as I lifted my head, Xin was there, shifting a mumbling Blood aside with Daire to make room. The ghostly silver wolf glinted in Xin's eyes, all predator. He'd killed for me tonight, when he'd feared he'd never be able to use his gift again. They'd all killed for me in one way or another.

He lunged for my throat, teeth flashing. I didn't flinch back. Not from him, not from any of them. I knew he'd never hurt me.

His fangs sank deeply into the front of my throat, his jaws gripping my windpipe, though there wasn't much room for his head against me, not with the twins on either side. He could tear my throat out if he wished. So could one of the twins. Instead, they simply held me, their fangs buried in my throat. My blood trickling into their mouths, stirring their appetite for more.

Rik surged up inside me and it was my turn to simply surrender. To give myself over to the rising pleasure inside me. Power flowed up through me into them through our bonds, a rush of moonlight and sparkling diamonds. Distantly, I felt Mehen and Guillaume above us. The dragon gnashed his teeth with fury and flopped aimlessly on the hard floor. He wanted to shift so badly. He wanted to be here. With me. Wallowing in my desire.

I wasn't sure if I could heal a stuffed stomach, but I sent a wave of power to him. Hopefully my magic could work in him somehow. If nothing else, maybe he'd be more comfortable, even if he couldn't shift back yet.

Rik tightened his grip on my waist, powering up harder into me. Climax rushed at me like a massive cliff. I wanted to hold back and make it last, but my own desire swept me closer and closer to the edge. I felt the moment Xin withdrew his fangs so he could drink fully. The twins and Llewellyn immediately mirrored him. Suddenly my head felt like I was going to float away into the clouds, my blood a fountain for these four magnificent men.

"Enough," Rik growled at them. At me. I wasn't sure which.

My feeding Blood immediately released me. He sat up and slid his fingers through my hair, turning my face into the hot curve of his throat. His skin burned against my face. His scent rolled through me. Hot rocks and iron. My blacksmith rock troll. I had to get him a smithy set up in my manor.

He tightened his fingers in my hair and pressed me harder against him. "We'll worry about that later. Right now, I need you to feed, Shara. Sink your fangs in me as you climax, so we can go together."

I wanted to, I really did. But my brain was so fuzzy. And he was so warm and hard and strong. Everything inside me tightened. My heart stuttered a moment, as if my body's electric system was overwhelmed. They pressed closer. My twins against my back. Xin and Rik in front of me. Llewellyn. Their hands anchoring me to this plane, even though my head seemed a million miles away.

"Shara!"

I sank my fangs into Rik's throat ever so slowly. For the first time, I managed to control the bite. I enjoyed the way his skin gave way to me, layer by layer. The muscle underneath felt different. Meatier. Then the vein. The motherlode. His blood filled my mouth and my head exploded. I was gone. My pleasure blasted through our bonds, and I felt my Blood coming with me, even though I hadn't bitten them all. Flying through a midnight storm on massive silent wings, I sought my prey. My thirst burned like a wildfire through my veins. I needed to feed. I needed more. So much more.

I heard hooves. The pounding of a stallion racing to my call.

I lifted my head and Guillaume eased Rik down to lie on the mattress. "Shara," he whispered, pulling me toward him. "I think your alpha has had enough tonight."

"Give her to me," Mehen retorted behind me.

I thought I was mistaken. He'd been unable to shift. The dragon's belly was too full of Skye sibs. Wasn't that what he said? But the hard, demanding tug of his hands was familiar as he yanked me up off Rik and slammed into me.

Bliss. Goddess. He flowed through me like an endless river, deep and dark and yes, dangerous. Staring into his glittering emerald eyes, I thought I should probably be a little concerned. Not afraid, because I could obliterate him with a thought if I needed to. But he'd never had free rein with me before. Rik had always been there to even him out. To even them all out and keep them controlled.

"Dragon..." Guillaume began in a low, warning tone.

"I fucking know what I'm doing," Mehen snarled back. "You can't stop me. You wouldn't dare."

My brain was trying to function on diminished capacity, but my body thought that this was a grand idea. I wasn't afraid of Leviathan. I certainly wasn't afraid of Mehen, the man. I dug my claws into his stomach, puncturing his skin.

Just so I could smell his blood. Such a sweet torment.

"Yes," he hissed. "G can take your back while you ride me."

"No." Guillaume seized me by the waist and pulled me up so quickly that I couldn't react. Mehen snarled and grabbed at my hips, trying to pull me back, but G shifted me around to face him. I smelled Guillaume's blood too. Mehen had shifted enough to use his talons to shred at the Templar knight.

I glared at him. "Why did you interrupt? I was fucking the fucking dragon."

His lips quirked and Mehen's fury settled some with the assurance that I wasn't refusing him. "You remember my size, right, my queen? I thought you'd rather I take the front and let the dragon have your ass."

"Why the fuck didn't you say so?" Mehen grumbled.

I smiled at Guillaume, and the amused grin he gave back told me I was still higher than a kite.

"Not high," he amended as he lay back beneath me. "Too drained. You need to drink deeply from both of us. We're the oldest. We'll get you back on your feet quicker than the others."

I licked my lips as he lifted me into position. "I intend to drink you all."

He started to push into me and my breath caught. He stretched me impossibly wide. Having him inside me at the same time as Mehen was going to be incredible torture.

"I can't fucking wait," Mehen whispered against my ear.

Yeah. Me neither.

Though I didn't think I managed to say that aloud.

9

GUILLAUME

I'd had the pleasure—and torment—of fucking many a queen in my day, many only at my former queen's orders, even while I dreaded the order of execution that would soon follow. Desideria loved to torture me by sending me in to play with the queen of a nest, only to order me to execute them all.

Shara fucking Isador wiped those memories from my mind. The sounds she made as she slid down on my cock almost made me spill before she could take me all the way inside her. She gripped me so tightly that I breathed hard and gritted my teeth, fighting back my need. I wanted to rut on her like a savage stallion lost in a mating frenzy.

"Yes," she settled on my groin with one last excruciating

twist of her hips that made sweat break out all over my body. "Please do."

"Do what?" Mehen asked as he moved over her back.

"He was thinking about rutting."

"Sounds good to me." He gave her more of his weight, pressing her down closer to me. Eyes blazing with hunger, she lunged toward my throat, but Mehen grabbed a handful of her hair and kept her back. "Not yet, Shara. If you bite him now, you won't have the pleasure of us both inside you."

"Bite me, my queen," Xin offered his throat, sliding closer on his knees.

She tried to lunge for him too, but Mehen kept her head pinned back against his shoulder. "You come to her, wolf."

I glared at Mehen, but he ignored me. Not that I was surprised. I didn't like to see him manhandling our queen in any way, although at the moment, she didn't seem to mind. It was a game, so far. If he wanted to dictate who and how she fed, it was up to her to tell him to go fuck himself. I had no doubt she would, when she tired of the game. Part of me had to admit I was interested to see how far she'd let him push.

And even more, I wanted to see what she'd do to him when she'd had enough of his commandeering bullshit.

Xin slid closer to us, leaning down with an elbow on my chest so he could offer his throat.

"Slowly," Mehen whispered with a glint of malice in his eyes.

Xin didn't bother with a response, but immediately pressed his throat to our queen's mouth. Mehen's hiss of displeasure was almost lost beneath Xin's shout of release. She jammed fangs deeply into him. If those fucking fangs got any larger, they'd protrude out the back of our throats when she fed.

Not that we'd care.

Her thirst. Goddess. I'd never seen a queen drink like she did. Her capacity was astounding, not just physically, but magically. She'd already managed to drain four Blood, including her alpha, to unconsciousness. Four large, able-bodied men with gallons of blood apiece. Granted, she hadn't drained them completely dry, but still. That was no small amount of blood. Where the fuck was she putting it?

I placed my palm on her stomach, trying to feel for any distention or pain, but she seemed fine. Certainly nowhere close to the misery the dragon had been in after chowing down on so many hapless sibs. I could feel her period blood coating my dick like liquid fire. No wonder I had so little control. I had the crazy thought that maybe her body took our blood and immediately bled it back out.

And no wonder the dragon had wanted to be inside her too. We all wanted to feel that precious blood scorching our dicks with her need. Our queen bred. We would service her as long as we could stay conscious. It was our instinct, even if she wasn't truly trying to conceive.

She pushed Xin away and licked her lips, her long, brutal fangs exposed. I swear, they got fucking bigger every time she fed on one of us.

"Almost as intimidating as that big dick of yours, huh, knight?" Mehen said with a smirk. "You said you wanted to spare the gryphon, so there's only two other Blood left to feed you, Shara. Do you want them now, or after you've had a taste of us?"

She turned her head and reached out toward the twins, drawing them both closer. "Touch me," she whispered. "While I hurt him."

I wasn't sure what she meant, but Tlacel smoothed his palms over her skin reverently, tracing the curves and hollows of her body. He lifted each breast to his mouth for a gentle kiss. She sighed softly and shoved her fingers deeply into Itztli's chest.

Even the dragon hissed with shock. He leaned back and pulled her with him to survey the damage she'd done to the Blood.

Itztli braced with a threatening growl that rolled from his chest. His shoulders bunched, his hair crackling up along his scalp like a ruff. "You would deny me the pain she's willing to give?"

I hadn't realized that Itztli was a masochist. Not really. She'd fucked him and Tlacel both a few times since she'd claimed them in Mexico, and I couldn't remember anything unusual about those sessions. But the memory of how she'd sacrificed him on the tree in Zaniyah's nest should have warned me. It should have warned us all.

Our queen was nothing but generous with her desire, and above all, consensual. She never wanted to do anything to any of us that we weren't into, no matter how hard her thirst and desire rode her. She'd never done anything to one of us that we didn't desperately want and would gladly beg her to give.

So, if Shara hurt Itztli, even seriously, it was only because that's what he truly wanted.

Mehen shrugged and loosened his grip on her hair. "It's your skin."

"No knives," she whispered, looking back at me. "Don't let me use a knife on him. Not unless Rik is awake and able to make sure we all stay in control."

"As you wish, my queen."

She looked back at Itztli. "The harder he fucks me, the more I'll hurt you."

Itztli growled like a rabid dog. "Then fuck her hard, knight."

10

SHARA

I'd fed enough that at least my head wasn't trying to float away, but now I felt buzzed, as if I'd thrown back a dozen shots of tequila. So much blood burned in my body, blending together like the finest wines mixed by a world-famous sommelier.

I had a few more Blood to savor, and then I'd be done. I'd be out. The rest of my Blood were still unconscious or weakened. The nagging worry whispered in the back of my mind that they wouldn't be enough.

I needed more. I needed more Blood.

I still had to face Ra. I still had to deal with the Triune.

And while I loved my ten Blood dearly...

I needed more, so I didn't drain them too much.

Itztli groaned roughly, drawing my attention back to him.

My fingernails glistened like silver daggers. I wasn't entirely sure how I'd done it. They weren't the winged jaguar's claws, nor the wyvern's. My stomach quivered at the thought there might be some other massive creature ready to crawl out of me.

I didn't want to hurt or kill anyone again. When the cobra had come to me the first time, I'd killed Rik. Sometimes when Daire looked at me, I still felt his horror at what I'd done.

Itztli pressed against my nails and dragged himself back and forth, letting me tear deep furrows into his flesh.

The scent of his blood fanned the fires of my hunger, but I sank my fangs into Tlacel first. The green jungles of his homeland filled me. Lush towering trees, thick undergrowth, large golden eyes flashing in the murk. The elegant swipe of wings as his feathered serpent brushed through my soul. They did everything together. It made me wish I could figure out how to get a fang in each of them at the same time.

"You did," Itztli rasped, shaking with release.

I rolled my eyes to the side, surprised to feel his pleasure pouring through the bonds. His come splattered me along with his brother's. A hot intoxicating mixture that my skin readily gulped up as eagerly as I drank their blood.

And I was drinking their blood. Both of them. I could taste Itztli's dark, spicy chocolate and smelled the warm, comforting scent of his black dog. But how...?

"Your fingers." He shook against me, each spasm of his body driving my fingernails harder into his skin. Deeper. He'd impaled himself on my silvered nails, and I could definitely taste his blood flooding my system.

"How is this possible?" Afraid, I looked wildly for Rik, and found him still out cold, one big arm slung over his head. Daire and Nevarre were tumbled in a heap beside the bed on the floor. Ezra sat on the floor beside them and managed to lift his head a bit, but he moaned and dropped his chin back down to his chest. Xin had fallen on the other side of Tlacel.

My Blood, brought down one by one.

By me.

And now I had this terrible power to grapple with. It wasn't bad enough that I had gigantic fangs that gave even Guillaume pause, but now I also had fucking *straws* for fingers?

It was..

I couldn't...

"Shara." Llewellyn's graveled voice broke through my panic. He cupped my cheek. Had I fed on him already? I couldn't remember. "An early Isador queen had this gift. I'm sure I read about it in the journals somewhere. It's not unexpected that you, as the last living heir, would gain some of these lost abilities. You have a great hunger. Your body is adapting to allow you to feed better and quicker."

I gulped and almost choked. I didn't even remember that I still had fangs in Tlacel. Despite my shock, I was still drinking from him, and his brother. My thirst wouldn't let them go yet.

"Where is she putting so much fucking blood?" Guillaume asked. "I don't see how she can even hold so much. Not after what Mehen went through tonight."

"Again, this is only something I read in the journals once. Ages ago, it seems. But I'm sure I read that some queens can transform blood into pure energy and store it. It happens so automatically that you don't even realize you're doing it."

:Storing it where?: I asked, trying not to freak out. I gave a tug on my alpha's bond, even though he was still unconscious. Maybe he'd wake up quicker if he felt my urgency.

"You have reserves. They're inside you somewhere. As your power has grown, your body has been trying to fill and establish those reserves. It's like you have three or four gas tanks to fill."

Guillaume grunted in agreement. "That could explain her hunger and her tiredness. When her reserves are spent, she blasts through us all like kindling."

Itztli collapsed first, falling back against Rik's legs. I'd gouged deep grooves across his chest.

Tlacel fell back and Llewellyn eased him off to the floor, so he could join us.

Three Blood remained. Really, two, because I couldn't risk hurting Llewellyn so quickly after he'd been tortured.

Hunger raged inside me like a thousand vicious, starving wolves howling at the moon as they charged after a wounded deer.

Mehen snagged my left hand and lifted it back over my shoulder. His tongue touched my nails and he sucked in a breath. "They're nice and sharp. Put these beauties in me, Shara."

11

SHARA

Fucking straws. I had straws in my hands. Both hands? I wasn't sure. I jerked my hand up off Guillaume's chest before I started feeding on him before we were ready.

Goddess. I had no idea that this was possible.

At least he didn't seem to be worried. Not if his erection was any indication. He still filled me almost to the point of pain, where on one hand, I instinctively wanted to lift up away from him to gain some space, but on the other, I wanted to shove him deeper and grind against him with delicious agony. Mehen still hadn't pushed into me yet, or I probably wouldn't be able to think about this strange new revelation. Let alone worry about what would happen if I drank from all my Blood and still needed more.

The more I fed, the more I wanted. It was like a vicious addiction, only instead of a single snort of cocaine, I needed a dump-truck load to satisfy the craving.

Llewellyn's eyes started to spin with fireworks. "Sometimes sex can help slake your hunger for blood."

Mehen snorted. "Not our queen. She's had us all before and still wanted more."

I swallowed hard, my cheeks suddenly burning with embarrassment. He made me sound like... like...

An insatiable vampire with a thirst for blood and sex.

Exactly what I was.

"Bring it the fuck on, Shara," Mehen growled as he slid his palm between my legs. He lifted me up off Guillaume a little, enough to gather my blood with his fingers. He smeared it like lube, only with this lube, he licked his fingers as he started to push inside me. "I'm going to fuck your ass so hard that you won't be able to move, much less still ache for another dick."

"Promise?" I retorted back at him. "Because right now, I only see three dicks and I don't think that's going to be enough."

"Watch me."

Despite his crude words, he took his time sliding into me, slowly deepening his thrusts. I'd taken several of my Blood anally before, but he wasn't a small man. Combined with Guillaume's size, I was stuffed so full I couldn't seem to get my lungs to work.

Eyes heavy-lidded, Guillaume dipped his fingers between my thighs too, brushing his thumb over my clit in the process. I twitched and groaned, unable to bear the intense sensation. Not with them both inside me.

"Do it again," Mehen said roughly, his breath hot against my neck.

I groaned again but I didn't deny them. It felt great. Even though I half-dreaded it, too.

Guillaume rubbed his thumb against me and I came apart. I screamed. I shook. I clawed. I smelled their blood, and I knew I was hurting them. I had to be. These fucking crazy nails...

Panting, I tried to calm the raging desire consuming me. Before it was too late. Before I seriously hurt someone. Rik wasn't awake to protect them.

Blinking furiously, I forced my eyes open. Mehen had his forearm locked around my throat, pinning me back against him so I couldn't bite anyone and end the delicious torment. Guillaume held my gaze as he licked his fingers.

"Do you honestly think you could injure the headless knight or Leviathan, king of the depths?" Mehen's fangs skated across my skin teasingly. "I've slaughtered and eaten dozens of queens in my lifetime. So has G. Unleash your darkest desires on us, Shara, because you couldn't kill us if you tried."

"You wouldn't stop me." The pressure on my throat made my words rough. "You'd let me do anything to you, and then I'd regret it later."

"You could bite his dick off and heal it." Guillaume chuckled, but his eyes were dark and heavy with all the things he'd seen and done in the centuries of his life. He didn't have to tell me how many queens he'd killed over the years. I could see the weight of their blood in his eyes. "You could tear my head off, and I'll just grow it back. What's the problem?"

"But I don't want to hurt you. I don't want to be that kind of queen."

Guillaume's gaze slid to the man behind me. "I think more of a demonstration is in order."

He didn't wait for Mehen's response but pressed his fingers against my clit again. Timing it perfectly, Mehen shoved deeper, his mighty body flexing against me. Guillaume tipped his hips up. Just a fraction of an inch. And everything inside me exploded again.

When I could hear again, I heard Llewellyn's heavy breathing nearby. "I'd sell my soul back to Keisha Skye for a taste. Shara. Please. May I?"

I appreciated the fact that he asked first, but I was beyond words. I tried to nod, but with Mehen's grip on me, I wasn't sure if they understood. Instead, I reached for Llewellyn's bond. His gleamed more golden than my other Blood bonds, so he was easy to find. I sank into his bond, letting his feathers and fur brush through my body.

Groaning roughly, he dropped down on his stomach beside us, so he could wedge his head in between my body and Guillaume's. I had a moment to worry that my knight may not care for another man's mouth so close to his dick, but then he hoisted me up enough to give the other man better access, drawing all that incredible girth along my nerve endings still screaming with sensation.

I hung there, half impaled on his massive dick, pinned against Mehen, still thick and deep in my ass, while my newest

Blood licked the blood dripping from my body to coat G's cock. And I came again. And again. They didn't have to thrust an inch.

I swear Llewellyn's tongue was abnormally long and wickedly agile. He did things with his tongue that even Daire couldn't do, and he didn't hesitate to lick anything he could get his mouth on. I could feel him teasing Mehen's cock in my ass. Guillaume's base and the inches bared by lifting me off his groin. My blood sizzled in them. Volatile. Destructive. Over-whelming.

They should have pinned my hands. They should have tied me up and gagged me. Maybe then I wouldn't have shoved those sharp nails back into Mehen's side, at the same time that I gouged Guillaume in the throat. Their blood bubbled up from the wounds, flooding me with more power.

So much fucking power. A mortal shouldn't have this kind of power at her disposal.

:Who told you we were mortal?: Llewellyn said in my head. *:My queen is a fucking goddess.:*

Mehen plunged against me, pushing me up with his thrust so Llewellyn could keep tormenting us all with his tongue. I licked my face, tasting Guillaume's blood. The wounds I'd made fountained blood all over me and the bed. Buried inside his throat, my strange nails sucked up blood directly from the source. I could feel the hot, wet flesh of his body around my fingertips.

:You're inside me,: Guillaume whispered in our bond. *:As I'm inside you. Fuck me, Shara. Fuck us both. Suck us down and use us. That's why we're here. That's why we exist. For you, and you alone.:*

Their hearts thundered in my head. Guillaume's warhorse reared and released a strident challenge. Leviathan swooped and dipped inside me, winding tighter into the death spiral he'd used to try and kill us both. Llewellyn's gryphon shrieked, and flames dripped from his massive paws as he padded through my mind.

Strong. Fierce. Unafraid. Even as I fucked them to death.

RIK

My vision was too fuzzy to make sense of the scene unfolding just feet away. I blinked and forced my eyes to focus. Shara. Goddess. She was coated in blood, like she'd slit someone's throat.

Her fangs glistened, bared ivory curves that could definitely tear a Blood's throat out if she chose, but something told me that wasn't the cause of so much blood.

Mehen roared with release, heaving them both backwards in a vicious arch. I could clearly see Guillaume's big dick inside her, while Llewellyn licked them both. She jammed her left hand back harder and the dragon's roar went up another notch. His exquisite pain made me suck in a hard breath, though it was mixed with overwhelming pleasure, too.

"Shara," Guillaume gurgled. "Finish me."

I scrambled up to my knees, but I didn't interfere. Not yet. I couldn't imagine her being able to seriously injure the headless knight, even in the throes of her worst thirst.

Mehen slumped down over her, a heavy weight that seemed to piss her off. She gave a sharp tug with her left hand and effortlessly dumped him off to the side. Her hand was coated in blood and squelched as she pulled her fingers free of him.

At first, I thought she carried several of G's silver blades. They weren't talons, but definitely gleamed like metal. Her head fell back as she settled deeper on his groin. Llewellyn came up for air and saw me alert.

"You don't even know what you fucking have, do you?" His face tightened, his eyes blazing completely red-gold. "I served her mother for centuries and never once tasted her menses."

I didn't think he was angry with me, not exactly. How could I have anything to do with Shara's miraculous ability to have her monthly period? And if he thought even her alpha could demand that she stay in the nest while she bred and hide from her many duties, then he could be the next one to attempt such an order. I'd sit back with glee and watch her rip *his* throat out.

Shara panted, her breath catching on a groan. "Why not?"

Llewellyn turned back to her, curling around her hips so he could work his tongue back down to her clit. :*Because she couldn't. She never bred. Not once. This gift is entirely yours, my queen. Goddess help me, I'll lick every drop that your alpha doesn't take for himself.*:

"Hey," Daire mumbled, turning over in a reckless sprawl of limbs and hair. "That's my job."

:*Bite me, asshole,*: Llewellyn retorted in the bond.

:*Gladly, birdbrain.*:

Shara's head fell back on a deep, guttural cry. She kept her right hand on Guillaume's throat. I assumed she was trying to control whatever wound she'd dealt him.

It didn't dawn on me that she was feeding from the wounds until he quaked with release, and then slumped. Drained.

Dead to the world.

"G," she whispered, her voice breaking. "Rik, I think I killed him."

I came to her, then, enfolding her against my chest, though Llewellyn's head remained between her thighs. "You forget who he is, my queen."

"Please," she sobbed against my neck. "Help him."

I reached down to check his pulse despite the five jagged, deep punctures in his throat. "He's fine. Sluggish and weak, but he has a pulse. He's no worse off than me or Daire were earlier."

Cautiously, she lifted her head. "He's alright?"

G stirred, his eyes fluttering as he sensed her worry. "Fine," he mumbled. "Sleepy."

"You've seen us heal before," I reminded her as I lifted her fingers closer. "If anyone can walk, flip the lights on."

Llewellyn ran his mouth down the full length of her slit, making her twitch and groan in my arms. Then he shoved up out of bed and stomped over to the wall to hit the light switch.

I turned Shara's hand over and examined the silver tips of her nails. They were two inches long, wickedly sharp, with tiny holes near the tapered ends. "I've never seen such a wonder before."

She tugged on her hand self-consciously, but I didn't release her. "They suck up the blood somehow."

I raised her index finger and sucked the tip into my mouth, running my tongue all over the gleaming nail to clean it. "I've heard that some of our kind can suck blood through their fangs too, but this is much more efficient."

Her mouth sagged open a moment. "Efficiency? That's what you care about when I've decimated my entire Blood?"

"Not quite," Llewellyn retorted as he plopped back down on the mattress beside us. "You didn't feed on me, Shara."

He started to lean back down toward her pussy and the tantalizing blood, but she stopped him with her other hand on his chest, mindful of her nails. "You need time to heal first before I drain you like I did them."

"Not with this blood powering me. Don't you feel the difference in me? After tasting you earlier, I was strong, yes. But now, I'm a fucking unstoppable beast."

She curled her fingers slightly, deliberately digging the silver tips into his skin. "I know you were my mother's alpha, but Rik is mine. I won't have any challenges to his authority. Do you understand?"

He leaned closer, piercing his skin on those sharp tips. Not deeply, but enough that his blood scented the air. "I understand, my queen. He got to you first. It's his right. But you can't fault me for wishing that I could have flown out from Skye Tower and searched for you myself."

Her eyes glittered and the fine hairs on my arms prickled. Her power sparked around her like static electricity. "You didn't even know that I existed."

"I did. I knew. I couldn't feel you, not in Skye's nest, but I knew you were loose on the world somewhere. It was the only thing that kept me sane."

"How?" She whispered, her eyelids fluttering. "How did you know?"

In her bond, I felt the first taste of his blood hitting her system. Her fingers burned and pulsed, drawing fresh blood up those long nails to feed her magic. She could taste his fur on her tongue, flavored with the scent of supple leather, even though his blood wasn't in her mouth.

Llewellyn leaned closer, pushing her nails deeper, and pressed his forehead to hers. "Because an Isador queen is always successful in what she sets out to do."

SHARA

I stood outside in the street. It took me a moment to realize that I was dreaming. The streets of Manhattan were never completely empty like this. Streetlights lined the road outside the Isador house, but they didn't interfere with the glorious sprinkling of stars across the dark sky. No moon tonight. No clouds. I wasn't sure what that meant, if it meant anything at all.

I hadn't dreamed since Snake Mountain. Just remembering how I'd met Coatlicue and gained the glittering red serpent around my throat made me shiver. I hoped it wasn't that kind of dream. Not now. I already had too much to do, and goddess help me, I couldn't bear to lose anyone else. I already feared I wouldn't be able to endure such a loss.

The sky brightened far off in the distance. A red glow slowly approached. It looked like a wildfire, although I was pretty sure the Atlantic Ocean lay in that direction. Something was coming to me from the east over hundreds of miles of water.

Light wasn't necessarily a good thing with the sun god gunning for me, but I wasn't worried enough to try and wake myself up. The reddish glow was warm and inviting. As it neared, I could see flickering blue and white flames too. It burned too brightly for me to tell what was inside the blaze, but the ground thudded heavily as it landed. It was big. Maybe not as big as Leviathan, but definitely something powerful.

I watched as the flames slowly died. For a moment, a massive red-gold bird with sweeping wings stood before me. A phoenix. So beautiful.

The flames banked, leaving behind a woman.

Tall and statuesque, the woman strode toward me confidently. Her ebony skin gleamed in the soft lamplight. Her hair swept down around to her waist, from black near her scalp to deep crimson and then brilliant orange-red fire. The long strands flowed around her shoulders like flickering flames, catching and reflecting the light. She wore black leather from head to toe with a silver chainmail chest piece over the top. Two sword hilts crossed on her back, rising over either shoulder.

She made no move to reach for her weapons. Her dark eyes sparked like the deepest blue of a gas flame as she dropped to one knee before me.

"My queen, I come in answer to your call."

Slowly, I reached out toward her cheek, but I paused and dropped my hand. I didn't want to injure her with the silver tips. "What's your name?"

"Vivian." She winced and dropped forward to her hands and knees, her glorious hair dragging on the ground. "You don't want me, then. It's hard to find a queen willing to take on a woman as Blood. Only Keisha Skye made a habit of calling female Blood, and I swore never to fall into her hands. I'd burn myself up in a fireball before I'd call that woman my queen."

"Not wanting to serve Keisha Skye is definitely a bonus. She's dead anyway."

"Yes, I know. You killed her, so they say."

"Who says?"

She only bowed lower, dropping her face so low she was almost touching the ground. "I have no interest in your males. I swore long ago to gut the next man who laid a finger on me, and I meant it."

I laughed softly. "That's not a problem, then. I'm a jealous queen. I don't want any other woman touching my Blood."

She threw her head back so suddenly that her hair seemed to explode around her. Her eyes flickered with flames. "Don't tease me, Your Majesty. I can't bear it."

My nose caught her scent and my fangs pulsed in my jaw. She smelled like burning cinnamon and herbs. Pungent but not unpleasant. I opened my mouth, letting my fangs descend. "Maybe I'll be the one to scare you away. My hunger is immense. Are you so sure you want to swear to me?"

She closed her eyes and a faint tremor rocked her shoulders. Then she launched at me, burying her face against my stomach. "Please, please, don't send me away. You don't even have to touch me much. Just enough to make the Blood bond final, and the occasional feeding to keep my flames alive."

Gently, I used the tip of my index finger to lift her face up to me. "Mayte."

Her eyes narrowed, her brow wrinkling with confusion. But suddenly my first queen sibling, Mayte Zaniyah, stood beside me, looking around her with interest.

"Is this where you are, my queen? Oh." She noted the woman on the ground at my feet and gave me a sultry look that made my breasts ache. "Is this number ten?"

"Eleven. She doesn't believe that I would want to touch a female Blood."

Mayte's lips quirked and a dimple appeared in her cheek as she sidled closer. "Surely not, my queen. Why would you want a woman when you have ten strapping men at your beck and call?"

She leaned in and pressed her lips to mine. So soft. Goddess. I wanted to wallow in her warm scent of flowers.

With a sigh, she leaned against me, tucking her face against my throat. "I'm so glad you're safe. I felt..." She shuddered, squeezing me tighter. "I can't imagine how bad it was for you and Rik."

I swallowed the tears that wanted to fall again. "He's perfectly fine now. I'm just..." I couldn't say it. My throat refused to utter the words that one of them would die. Or Mayte herself. Or Gina...

"I know," Mayte whispered softly.

The woman on her knees made a small noise that drew my attention back to her face. I thought to tease her a bit longer, but the abject longing on her face pushed me to action. I held out my hand, bending my fingers to show the silver tips. "I gained these tonight and severely injured several of my Blood while I was feeding. I didn't want to hurt you. I'm still getting used to them."

"Oh," she whispered. "So you don't... You wouldn't..."

I cupped her cheek and pressed the tips against her, just enough to lightly dimple the skin so she could feel how sharp and vicious they were. "When you're here, I'll accept your bond, my Blood."

"I'm here, my queen."

I sat up sharply, my senses immediately reaching out into the night. Rik jerked awake from a light dose. "What is it?"

"I've called a new Blood."

"Good. We could use the help."

My lips quirked, and I couldn't resist teasing him a little. "I hope you like her."

His eyebrows rose but all he said was, "If you like her, then I will too."

"I do. She's a phoenix." His eyes tightened slightly, making me ask, "What?"

"The phoenix is always associated with the sun."

I blew out a sigh. "Shit. I didn't sense anything off about her."

He settled back against the headboard and drew me against him. The rest of my Blood lay tumbled on and around the bed like we'd just had a drunken orgy. Which, yeah, we had, pretty much, though all we'd drunk was blood. That was some powerful shit.

"I wish at least one of us was fit enough to act as sentry."

Someone tapped lightly at the door. "Your Majesty?" Winston called softly. "You have a visitor. She's adamant that she needs to see you."

"Thank you, Winston. Vivian, come in."

Shaking his head, Rik let out a grunt of disgust. "That's why I will never trust anyone not Blood with your safety. Winston means well, but he should never have allowed a stranger into your house."

The door opened and the woman from my dream stepped into the bedroom. She looked the same, though her hair didn't seem to be living flames. She shot a hard look at Rik that caught me by surprise. "Some alpha you are. She doesn't even have a nest."

Rik's voice rumbled so low that my bones vibrated. "As you see, all her Blood are here. We'll die to the man to keep her safe, so there's no need for a guard at the door."

"I'll die to the woman too."

He relaxed against me and gave her a nod. "Then you're welcome, Blood. Our queen needs you desperately."

She stepped to the edge of the bed, weaving her way carefully around downed Blood. "I don't do men. Not even alphas."

He snorted. "Good. I don't do women, other than my queen."

She searched my face, her eyes softening with reverence. "I'd rather not do any women but our queen, either, but if you order me to fuck one of your queen sibs, I will."

I nudged Daire with my foot to get him to move aside. Even in a heavy sleep, his chest vibrated with a low humming purr that deepened a moment as he shifted to his other side. I held my hand out to her. "In House Isador, no one is ordered to fuck anyone. Not even me."

She planted a knee on the mattress and took my hand. Her grip was firm, her palms calloused from wielding the swords on her back. "You should know that Ra is my father. My full name is Vivian Helios, but I changed my name to Smoak when my power emerged."

"Would you rather I call you Smoak then?"

Eyes round, she cast a quick glance at Rik as if to say, *"is she for real?"* "My queen can call me whatever the fuck she wants. You don't care that Ra sired me?"

"When the Great One sends me a Blood, who am I to question Her gifts?"

Rik wasn't so easily persuaded. "Do you have any ties to him that we need to worry about? Have you taken his blood recently?"

She grimaced as if he'd rubbed her nose in something foul. "Not since my cursed birth. He doesn't give his blood to anyone, especially his children. He sired me by rape, and I haven't even seen him for nearly five hundred years. Fuck Ra. I'll swear my life to House Isador in a heartbeat. If you manage to eliminate his taint on this earth, then I'll fucking worship the ground you walk on."

"I already do," Rik said mildly. "We all do."

Vivian let out a long, soft breath that tugged on my heart-strings. "I can see that. I don't know why it wouldn't be the same for me, as long as you and I come to an understanding, alpha."

"I understand you perfectly, even before you taste our queen's blood." She looked at him doubtfully, so he held up his hand and ticked off each statement. "Even if our queen takes another woman to her bed, she has asked us not to touch anyone but her. So there's no reason for you to worry about any of us so much as laying a finger on you. Our queen wants you, and what our queen wants, she receives. I'm alpha and I never leave our queen's side unless she orders it. As long as you don't challenge me, we're good. Any other questions?"

Vivian turned back to me, her eyes blazing bluer, as if someone had turned up the flame inside her. "You want me, my queen?"

I tugged her closer, inhaling her scent. "You smell so good. Different. I recognize the cinnamon, but what else is it?"

"Myrrh. According to legend, the phoenix makes a nest of these herbs and then dies in the raging fires to be reborn every thousand years."

I clenched my jaws, fighting down the instant pain, regret, and desperate hope that burned through me as brightly as her flames. Coatlicue required a life. If She took Vivian's life, so she could be reborn... Maybe my other Blood would be spared.

Guilt twisted my heart into knots. I didn't want to accept another Blood, only to see her die. It wasn't fair to her. To any of us.

She must have read the turmoil and regret in my eyes. The chiseled planes of her face hardened, so coldly gorgeous despite the blazing fires in her eyes. "I'll die for you. Gladly. Especially if it's to stop Ra."

"Because fuck Ra." Daire sat up, delightfully mussed with a sleepy, sexy look heating his gaze. "Hey, Nevarre, another bird for you to play with."

"Everybody out of the bed," Rik ordered, giving a snoring Mehen a shove to wake him up. "Our queen has some serious shit to do and she doesn't need helpers for this one."

Lightly, I ran my other hand up her arm, feeling her strength. She was built like Llewellyn, though not as tall. Long legs, slim hips, and a muscular physique that spoke of her training with the swords she carried. There wasn't anything delicate or soft about her. Even her breasts looked imposingly hard, though maybe that was the chainmail.

Her eyes were ice-cold or blazing hot—I wasn't sure which.

She leaned down slightly, and her vibrant hair slipped over her shoulder to tumble onto my lap. My eyes flared wide at the sensation of liquid fire moving over me, though it didn't burn. Tipping her head to the side, she offered me her throat.

I wasn't sure if my silver-tipped nails would cause her to orgasm the same way as my bite. Itztli had come hard with my nails planted in his chest, but I suspected that had to do more with the pain than the way I was feeding. "Do you—"

"Please," Vivian said roughly, her breathing loud and ragged. "Please, take me."

I leaned closer and brushed my mouth over her skin above the high neck of her leathers. "My bite will make you come, though we can easily do this other ways, too."

"Bite me hard, my queen."

13

VIVIAN

Desperation burned in me hotter than the deepest pit of hell.

Please, take me, as far as you can. Before it's too late. Before you change your mind. Before you realize...

Her fangs sank into my throat and my spine bowed. White-hot sheets of pure light blasted through me. Every muscle in my body spasmed and I thrashed against her. My cunt clenched desperately in a vicious ache of need. I wanted her pleasure.

Her blood.

Her scent.

Burning, blowing sands of the desert, softened with night-blooming jasmine. Pure, sweet water. Crystal moonlight. A balm to the punishing, blistering fires that raged inside me. She pressed her lush body closer, an oasis of touch and welcome that I'd never dreamed possible. She lay back on the pillows and drew me with her, her mouth locked to my throat.

My queen. On her back. Taking the lesser position. A queen of such power.

Ra must be thrilled.

It's too late, I told myself as she cupped the back of my head and pulled me into the cradle of her thighs. I couldn't turn back now. All I could do was hope that she could spring the trap.

I felt the moment she realized something was wrong with my blood. The pleasant heat curling through her burned a little too hot. A little too painful.

The alpha growled, baring his teeth at me. "What did you do to her?"

I closed my eyes, praying. *Please, goddess. Great One, whoever you are. Please. Help her be the one to free me.*

My flames licked through her body, burning hotter every moment, fueled by her own power. And oh, this queen had so much power to burn. Smoak screeched with glee inside me, reveling in the scorching heat.

Her alpha seized the harness holding my weapons and tried to haul me up off her. She refused to let me go, though she did lift her mouth from my throat.

"Rik." Her voice rasped with pain. "I've got this."

I didn't want the rest to happen. I'd seen it so many times. A queen, burned from the inside out. A nightmare of screaming. Blackened flesh. Ash. Charred bones crumbling to dust. While Ra whispered in my head, *"Burn the witches. Every last one of them."*

Her Blood roared and thumped and slammed around us,

unable to help her. Forced to watch as she suffered, their furious fear fanned the flames inside her.

"Shara!" The door slammed open and a woman cried out, though I didn't know who it was. "Goddess, no," she moaned, her voice breaking. "It's too late."

Shara. At least I knew her name, now.

The alpha jerked on me harder and I felt a rush of power sweep by me like I was a gnat. Her Blood stilled immediately, unable to act against her will.

"I've got this," she repeated. Calmly. While she burned.

I tried to ignore the way her eyes clenched shut with pain. The blood that welled from her lips, spilling down her chin. My blood, mixed with hers. She'd gnashed her own lips with the biggest fangs I'd ever seen.

Her hand tightened on my head and she pulled me down into a kiss. Her blood smeared on my lips. Intoxicating. So fucking powerful. I sucked her bottom lip into my mouth and fed through the tears she'd made in her own flesh. It probably hurt her, but I couldn't find it in me to care. Not with the wealth of power flooding my system.

I'd never tasted a queen's blood before. They always died before they had a chance to fully bond me. Besides, I didn't have fangs. They would have been useless in me. My sole purpose was to destroy any queen who attempted to claim me.

Her blood. I never dreamed a queen would taste so good. I couldn't get enough of her. Even Smoak was shaken by the taste of her, pausing from her cackling fury to lap up the queen's offering. A queen's sacrifice.

The eternal flames inside me dimmed. Flickered. Banked to

a low roar. And then went out like a candle blasted with a gust of winter wind.

I quivered, my mouth falling open. Blood dripped from my gaping lips back onto Shara. She hummed softly and licked the blood from her chin.

She fucking *hummed*.

Frozen, I blinked. Waiting for Smoak to come pouring back in rage and hellfire. But she curled up and dropped off to sleep, basking in our queen's blood.

Fucking phoenix. Asleep.

I couldn't even. I didn't know.

Shara laughed softly. "There. That's better, isn't it?"

"She hurt you," the alpha growled, but he released the harness and allowed me to drop back against her.

She shrugged and combed her fingers through my hair. "Love hurts sometimes, doesn't it, Vivian?"

"You…" My voice cracked and I paused, breathing hard. No, that wasn't my voice cracking. It was my ribcage. My heart. Into a thousand pieces. "How?"

"I could see the flames inside you as they poured into me. Magic didn't douse the flames, so I used the next best thing."

"Blood."

She nodded, wincing a little. I felt the pain inside her like a raw open wound tearing muscles apart inside me. Thousands of nerves screamed throughout my body, making me groan like I was dying. I'd hurt her. Terribly. A Blood was never to hurt the queen.

"I'm going to need to feed from you to heal this completely, though I should warn you, first. That's why all my Blood were out when you arrived."

She'd fed on them *all*? Until they'd passed out? My mouth fell open again with awe. "I thought they were asleep."

One of the others made a low sound of disgust. "Blood never sleep, unless we've fucked ourselves into oblivion."

"Or our queen has drained us to unconsciousness," another said.

"Or both," one man said with a deep, rumbling purr in his voice.

No wonder the air in here was thick with the scent of sex and musk. Yet she'd still called me. A female Blood with a terrible curse that made me Ra's most prized assassin.

Her cheeks turned a soft, delicate pink. "I called you because I need more blood. My thirst hasn't been quenched tonight despite their best efforts."

"I should take this new Blood outside and pound her into a bloody smear on the asphalt for what she did to you." The alpha's voice rumbled with fury. "The risk, Shara. We can't lose you."

The other woman sat heavily beside us on the mattress. She wore an old-fashioned long, white nightgown and cap. Breathing hard, she fanned her face and swayed like she was going to pass out. "I told you, Shara. I need to be close. If I'd been here, I could have told you the probabilities that you'd die if you attempted to take this Blood were beyond scary."

Shara huffed out a laugh. "Then I'm glad you weren't here to tell me how bad the odds were. I had no choice. Isis sent her." Tightening her thighs around me, she gave me a sultry look of invitation. "I sprang Ra's trap. Now I'm going to use his own weapon against him."

SHARA

My intestines felt like they'd been scorched with a blowtorch, but for her, it was worth it.

Her hair flowed down around us like a silk curtain, fragrant and almost hot to the touch, a testament to the flames burning inside her. Rik's bond still raged like an angry forge. He wouldn't soon forget how quickly her gift had become deadly. Her memory of charred queens flickered through my mind, but I firmly pushed them away. She had enough of my blood, now, that I could feel her sincerity. Her horror. She hadn't been a willing party to the death of those queens.

"Why don't you take off your weapons, at least."

Her eyes widened but she hastened to obey, scrambling up on her knees between my thighs. I knew the picture I made for her, because I could see myself reflected in her mind. My eyes blazed with hunger, and not just for her blood. My skin gleamed like burnished metal, still lit from within by her fires that were now mine to call. They mingled with my own gift, creating a viciously combustible mix of liquid hellfire.

My fangs had receded a bit, but they were still long enough that I couldn't shut my mouth fully. I ran my tongue over my lips, searching for any lingering blood.

Her gaze dropped down to my breasts, my stomach, and then my pussy, where she sucked in a hard breath. "Goddess! You're fucking *breeding*? Does Ra know?"

"I hope to fuck he doesn't," Rik muttered darkly. "He won't, unless you've warned him somehow."

"I haven't spoken to my sire in hundreds of years. Like I said before—"

"Fuck Ra," Daire called from the other side of the room.

"Yeah. But shit. I mean, my queen, surely you realize how rare this is."

I wasn't prepared for her to slide one of the swords out of its sheath. She pointed the slim, curved blade at Rik's throat. "You're the biggest fucking moron of an alpha to ever answer a queen's call, and one lucky motherfucker that she's still alive. No nest. Out in the open in fucking New York City. Are you mad?"

I started to sit up to settle her down, but Rik gave me a smoldering look. "I've got this, my queen." Then he focused on the newcomer. "I applaud your determination to protect our queen, but you'll soon figure out that Shara fucking Isador does as she wishes. If I tried to stop her from completing her goddess's will, she'd blast me into kingdom come, and rightfully so. No Blood commands his queen, not even her alpha. Certainly not you."

Vivian tightened her grip on the sword, eyes narrowed. The way she held herself, and her confidence in facing off against probably the biggest and strongest Blood she'd ever seen in her life, told me she had to be very skilled with her swords. She truly thought she could beat him, or at least prove her point.

Rik laughed. "Go ahead, Red. I hope you don't like that pretty sword much, because I'll take it from you and break it in half like a twig. Or better yet, I'll sit here, not lift a finger, and watch you shatter it into a thousand pieces on my rock troll's hide."

He shifted just enough to give her a glimpse of the massive stone gift he carried.

Grudgingly, she lowered the sword. "Like I've never heard that before. At least come up with a better nickname for me than the color of my hair."

He scooted a bit further away toward the middle of my huge bed, leaving plenty of room for me and the new Blood. "If you don't hurry up and satisfy our queen's hunger, *Smoak*, I'll take care of her myself."

Vivian leaped into action, quickly unbuckling her harness and tossing her weapons off the side of the bed.

"This is my cue to leave," Carys said as she pushed up her to feet. "For goddess's sake, try not to get into any more trouble tonight, my queen."

I grinned at her. "I'm not making any promises."

Vivian pulled the chain-mail vest over her head and tossed it over her shoulder. It landed with a soft tinkling like chimes on the floor. Her hands stilled on the tight-fitting jacket's zipper. "Did you want me to take everything off? Or just the weapons?"

I looked up at her, listening to her bond. She still didn't quite believe that I'd truly called her. After centuries, she was finally Blood to a queen who fully intended to embrace all that could mean.

"That depends," I said slowly, drinking in the long, lean lines of her body. "On whether you want to fuck or not."

14

SHARA

mused, I watched as she hopped off the bed like it'd suddenly caught on fire. Bending down, she tugged impatiently at the laces of heavy motorcycle boots so she could kick them off and shimmy out of skin-tight pants and thong. Her long red hair hung down around her, swaying with her movements. Almost as mesmerizing as staring into a fire. So gorgeous against her luminous black skin.

Under the leather jacket, she wore a simple crimson tank that hugged her curves. She stripped it off and turned to face me, pausing so I could drink my fill. She'd shaved most of her pussy, leaving just a delicate, trimmed triangle to point the way. Not that I needed any help. Gray scars that looked like old burns covered her midsection, with a few on her arms and thighs. Maybe from her phoenix? Though I didn't think a goddess-given gift would hurt her like that. Some of them were perfectly round, though of varying sizes. It had to have been a hell of a burn to leave that kind of scar, but maybe her last queen hadn't been strong enough to heal her.

"I've never had a queen. Not really. They always died before they could give me their blood and complete the bond. These scars are so old, I don't think even you could heal them."

Old scars. That made me wonder so much about her past. Her childhood.

She averted her face but didn't duck her head. In fact, she stood straighter. Prouder. Though inside her, I felt a brittleness, like a sword that had seen so many battles, that it was close to the point of shattering.

"Growing up Helios is a nightmare that never ends," she whispered hoarsely.

Keeping my touch narrowed to Daire, I asked, :*What do you know about Helios?*:

:*Nothing*,: he replied. :*It's not an Aima House.*:

"Who was your mother?" I asked out loud.

"I don't know. I wasn't allowed to know. I have no idea of my heritage, other than the fires that have burned in me my whole life."

I leaned out enough to snag her hand and pulled her gently to me. She came to my arms readily enough, her piercing eyes locked on my face. "I was made to destroy you. Maybe not you in particular, but queens like you."

I stroked my fingers down her back, learning the texture of her skin. She was so lean and hard. Not like Rik's stone, but like metal. Forged steel, tempered by her phoenix. Her skin felt hot against mine, another testament to her gift. Even in my arms, she didn't relax. Her muscles quivered faintly beneath her skin, ready to leap up into battle at a moment's notice.

She tipped her head to the side, baring the punctures that still dribbled blood down her throat. I definitely wanted more, but I wanted to know her better first. I wanted to understand.

I could feel the rough texture of scars more heavily on her back. I couldn't imagine how bad each mark would have had to be to still be scarred over. I didn't want to hurt her more by pushing her to reveal a painful past, but I needed to know as much as possible. I felt as though there was a secret key inside her that would give me every single thing I needed to defeat the sun god. Her father.

"He's not my father," she retorted, her eyes flashing. "He sired me. That's it. Helios is what he calls his breeding grounds. It's where he takes young Aima queens stolen from their nests. They're raised by…"

She shuddered, her breathing ragged. I kept up the steady, slow circles on her back, letting my touch soothe her.

"Demons, called sunfires. He likes to take the queens as early as possible. Before they can come into their power and protect themselves. Then he and his vizier break them. If they die, the demons feast. If they don't… he tries to sire a child on them. If that fails, then he gives them to the sunfires as prizes."

She buried her face against my throat and I hugged her closer. My stomach quivered with dread. No wonder he'd tried to take Xochitl. The thought of what she would have suffered on the other side of that portal…

I reached for Mayte's bond. *:Keep Xochitl inside your nest at all times until I succeed in killing Ra. It's urgent.:*

I felt her in bed sandwiched between her alpha, Eztli, and her god who'd sired her daughter, Tepeyollotl. By the pleasure simmering in her bond, I'd caught them at a most inopportune time.

:Oops, sorry.:

She let out a husky laugh in my head, her sweet flower scent winding through me. *:Next time, maybe you and Rik can join us. I've kept Xochitl inside the nest since you left, although there has been a development with her. I've been meaning to tell you, but I didn't want to distract you from Keisha.:*

:A bad development?:

:Not at all, though it has been... interesting.: She paused a moment, and then she laughed again. *:So you did call a female Blood.:*

She really had been there? *:You remember my dream?:*

:Another queen used to come to me in dreams over twenty years ago. She had a way of making me forget. I never knew her name, but...: She sighed softly. *:I think she was your mother.:*

I closed my eyes, swallowing down my emotions. Longing for the mother I'd never known. Sadness and grief that Mayte had known her, but then the spell had wiped her memory. And yeah, a bit of heartrending awe that Esetta had set so many plans into motion long before I was ever born.

:Did the new Blood tell you something useful about Ra?:

I breathed in Vivian's scent of cinnamon and herbs, my mouth watering. *:Yes. I know why he tried to take Xochitl and it wasn't just to kill her. It's horrible. Please, keep her safe.:*

:Do you even know where he is?: Mayte asked.

Vivian lifted her head and stared into my eyes solemnly. "Are you going to kill him?"

Without hesitation, I replied, "Yes."

Lingering tension bled out of Vivian until she lay soft and relaxed in my arms. "Then I will tell you everything I know. Including how to find Heliopolis."

SHARA

I closed my eyes a moment, battling down my dread. Not because of Ra—but because of the price I would have to pay. Knowing the horrors he was committing on young women... How could I not pay that price? I had to stop him. No matter what. No matter how many of us died.

If he'd managed to take Xochitl...

Thank you, Great One, for allowing me to save her. Please help me save them all.

"He hates us," Vivian whispered, her voice raw as the words tumbled out of her. "Queens especially, but all women. He allows his minions to torture even the youngest, because he honestly does not care if we live or die. No, that's not true. I think he wants us all to die, especially his children, because we're a reminder of what he did to sire us, and his failure to sire a queen of his own. Not one of us are queens. We only carry his foul blood.

"For all the hate and filth that he spews, his desires are infinite. I've seen him fuck every female in the main temple and then walk naked and still erect through the breeding grounds, looking for anyone he might have missed. I think that's why he hates queens so much. They remind him of his weakness. His desire. He doesn't want to desire a queen, but he fucks like he'll die if he doesn't come."

"Is he always there? How many queens does he have?"

"He stays away as long as possible. His priests are always trying to cleanse him of his thirst for Aima pussy like it's some kind of poison or curse. He distracts himself with humans as long as possible. Sometimes it's a day, or a week, maybe even a month. When I was a child, we sometimes were free of him for even a year at a time. But inevitably, his desires overpower him, and the longer he has denied himself, the worse it is for anyone in his city. The last time I was there, he only had two queens left, but that was over a hundred years ago. The rest of his captives have died, and Aima queens aren't born often enough to satisfy his perverse pleasures. The sunfires rage all the time, desperate for flesh. It's all he can do to keep them from breaking loose and ravaging the humans. But he dares not let them kill his last queens, for fear that he won't be able to find another to take their place, if he hasn't already killed them himself."

I swallowed hard, inwardly shuddering at how close Xochitl had been to that horror. Or even myself. Maybe that was why my mother had decided to have me in secret. Not because she

was afraid of what Keisha Skye or the Triune would do to me...
but to keep me out of Ra's grasp as long as possible.

I rubbed my thumb in one of the pockets of scar tissue in
her back. "What are these from?"

She shrugged like it was no big deal. "The sunfires burn
when they touch you. They like to drip their essence on us,
sometimes as punishment, but sometimes just because they
liked watching us scream. It burns like acid. Sepdet can make
his arms into burning, liquid sunlight whips that curl around
and dig into your flesh. That's the worst. But they all can
burn us."

"How many sun demons does he have?"

She shook her head, her mouth a grim slant. "Too many. At
least a thousand."

Ideas exploded in my head rapidly, alternatives that I
considered and quickly dismissed. If they were liquid sunlight,
I didn't think water or rain would affect them. Fire, I could
smother. Maybe with darkness, somehow? My cobra wouldn't
be able to deal with them. Wings wouldn't help me. My mind
ticked through each Blood. Rik's rock troll might be okay
against sun demons, since he couldn't melt, and probably
Leviathan. Surely his hide would protect him. But the
others...

Vivian brushed her lips against mine, drawing my attention
back to her. "Maybe that's one reason your goddess called me,
my queen. You can fight fire with fire."

I settled against the pillows, deliberately letting my thoughts
turn to sex and blood. I couldn't defeat Ra this very moment. It
wasn't time. Not yet.

I had to get stronger. Taking this new Blood would help in that regard.

She felt me softening against her and her eyes blazed brighter. "You hunger, my queen. May I have the pleasure and honor of feeling you come while you feed from me? Or have you had your fill of sex already this evening?"

Somebody snorted. Loudly. I didn't have to look to know it was Mehen.

"Everybody out," Rik said, giving a hard, no-nonsense alpha push toward the door. "Work in pairs and secure the building. Guard the main doors on the first floor. Mehen and Nevarre to the roof, and the rest of you fuel up. Our queen may yet have need of you again before she handles the rest of Skye business."

I didn't wait for them to leave. I locked my mouth to the punctures I'd already made on her throat. We Aima healed quickly, but when I sucked on the two wounds, her blood filled my mouth as if eager to hear my call.

She shifted closer on my left side and ran her palm down my flank in one smooth, confident swipe that brought my body to life. While I'd enjoyed my time with Mayte, we'd both been inexperienced in how to please another woman. With one touch, Vivian told me she could send me to the heavens as many times as we wished. Though she kept a wary eye on Rik on my other side, as if she didn't quite trust that he wouldn't interfere.

I didn't have to ask him to give us a little space. He rolled from the bed and quietly paced around the room, checking the windows to make sure they were secure.

:Better?: I asked her.

152 | JOELY SUE BURKHART

:I'm sorry, my queen. It's not that I don't trust you or him. It's just—:

:I understand. You have no reason to trust men at all.:

Her blood sparked inside me, stirring up my own gift of fire, though this time, it wasn't painful. Her fingers trailed up between my breasts and she paused, her hand over my heart, feeling it beat beneath her skin.

"There's something incredibly exquisite about giving a lover blood and pleasure at the same time," she whispered against my temple.

:The only thing better is tasting the pleasure in the blood, so feed more if you like.:

I felt her surprise in the bond, though she didn't say anything as her fingers glided over my breasts. Rik had told me before that most queens didn't feed their Blood very often. Once the initial bond was made, a Blood may never taste his queen's blood again.

She squeezed lightly, reveling in the soft curve of my skin. Through her bond, I felt the throb of her desire, and my inner muscles clenched in response. She wasn't in any hurry. Her touch on my skin was hard to describe. Unique. Her hands were smaller than any of my men's, so her touch was delicate and feminine, though I felt the promise of strength too. She wasn't hesitant or shy, but she touched me with reverence and a full sense of exactly how each stroke of her fingertip felt on my body, because her body was so similar. She knew how it felt without relying on our bond.

I spread my thighs wider, inviting her to explore as she wished. She didn't dive right in to my pussy, which I appreciated, though I wouldn't have minded, either. She ran her hand down my thigh to my knee, and then lifted my leg up over her hips, turning me more fully toward her. My breasts rubbed against hers and I felt the soft sigh of her breath in my hair. She was so warm that sweat glistened on my skin. Her touch firmed as her fingers roamed back up my thigh.

Sucking harder on her throat, I pressed closer, deliberately rubbing the hardened tips of my nipples against hers, which were just as hard. Her desire matched mine. It was such a small thing, but a delicious pleasure that none of my other Blood could give me. Tingles spread through my breasts, making them feel heavier, spreading the ache of need through my body.

Her fingers delved between my thighs and she sucked in a hard breath, her body going rigid. I started to pull back from her throat to see her face, but she cupped my nape with her other hand, keeping my mouth to her skin.

"Such a miracle," she whispered, her voice lowering to a husky growl. "I never expected to find a queen who'd actually bond me as Blood. Let alone a breeding queen. I can't even comprehend the fact that I'm here, touching you, feeling your blood on my fingers, and your alpha isn't ripping my head off for taking liberties when he should be helping you conceive."

:I'm not ready to have a child yet. I won't even consider it. Not until I've dealt with Ra.:

Her wiry body vibrated with intensity. *:Do you... Do they...:*

I listened to her bond, trying to understand why she shook so hard. What she fought against. Then I smiled against her throat. *:Yes. They have. I do.:*

She let out a rough groan and lifted her bloody fingers to her mouth. I should have warned her. But she did it so quickly...

Her back arched and she let out a guttural cry. I tightened my thigh across her hips, gripping her as she came. Her fiery blood turned to warm, thick honey in my mouth. Sweet and luscious with pleasure. I sank my fangs into her again, pushing her climax even harder. Just because I could.

Gasping, she reached between my thighs again, sinking two fingers into me. She didn't thrust inside me, but stroked, swirling the pads of her fingers against tender nerve endings that screamed with sensation. In seconds, I climaxed too, quivering against her. Though I never let go of her throat.

She curled around me, tucking me close. And this time, when Rik slid in behind me in bed, mindful as always to not touch another woman as I'd asked, she didn't tense or even spare him a look.

Not when she had my blood to lick from her fingers.

16

DAIRE

My queen filled my head and I immediately froze, gripping a knife loaded with mayonnaise in midair. *:Is the sandwich king perhaps making a sandwich?:*

I rumbled out a low purr in her bond. *:Would my queen like one too?:*

:I'm starving.:

:Give me five minutes, and I'll make you the biggest sandwich you've ever seen.:

I pulled out another long loaf of freshly-baked bread, and Magnum arched a brow at me as if shocked. Okay, maybe I had already eaten three sandwiches, with a fourth in progress. But after the way Guillaume and Llewellyn had emptied the fridge, she could hardly be surprised. The only Blood who hadn't fallen on the kitchen like a pack of starving wolves was Mehen. Shara had managed to heal him enough to let him shift, but he'd muttered under his breath that he wouldn't eat for at least a week.

Nevarre and I had a private bet. I had Mehen eating tomorrow. Nevarre thought it'd take him at least three days to eat again. But I knew the dragon's appetite better than anyone but our queen. He'd be rummaging around in the kitchen in no time, complaining that none of us heathens would know fine dining if it hit us between the eyes.

But the dragon had a point. If our queen had New York City at her disposal, why would she want a simple sandwich? I turned to Magnum. "Our queen said she's starving."

Magnum's eyes widened, and she leaped to the fridge, shoving me out of the way like I was an annoying house cat rather than a formidable warcat. "Goddess! Does she like seafood? Her mother did. I wasn't sure, but I've stocked all her mother's favorites. Lobster bisque, clam chowder, smoked salmon, grilled trout... Though that might take too long."

"I told her five minutes. As far as I know, she likes everything. She hasn't turned her nose up at anything we've brought her yet."

So I found myself carrying up a massive tray of soup, smoked salmon quiche, a tea kettle with half a dozen varieties of tea bags, juice, and my sandwich, though Magnum had insisted on cutting it up into little triangles. Guillaume opened the bedroom door for me, and I stepped inside quietly.

Shara sat up, carefully untangling herself from the new Blood's long-ass hair that put us all to shame. Rik lifted her up and set her down at the foot of the massive bed. Vivian was still out cold. Had she managed to shift with her power? The bed didn't look scorched. Yet.

We'd all felt the flames flickering in our queen as she'd bonded the new Blood. I still felt like if I opened my mouth, a puff of smoke would escape. Damned phoenix had nearly burned us all to a crisp. If anyone was going to blast us with fire, I would've expected that it'd be Leviathan.

The bed was large enough that the three of us could sit at the foot without disturbing the sleeping Blood. Shara sampled everything, declared it fantastic, and then loaded both hands with triangles of my sandwich.

Goddess. I loved her so much that I almost embarrassed myself by getting weepy over a fucking roast beef and rye. Granted, it was freshly baked bread, but still.

It was almost like those early days, when it'd just been me and Rik at her side. When everything had been strange and exciting for her as she faced a brand-new world. The worst thing after her was some thralls, which we could tear apart without even having to shift. There hadn't been any mad queen with a demon child, a magic-mirror Triune queen, or a fucking asshole sun god after her.

I didn't begrudge her one moment with any of her Blood. She needed us all. In fact, she needed about ten more. Maybe twenty. Who the fuck knew where her upper limit of power even was yet? But still...

This quiet time with her was fucking priceless.

"Do you still want to ride the motorcycles back to Eureka Springs?" Rik asked.

She smiled, her eyes brightening with excitement. "Definitely. Though only you and Daire have bikes. What will everyone else ride or drive?"

"G had a fucking 1967 GT500 Mustang," I replied. "Did you hear that beast? She purred almost as loudly as I do. He'll have every cop between Kansas City and Arkansas chasing us to the state line."

"Your mother's car is still there too," Rik reminded her. "I could see Mehen driving a Jaguar."

Her head tipped to the side, a smile tugging on her lips.

:What the actual fuck?: Mehen roared in our bonds, making me choke on a bite because I tried to laugh and swallow at the same time. *:What did I ever fucking do to you to deserve such an insult?:*

:You bit our queen's arm and broke it, asshole,: Rik retorted, though without any real heat. Water under the bridge and all.

:If you could drive any vehicle in the world, what you drive?: Shara asked.

:Aston Martin Vantage in British racing green,: he replied immediately. *:It'll match my scales.:*

:Very nice,: she replied in the bond, though to me, she mouthed, "I have no idea what that is." *:Nevarre, what would you drive?:*

:Why ride when you can fly? I prefer to guard from above anyway.:

:Like a helicopter?: She asked him.

:Blackhawk would be nice.:

Ezra didn't wait for her to ask. *:I have my truck stored near the tower. I won't drive anything but it.:*

:Xin?: She asked.

:Ducati. Matte black. Sleek and deadly.:

:Same,: Itztli and Tlacel replied at the same time.

:Llewellyn?: She asked.

:I don't drive. Some poor bastard will have to give me a ride.:

:You,: Guillaume and Mehen both retorted at the same time.

:You can draw straws later,: Rik said with his alpha rumble.

Shara looked over at the sleeping woman in her bed. "Any guesses what she'd like to drive? Or would she rather fly like Nevarre? I need to make sure Gina has time to hunt down everything for our trip home."

We hadn't been loud at all, but Vivian raised her head, her stunning eyes flickering with blue flame. "Hummer all the way with military-grade bullet proof glass. That way if we run into trouble, Rik can throw you inside with me."

"There won't be—" Shara froze, her eyes going distant and unfocused.

I scrambled off the bed, ready to fight. Rik pressed against her, a formidable wall of stone. Vivian was suddenly on her other side, her hair flying like a banner in her urgency.

Blinking back into focus, Shara whispered, "Trouble. Now."

And the wall-to-wall windows suddenly shattered.

17

SHARA

I screamed instinctually, even though Rik and Vivian both shielded me so well that not even a single splinter of glass struck me. It was habit, that old childhood fear. So many nights, I'd lain awake in dread while the monsters tried to break into the house. I'd taken the dark tower room in the attic, simply because there weren't any windows.

I knew my Blood could handle this threat. Easily. For fuck's sake, it was only thralls. Even if there were a hundred, I could incinerate them in a heartbeat if I was bleeding. I wasn't powerless and scared any longer. I was the fucking queen of Isador. Last daughter of Isis.

But there was still a small part of my heart that wanted to throw the covers over my head and curl up in a ball on my bed.

:There's no need for you to bleed,: Rik growled in my head, his

arms locked around me. *:Allow us to protect you. This is what we live for.:*

:I know.: I squeezed my eyes shut and pressed my face to the hot, bare expanse of his chest, allowing the thunder of his heart to drown out the chittering screeches that made me want to clamp my hands over my ears.

Something tickled in the back of my mind. Despite Daire's roars and the rush of Blood surrounding me and leaping out the two-story-window to take the battle to the street, I heard something soft and quiet inside my head. Like a squeak. Small, but urgent.

It wasn't words, so it took me a moment to realize that it was the rat I'd set to guard Huitzilopochtli's resting place. I sat straight up and met Rik's hard, furious gaze. "It's a distraction. There's something going on at the tower."

I reached for my new bond with Gwen and touched Gina's at the same time. *:Take our most powerful shifters down to the basement. I'll guide you to the location. We have intruders in the tower.:*

Focusing on the small squeak, I tried to slide deeper into my rat friend's bond. She had my blood, even if it was a drop. If I was careful…

Goosebumps flared down my arms and I was there, in the basement. I heard the soft whisper of soles on the floor, headed down the hallway. We were high up in the vent, giving me a good vantage point.

Three men approached. She bristled, sharp teeth bared, but I held her quiet, safely hidden in the vent. *:Do you have some friends who can help us?:*

She squeaked and her—my—nose twitched in agreement. I

couldn't tell how many rats might be close, but I trusted that they'd come and do whatever they could until Gina and Gwen arrived.

"Which one is it?" One of the men whispered.

"I don't know," another replied. "The report said there were rooms deep in the basement that we should check. That's all I know."

"He's got to be here somewhere."

He. My heart thudded heavily. *:Rik, they're after Huitzilopochtli.:*

:Fuck,: he growled. *:The last thing we need is an Aztec sun god running around the city.:*

I felt for Gina and found her waiting on the service elevator, impatiently tapping her toes but still looking incredibly elegant in shoes I would have kicked off hours ago. She was on her phone, likely calling Frank's team that'd be taking over security of the building. Gwen stepped off the crowded elevator with a couple of people who immediately shifted. A wolf took the lead, using his nose and stealth to track the intruders. Two lions and a tiger prowled after him.

Gwen paused a moment in the hallway and used something hanging from her throat to puncture her wrist. I wasn't sure what it was, but the rat smelled her blood. I felt her power rising, and a soft, glowing white light filled her. She shone like the full moon.

House Findabair, the White Enchantress.

:What weapons do these men have?: Guillaume asked.

I focused on the men, watching as they checked each door down the hallway, and let that image filter through my bonds.

:They each carry a 9mm handgun and extra ammunition,: Guillaume said. *:Looks like a hunting knife on the lead man's thigh. He walks like a soldier. Special Forces, maybe Green Beret. The other two are GRU.:*

:What's that?:

:Russian Intelligence.:

I didn't bother asking how he knew. He'd probably tell me he smelled the guns again, though I didn't know how that was possible. With that thought, I was sure the rat smelled gunpowder and a hint of metal. *:Who told them about Skye's basement secrets? Gwen, that's something else we have to ferret out, unless they already fled.:*

:I agree,: she replied. *:There are several houses that may have been disgruntled enough with Keisha to supply information to Ra. Certainly several queens were Marne's eyes and ears inside the tower.:*

My stomach tightened. Had Marne managed to plant a spy in my court? But who? Everybody close to me was sworn to me. They were either Blood, and impossible to corrupt, or human, and so above reproach and dedicated to Isador that I couldn't imagine them betraying me. Accidentally putting me in danger, like allowing a stranger inside the nest, was one thing. But deliberately supplying information to a queen that wanted to eliminate me?

I pushed those anxieties aside. I couldn't deal with Marne Ceresa right now. But I could do something about these three men that now stood below me. They noted the protections on the door and looked at each other. The leader nodded and stepped back, hand sliding down into a utility pocket on his cargo pants. One of the other guys drew his weapon and took up position on the other side, while the other jiggled the door.

They looked at each other again suspiciously when the door opened easily. We'd already unlocked it earlier. The door creaked open and they cautiously stepped inside.

The rat slipped out of the vent and crept along a tiny ledge, ducked inside the door, clinging to the door frame and inching along until she grabbed on another small ledge on the inside of the room. She balanced precariously in the corner of the room but didn't seem to be straining or fighting to hold the position.

"Bingo," the lead guy said.

"You sure?" One of the others asked.

He snorted derisively. "The witch was just as scared of him as the vizier. Come on, let's get it done."

What did they even think they could do? They were human. I didn't sense any Aima blood or power in them at all. So they couldn't resurrect him. Maybe they were going to smuggle the mummy out of the building.

The leader pulled out a silver lighter. It looked ornate and antique with lots of fancy engraving. He flicked it open and started spinning the starter, but it didn't light right away.

It finally dawned on me. They were going to burn the mummy. Not resurrect him. But why?

He finally managed to get a flame and started for Huitzilopochtli's carefully-wrapped body. The rat tensed, ready to send us flying down on top of the nearest man.

:Now.:

She leaped out at the nearest man and sank her teeth in his ear. He let out a shriek to raise the dead.

Suddenly, it was raining rats. They dropped from the ceiling and poured up out of tiny cracks in the walls and floor like a horror movie. The men yelled and kicked at the vermin, scrambling away from vicious teeth.

Only to find Aima shifters waiting for them outside the door.

:*Don't kill them,*: I ordered, hoping Gwen could relay the message quickly enough. :*I need answers.*:

The leader whirled and tossed the burning lighter toward the mummy.

Old, desiccated flesh and fabric would go up in flames in a heartbeat. I didn't know why they wanted Huitzilopochtli destroyed, but I couldn't allow it to happen. Not before I understood why.

My rat leaped toward the table, scurried up the leg, and launched herself upward impossibly high. I didn't know if a single drop of my blood was enough to power that kind of jump for her, or if that was her natural ability. She knocked the lighter off its trajectory. Flames scorched her fur and she screeched in pain, falling toward the hard ground.

I felt the searing flames. I smelled her scorching hair. But I didn't pull back from our bond. I'd suffer with her, though I strained to stop her fall, or at least slow the tumble.

She fell into soft palms. Gwen cradled her gently while snuffing out the smoldering patches of fur. "Well done, Your Majesty."

Soft moonlight wrapped the injured rat in cushions of airy silk as Gwen healed her.

I let my awareness fade from the rat, but I sent her a warm, gentle wave of appreciation. *:Thank you, my friend.:*

Gwen focused on the intruders and sent me an image of one man dangling by his arm, trapped in the wolf's jaws. The tiger had a big paw on one man's chest, and the other man, the leader, slowly backed away from the two prowling lions.

As he shoved his hand into his pocket, he screamed, "Lord of Heaven!"

Molten solar energy shot up through him to blacken the ceiling, obliterating him into a handful of ashy motes that slowly drifted down to the floor.

Stunned, the tiger didn't react quickly enough when his captive did the same thing. Liquid sunlight flared up his paw and he roared with pain, jumping back before his entire body went up. The wolf dropped his prize just in time as the man dissolved into a small pile of soot.

"Fuck." I opened my eyes and pushed up out of bed. "They killed themselves, the same way that Ra agent did when the attack on Xochitl failed. Though at least this time, the fireball was contained. They could have brought down the entire building."

"Fucking boobytrapped pussies," Mehen growled, striding naked toward me. "We saw a large box truck parked down the street that seemed out of place. Nevarre flew down to investigate, and they drove off in a hurry."

My Blood gathered closer. Nevarre was still his massive raven, and Daire padded toward me as the warcat. Glass sprinkled the floor, though the crisp winter air slicing into the damaged room actually felt nice. The cold had never bothered me.

What did bother me was the idea that someone could control thralls. That they'd actually loaded up a bunch like cattle and brought them here to attack me.

I'd been hunted all my life by these monsters.

Had someone been directing them from afar all this time? A master thrall like Greyson? No. I didn't think so. This was too thoughtful. Too coordinated. Greyson had been driven by his urges, while this plot spoke of planning and coordination.

I rubbed my arms briskly. It wasn't the cold that made me shiver, though I didn't complain when Rik wrapped me in a blanket and pulled me into his arms.

"Are you well, my queen?"

I nodded, still mulling over the implications of the attack. Humans, including Russian Intelligence, had broken into my building and tried to destroy the mummy I'd found locked away in Keisha's basement. I'd been too worried about Huitzilopochtli to wake him up, but maybe I should, at least before someone managed to destroy him. Or was that all a plot to trick me into doing exactly that?

"You haven't taxed your reserves?"

Hearing the surprise and faint worry in Rik's words, I turned in his arms and lifted my gaze to his. "I'm fine. Great, actually. I'm still hungry. We need to let Magnum—"

"Already here, Your Majesty," Magnum called from the door. "Oh dear. Let's get you comfortable in one of the other rooms until we can get the glass fixed."

Carys stood beside her, bleary-eyed and grouchy. "I thought I told you not to get into any more trouble tonight."

I grinned at her and slid out of bed. "I told you I wasn't making any promises."

"Humph. Maybe I should have stayed at the tower. At least I'd get some sleep."

Rik swept me up into his arms, ignoring my protests. "There's glass on the floor. You're barefoot."

"So are you."

"When you can turn your soles into granite, then I won't worry about your pretty toes getting cut up."

He had a point.

In a matter of minutes, Magnum had us stationed in another bedroom. The bed, regrettably, was nowhere near as large. Rik set me on the fluffy down comforter. Daire hopped up and curled around me. Winston handed Tlacel another tray of food and then quietly retreated. My Blood shut the door, enclosing us all in a sumptuously decorated room in golden silk.

But sleep couldn't be further from my mind. I touched Gwen's bond and found her healing the tiger's burns and securing the mummy's room once more. I touched Gina's bond and found her with Madeline, going over accounts. I wasn't sure why, but hopefully they could figure out where the intruders had come from.

I started mentally making a list of all the things I needed to do. Like secure the tower with a blood circle. Should that be just me? Or should Gwen do it? Or both? I wanted to tell Gina about my desire to ride home from Kansas City on the road. I still needed to talk to Dr. Borcht about my crazy reproductive cycle before I accidentally had a child. I needed to examine the legacy—

"Shara," Rik said, louder, as if he'd been saying my name awhile.

I focused on him and noted the furrow between his eyes. "I'm fine, really. I just have so much to do…"

"You aren't tired?"

"No, but I will take a chunk of that sandwich." He handed it to me and I dug in like I hadn't eaten in days. "Mmmm. It's good, but Daire's is better."

Daire purred louder and swiped his sandpaper tongue over my arm.

Rik dropped down on his knee in front of me and leaned closer. Cupping my chin, he stared deeply into my eyes as he ran his bond through me. It felt like he was examining my internal organs and lightly touching me deep inside. It wasn't unpleasant, but it made me shiver a little.

"What's wrong?"

He sighed. "Nothing."

I snorted and reached for the tea kettle. I poured a cup and added a cube of sugar, though I had no idea what blend of tea it was. It smelled perfumey without being too strong. "That's a good thing, right?"

"You were exhausted at the tower, even after you fed from several of us. I carried you to the car. I expected you to sleep heavily and long, like you did after Venezuela."

I listened internally to my body a moment and then shrugged. "I don't feel tired any longer. In fact, I kind of want to go to the tower now and see if Gina's found anything that might explain how those guys knew where to go."

"It's her reserves," Guillaume said. "You're filling them."

"Finally." Mehen smirked. "It only took draining eleven Blood to unconsciousness. Even our alpha."

"But you're still developing those reserves, or you wouldn't still be so hungry," Guillaume continued, though his eyes twinkled with amusement. "Adding another Blood tonight was the tipping point, though you certainly need a few more to ensure you can keep those reserves filled."

Rik searched my body again, using the bond like a gigantic flashlight inside me. With a sigh, he sat back on his heels. "I still don't know where you're putting all that power. All that blood. I don't sense any massive pools of power to tap."

Guillaume knelt beside Rik and held out his hand. "May I look, my queen?"

I slipped my hand into his. "Of course."

His bond didn't slide through me like Rik's. Guillaume's bond hardened, shining like steel inside me. Cold, hard, and brutally sharp, just like his weapons, though as he moved through me, it didn't hurt or cut.

His bond softened and he released my hand. "When you draw on your power, do you have a sense of where it comes from?"

"Not really. I just do it."

"What about when you're feeding? Do you have a sense of where the power goes?"

Now it was my turn to smirk. "I'm usually too busy to worry

about anything but coming thanks to you guys." I glanced at Vivian and smiled. "And lady."

She grunted with disgust. "I've been called many things, but never lady."

Finished with the sandwich, I leaned back into Daire's furry side and sipped my tea. Now that my stomach was pleasantly full, my eyes were a little heavy. Though overall, I still felt great. Fantastic.

"I'll try to pay attention next time." I tried to adjust my grip on the teacup, and I almost spilled it all over me. These stupid silver nails were way too long. I glared at them, silently willing them to disappear. The other shapes that Isis had given to me came and went as I needed them, and I didn't need to feed now. I didn't have fangs all the time. "How can I make these go away?"

Rik took my free hand in his and lifted my hand to his mouth. He pressed a kiss into my palm, and I couldn't help but note that my nails rested on his skin. His face. If they started to hurt him...

"You could never hurt me. In fact, I hope you use these on me next time, though I'll always love your fangs too."

"They feel fucking incredible," Itztli said.

"Agreed." Mehen and Guillaume both said at the same time.

I turned my glare on Guillaume. "How can you say that when I almost killed you with these fucking things? I buried them in your throat."

He tipped his head back a little. "Do you see any scars, my queen?"

I blew out a sigh. "No, you've already healed."

"Of course I did, because Shara fucking Isador is my queen, and your blood is so powerful that you can heal any of us in a matter of minutes, even from severe wounds. I only ask one thing, my queen."

I focused on his face, noting how young and healthy he looked, even though he was the last Templar knight. Every strand of hair on his head was dark, thick and curly. His skin was smooth without a single wrinkle, other than a deep furrow between his eyes. He'd come a long way from the terrible condition in which he'd first arrived weeks ago, nearly starved to death. "Anything, my knight."

My grim, deadly knight winked. Fucking winked. "If it comes down to a handjob with the nails, or a blowjob with the fangs, I'll take them both."

18

SHARA

This time, when I approached the building formerly known as Skye Tower with my Blood and Carys, my reception was markedly different. Two human guards —different from the rude guys who'd been here when I'd first visited—snapped to attention.

One moved quickly to the door and opened it for me. "Your Majesty, good morning. Ms. Talbott asked that I alert her immediately when you arrived. Is that alright?"

"Yes, of course. What's your name?"

He was dressed in a black polo shirt and khakis with a gold emblem embroidered over his heart. "Hammel, Your Majesty."

I stepped closer so I could make out the symbol, and my mouth fell open. It was a golden pyramid with an ankh in the center. *"House Isador"* was written beneath it in bold capital letters. "Oh my goddess, that's awesome! Are you one of Frank's guys?"

He smiled and tapped his chest proudly. "Absolutely. He's the best. It's an honor to work for Isador, Your Majesty."

He tapped an ear piece as we walked past. "Our queen is headed upstairs now."

Inside, all the gold furnishings were gone. The white marble floors and empty walls made the large plaza level seem cold, and our footsteps echoed loudly. Some color or textiles would help warm things up. Maybe a carpet of some kind? Decorating giant office buildings was not my forte.

A woman and another man dressed the same as Hammel stood at the elevator. "Good morning, Your Majesty."

"Good morning. Has there been any trouble today?"

"Not at all." The woman clenched her jaws and looked down at the floor. "I'm terribly sorry about the break-in last night. We should have taken over the guard shift immediately, rather than waiting until this morning. I guarantee there wouldn't have been any intruders if we'd been on duty."

"It's fine. We handled it. I'm glad to have Frank's people here."

It seemed like forever ago when Gina had hired Frank McCoy's security company to guard my Kansas City house. I missed having him close, but I'd needed to leave someone guarding the nest too, and I'd rather have someone of my blood there. If I concentrated, I could feel his bond and know if anything was amiss without a single phone call.

The elevator opened on the fourth floor and she inclined her head toward the other elevator across the plaza that would take us to the secure area of the building. "Angela is waiting to take you upstairs."

"Thank you." I knew the drill. I waited beside Rik while my Blood stepped out of the elevator and took up positions throughout the area. Then I stepped out with my arm tucked around Rik's and we headed for the other elevator. "This is where Keisha had her blood circle, isn't it?"

"Yes. She rented out offices in the first four floors, but the blood circle kept everyone outside Skye from approaching the secure elevator. She always had guards placed here, too, but it was the circle that kept everyone out."

Angela was one of Gina's assistants, though she was usually armed. When we'd stopped in Dallas to shop before visiting the Zaniyah nest, Angela had guarded my jewelry and crown.

"I love the uniforms."

She grinned. "I asked Gina if we could do something fancy, and she agreed. I hope we didn't overstep."

"Not at all. I love it."

As we stepped out of the elevator, Gina, Madeline, and Gwen waited for me. I smelled coffee and something sweet, which made my stomach growl again. Even though Winston had fed me at the house before I came over.

It was so loud that Gina laughed. "Good morning, Your Majesty. You're certainly up and around way earlier than I expected!"

"Me too."

Carys scowled. "You have no idea how many times we were up last night. It was like a fucking circus."

Her owl squawked and fluttered her wings in agreement.

"Gina, let me introduce you to my new Blood, Vivian Helios."

Gina was too much a professional to betray her sudden alarm, though I read her concern in her body language. Her shoulders tensed and her smile was hard, a flash of white teeth like a dog warning off a strange dog from her master. "Helios, huh? That's very interesting."

Vivian was dressed in her black leathers again, though she'd twisted her long hair into a tight cord, bound every few inches with gold bands. Her hair was so long that the ponytail hung down to mid-thigh. If she swung her head, she could use that tight cord as a weapon. "Interesting isn't an adjective I'd ever use to describe growing up Helios."

"I know what it means," I said softly, trying to assuage Gina's concerns. "Our goddess sent her to me."

Gina smiled a little easier and nodded her head at Vivian, though I sensed her hesitation. "Then all will be well. I have some details about the break-in last night that may interest you."

She gestured to the open door, so I followed on Daire's heels. The walls were paneled in glossy, dark wood with a huge desk and several comfortable chairs scattered throughout the room. A gas fireplace was lit in the corner, but I didn't feel any heat from it. The chairs were pulled around a low coffee table that was loaded with donuts, pastries, and most importantly, coffee. Daire was already pouring me a cup.

Three of the chairs already had cups and saucers with crumbs on them, telling me where the other women were sitting. I picked an empty chair, and Carys took another on the opposite side of the table. Probably to get as far away from me as possible. She'd been impossible this morning. I didn't know if she wasn't a morning person, or if she truly was angry about the excitement last night.

Rik stood behind me, his big palm warm on my shoulder. Daire handed me the cup and dropped down beside me on the floor. The rest of my Blood scattered around the room. I didn't fail to notice that three of them stood at the large, plate-glass window. It wasn't to admire the view, though from this high, we had a fantastic view of the city. They were braced for another attack through the glass, even at one hundred stories high.

Madeline sat on my left, and Gina on my right. Gwen sat across me beside Carys, who was feeding crumbs to her owl in between huddling over her own cup of coffee like it was the only thing keeping her alive.

A spark of fire caught my attention. I looked up and met Vivian's piercing blue gaze. :*There's something of Ra's in this room. His power calls to his blood that flows in my veins.*:

I didn't allow my face to betray me. :*Find it, so we can eliminate it as quietly as possible.*:

Madeline laid a stack of papers in front of me. "As soon as you took over control of the tower and made your wishes known to Gina, I started notifying all of our tenants that we were buying out their leases effective immediately. By eight last night, we'd bought out every single lease but one." She tapped the top page. "SLI."

Vivian made a rude noise as she passed behind me. "Sun Lord, Inc."

I shook my head. "He's full of himself, isn't he?"

"Very," Gina said grimly. "SLI had one room leased according to the contracts. It was only a small room, very innocuous, right? But we started going through the security logs last night. Keisha Skye may have had many failings, and we certainly found her guards to be less than professional. But they always managed to make a note of everyone entering the building."

I knew where this was going. "Let me guess. Someone from SLI accessed the building last night."

Madeline nodded. "It immediately set off red flags when I looked into their record, because they've never entered the building before, until last night."

I took a sip from my cup and let out a pleased hum that made Daire rumble a purr and rub against my knee. He always knew exactly how I liked my coffee. "So did Keisha know that she'd leased an office to Ra, even indirectly? Was it on purpose?"

"I don't think she knew, though I could be wrong," Madeline replied. "I wasn't privy to much that my former queen did. She had many secrets and she trusted nobody. There were rooms in this tower that I never entered, even as her consiliarius. Nobody was allowed to enter them."

"Even outside of the basement?" She nodded, and I took a deep breath. "Then those are the rooms that I need to see first today."

I waited a few moments, noting that Vivian had stopped behind Madeline's chair. The fire sparked inside her eagerly. She took another step closer, so she stood just inches behind the woman's chair, and the spark burned brighter.

I had to proceed carefully. Maybe Vivian was wrong. Maybe I could trust Madeline. Or, more likely, Vivian's sensitivity to Ra's corruption in humans was exactly the reason Isis had sent this new Blood to my side. "Do you know why she had that mummy in the basement?"

"I'm afraid not, Your Majesty. I had no idea those rooms even existed. I was terrified of Tanza, so I never went down there unless Keisha ordered me to accompany her."

She stood and moved away briefly, returning with several plastic bags carefully tagged like police evidence. With each step closer, I felt the pulse in Vivian's fire. "We recovered a little evidence from the men who tried to take it."

"G, take a look."

He immediately stepped closer and went through the bags one by one. "Glock, SIG Sauer, and this one's interesting. A GSh-18 semi-automatic pistol with armor piercing rounds." A melted mass of bullet casings was in another bag, the long hunting knife the leader had been wearing, and lastly, the lighter. "They might as well have come in naked."

I frowned. "What does that mean?"

My Templar knight waggled his eyebrows at me playfully. "How many weapons am I carrying on my person today, my queen?"

I ran my gaze down his body, noting the tight, faded jeans that hugged his thighs and the long-sleeved baby blue shirt he wore. Nothing seemed out of place on him, though I knew he had to be carrying the long knife down his back. He always wore it. And he had two wrist sheaths on each arm. Maybe a knife in each boot. Probably something in his pockets. Then I added a few to be safe. "Ten?"

His lips quirked. "Not even close. My point is that I'm armed to the teeth for any situation. I'm prepared to fight our way out of hell at a moment's notice. They came in with one gun each and a knife. They didn't plan to fight their way out if there was trouble. They were going to sneak in and out. Quietly. Or die in the process."

I touched the lighter inside the plastic. "They intended to destroy the mummy. But why?"

Guillaume's gaze flickered to Madeline briefly, the one person in the room not wholly mine. "They had to know who he was, and they would have been acting out someone's orders."

The spark in Vivian's bond was still there. A giant bull's eye on Madeline's back. Enough of this bullshit. I needed to bring things to a head. "You said last night that you were willing to stay on as my second consiliarius."

She set the cup down on the table. "Yes. It would be an honor to serve, Your Majesty."

Daire snarled at her beneath his breath. I bumped him with my knee to settle him. "Did Gina tell you what I would require to join my team?"

Her eyes burned brightly, almost as if she had a fever. "Yes. It would be a great honor, Your Majesty. I'm willing to do whatever you wish to ensure your trust."

Vivian's spark burned hotter, matching the heat in Madeline's eyes. Something was definitely wrong with her.

To be safe, I glanced at Carys. Her owl had hopped down off

her shoulder to peck at a crumbled scone on the table. *:What's the probability that Madeline will betray me in some way?:*

Carys looked at the woman beside me and twitched in her chair like someone had poked her. *:Shockingly high. She's not to be trusted.:*

I touched Gina's bond. *:I changed my mind. I can't trust her.:*

The consummate professional, Gina didn't reveal any surprise or disappointment. "Please excuse me," she murmured as she stood and moved aside. "I need to make a call."

"I wouldn't mind tasting your blood at all, Your Majesty," Madeline said, a little too eagerly. Even Gina, whom I trusted implicitly, had been surprised at first. It was a great honor, yes, but not something that most consiliari did any longer. At least that was the impression I got from her.

Daire casually shifted closer to Madeline, putting himself between me and any danger. He was already licking his claws, though she didn't pay him any attention. Her second mistake.

"Oh?" I drawled softly. "I didn't think it was customary for queens to make human servants nowadays."

"It isn't," she replied quickly. "But it should be. It's a smart choice, Your Majesty."

"Did Keisha give you her blood?"

"No, not at all. It wouldn't have occurred to her. She was too jealous of her power. She didn't trust anyone."

"How many years did you work for House Skye?"

"Only ten, Your Majesty. Her previous consiliarius had cancer, I believe, and passed away suddenly."

Rik growled in my head. *:She did die, I remember that. But I don't think it was cancer.:*

"Did she serve House Skye long?"

Madeline shrugged apologetically. "I'm sorry, Your Majesty, I don't know."

"Which house did you serve before you came to House Skye?"

Madeline blinked. "I didn't serve a house, but I worked in the best accounting firm in New York City for twenty years."

I sipped my coffee and blinked back at her, keeping my eyes wide and innocent. "I'm new to how the Aima do things. How did Keisha come to hire you, then? Gina worked for my family before I even knew anything about them."

"I came highly recommended."

I heard a bit of stiffness in her voice. I listened harder, letting my senses focus on her solely. Her heartbeat was rapid. I detected the flutter of her pulse in her throat. Her body temperature was also elevated. Sweat beaded on her brow.

"I didn't work directly for any house, but I had many previous dealings with House Skye and had interacted with the former consiliarius several times. So Keisha knew me."

I settled back against the chair, seemingly relaxed. "What did you have on her?"

"Excuse me?" Her voice rose in pitch. "I don't know what you mean."

"You had to have something on her. Some dirt she didn't want anyone else to know. So she hired you. What was it?"

She stared at me a moment, her eyes hot and bright, almost delirious. She hadn't seemed off to me yesterday. I would have accepted her as my second consiliarius on Gina's recommendation alone. If I hadn't been so tired...

"Please," she whispered raggedly. "I need this. Desperately. You're my only hope. I'll do anything. Anything at all. But I must be by your side."

"Why?"

"You wouldn't understand." Her voice cracked with strain. She gripped the arms of her chair, her nails dug in like a cat's claws. "Keisha was only a stepping stone to get here. To be close."

I let my breath sigh out softly. "Close to Huitzilopochtli."

Her eyes went wide, the whites shining. "You know? And you did nothing to stop him?"

"Stop who? He's dead."

"A god is never dead. You should know that better than anyone."

Daire's purr never changed. :*I've got her.*:

Behind the woman, Vivian glared at him. :*She's mine, dickhead. I noticed she was off first.*:

Mehen chuckled in our bonds. :*Oh, I like her. She fits right in.*:

"Why would I want to stop Huitzilopochtli? Why is he here, locked in Keisha's basement?"

Madeline shook her head, a rough, jerky movement as if she'd lost control of her bodily functions. "It's time. It needs to be done."

Sweat poured down her face and her eyes glowed painfully bright. She started to rise, her movements stiff and jerky as if controlled by something else. She rose enough to fall on her knees heavily. She crawled closer to me, wringing her hands. Her lips were cracked and peeling, her tongue slipping out to moisten them. Her eyes burned so hotly. Pleading for me to do something.

Vivian paced behind her and quietly unsheathed one of her swords.

"You have the power. I need it. Please," she whimpered. "You have to help me. You have to save me."

"How?" I whispered, pity welling in my heart. "What happened to you?"

Fat tears rolled down her cheeks, blistering her skin in red welts. "He doesn't want you to wake him up. That's why he wants him dead. I'm sorry. I thought you could cleanse me. But it's too late now."

Her voice broke and she wailed, her head falling forward. She wretched and heaved, her shoulders straining. Heave after heave, while her body strained and shuddered. Finally, she vomited out... something. I couldn't make out what it was.

Then it leaped toward me.

Rik jerked me up so fast I squeaked. Daire swiped at the thing in the air, knocking it onto the carpet. Vivian pinned it to the floor with the tip of her blade. She lifted the squirming thing up into the air, skewered on her blade. "Bingo."

It was one of the blue-green beetles that we'd seen devouring Keisha's body. I shuddered and looked back at Madeline. She'd collapsed on the floor, mouth open, her eyes... melting. Like her eyeballs had exploded. Fluids leaked out of her eye sockets.

"Goddess, above." Gwen whispered. "What the fuck happened to her? She seemed fine last night."

"Did I miss one?" I asked. "Could one of them have escaped?"

Rik wasn't taking any chances of another creature crawling out of the dead woman. He kept me locked high in his arms. "No. I didn't see one escape. Could she have been infested with one earlier?"

Vivian concentrated on the wriggling beetle and it burst into flame with an eerie screech. "This thing was probably planted in her years ago. That's how Ra works. He plays the long game, willing to wait for hundreds of years for his plot to come to fruition. She probably didn't even remember when he planted it in her."

Grudgingly, Rik set me back in my chair. In the attack, I'd lost track of my cup. It'd tumbled to the floor and spilled on the carpet, so Daire started making me a fresh cup.

Gina stepped back inside the room and gasped. "Oh, goddess. What happened?"

Vivian waved the crispy critter at her on her way out the door. "Ra's scarab. I'm going to flush it to be safe."

Gina looked at me, wringing her hands. "I'm so sorry, Shara. I had no idea. I feel terrible that I recommended her."

I shook my head and accepted the cup from Daire. "How could you possibly know? She was a smart choice. Who else on Skye's team do you think could step up and help us?"

"Going through her reports, I saw that many of them were generated by a single name, Kevin Bloom. I took the liberty of calling him up to join us."

Poor Madeline was starting to melt into the carpet. "I think we need to hire a really good clean-up crew that doesn't mind dealing with strange shit."

"I'm sure Skye already had several clean-up crews on staff to cover up for all her... um... less savory dealings." Gina hesitated and then lowered her voice. "Are you sure about Vivian? What if she's carrying one of those things inside her too? Can you tell?"

I shook my head. "I felt the spark in her bond and she warned me there was something of Ra's in the room. I don't think I would have sensed anything amiss, at least until Madeline started showing symptoms."

Vivian stepped back into the room. "We really ought to burn the body to be safe. I've seen scarabs hide for days and then burst out in search of a new host."

I shuddered. "Definitely, let's burn it, then." I started to press a silver nail to my wrist, but she laid her fingers over mine, stopping me.

"There's no need for you to bleed, my queen. Not when you have a phoenix at your disposal."

"You didn't shift after our queen took you," Daire said. When Vivian narrowed a hard look on him, he held his hands up. "Just curious. A Blood only gains his or her gift once the queen bond takes over. You said you'd never had a queen before."

Standing over the crumpled body, Vivian held her hand out, index finger pointed down. I felt her gift stir. Smoak uncurled from her slumber, spreading flames inside her. Holding her breath, she opened a tiny gate inside her and allowed fire to drip from her finger onto the body. It flowed like lava, hot molten rock that gleamed red and gold, sinking immediately into the body and catching flame. "I was born with this power, able to call Smoak at will. She's my curse and my gift. For most of my life, she's been my only friend. Though she's very hard to control."

Her voice quivered with effort. In her bond, I felt the phoenix's eagerness. Flames licked Vivian's ribcage. Sweat beaded on her brow as she strained to hold the tiny gate open without allowing Smoak to spread uncontrolled fires. Her instinct was to rage and burn. Not carefully dribble fire on a body to dispose of it.

I focused on my bond inside Vivian and glowed with power. Reminding them both of what I tasted like. What I felt like. The promise of pleasure and power in my blood.

Smoak subsided without another complaint. Vivian swiped at her forehead and gave me a weary smile. "Thank you, my queen."

Someone tapped at the door. Gina stepped over to crack the door and see who it was, then she glanced worriedly over her shoulder at me. "It's Kevin. Should I have him wait?"

I shook my head. "It's best that he sees what we're dealing with. If he can't handle it, I'd rather know now than later."

Gina opened the door wider and a beautiful young man stepped inside. His black hair was perfectly shiny and styled. His smile was dazzlingly white. His suit impeccable. His eyes were a brilliant blue, just a shade darker than Vivian's. He started to bow and then caught sight of the flames spreading across his former employer's dead body.

He froze, his eyes widening. Slowly, he straightened and looked warily around the room before his gaze fell onto me. He quickly bowed again, even deeper. "Your Majesty."

"We had a bit of difficulty," I said lightly.

"So I see. We have several professional cleaning crews that we've used in the past with utmost discretion. Shall I ring one?"

"Yes, please, but in a moment." I gave a gentle tug on Vivian and she stepped away from the body and closer to the young man. I listened to Smoak, waiting to feel any spark or hint that he'd been contaminated too. Vivian shook her head slightly, and I nodded, letting her return to her work. "Is there another room we can talk, Gwen?"

"Of course." Standing, she led us down the hallway toward another meeting room. I took my coffee cup, and so did Carys. Vivian, Guillaume, and Xin remained behind. Rik didn't have to tell me why.

They still didn't trust her. Not really.

:It's not that I don't trust her,: Rik said as I sat down once more. *:It's better to be safe than sorry, and I will always err to safety when it comes to you.:*

:You said a Blood couldn't be compromised.:

He grimaced slightly. *:So I did. But that was before you called a Blood sired by Ra.:*

Gina waited until we were all seated and then started the interview. Because that was actually what we were doing. Trying to fill a spot on my team. "I noticed that your work was showing up quite often in Madeline's files, so that's why I called you in. Her Majesty is in search of a second consiliarius, preferably someone who's familiar with the Skye legacy."

"Oh." He blinked and nodded his head slightly, his eyes dazed. "Oh my. That couldn't be further from my mind. I thought you were calling me up to take me to task for failing to do a background check on SLI. I swear, that wasn't my fault. I noted it in the file, but Madeline checked off on their lease. I let it go."

Gwen set the coffee service tray on the table and took a seat. "Now we know why."

He shuddered. "I don't know what happened. I don't want to know. But I can't say that I'm surprised that she turned out to not be... suitable."

That was one way to put it. I studied him, trying to get a sense of his character. He reminded me of a young Winston, probably because of his gorgeous suit. "Have you worked for Skye long?"

"Only two years, Your Majesty."

Gwen shook her head. "Fess up, Kevin. She doesn't know the houses. She wasn't born in a nest."

He gave himself a little shake. "Of course. I worked as a sort of intern for Byrnes. He's my grandfather."

The name sounded familiar, but I couldn't immediately place it.

"Byrnes is Marne Ceresa's American consiliarius," Gina added.

Oh shit. I didn't know which was worse. A consiliarius contaminated by Ra, or one who'd worked for the Triune queen.

Kevin grimaced too. "Yeah, I get that a lot. People are terrified of her, and rightly so. But she runs her massive house like a finely oiled machine, with the help of people like Granddad, of course. I'm grateful he allowed me to work by his side."

"For how long?" I asked.

He shrugged. "Pretty much my whole life. My earliest memories of Granddad were sitting beside him while he worked on the books. He taught me as much as he could, given that I wasn't sworn to House Ceresa."

"Why didn't you stay on as his replacement?"

Kevin laughed, shaking his head. "Replacement? Surely you're joking. Granddad won't be retiring anytime soon, and the queen made it clear that she had no intentions of hiring me on. She already has seven consiliari and has no need for a snot-nosed smart-aleck." He smiled. "Her words, not mine."

I laughed softly. "If you managed to irritate her, then I think you and I will get along famously."

"How much involvement were you allowed with the Skye legacy, though?" Gina asked. "I did see your name on many reports, but it wasn't clear to me how deep your knowledge went. Madeline may not have even allowed you to gain enough experience to make this a worthwhile endeavor."

His hands smoothed over his pants, flicking away an invisible piece of lint. "Well, to be honest... I'm a tad bit nosy. There's not much I don't know about the Skye legacy itself and I have an eidetic memory. When Madeline realized how much I already knew, she pretty much gave up and allowed me to take on more responsibility."

I took a deep breath and met Gina's gaze. The real question wasn't his ability or his knowledge of Skye matters, but whether he'd end up being eyes and ears for Marne Ceresa inside my own court. But I liked him. I liked his intelligence and his personality, at least so far. He wasn't contaminated by Ra, at least not the same way that Madeline had been. And we needed help. We needed to get through the Skye legacy as quickly as possible so I could head home.

:*What do you think?*: I asked Carys. :*Will he betray me?*:

She snorted and shook her head. :*Not that I can see. He's on the level of Winston as far as probabilities of doing a great job and being dedicated to you. Though that doesn't mean he won't still be eyes and ears for Marne Ceresa too.*:

I focused on Gina's bond. :*Let's give him a try, but slowly. Don't give him any Isador details if you can help it.*:

Aloud, I asked, "Would you be willing to assist Gina on a trial basis for a few days? Then if things go well, I'll add you to my team as second consiliarius."

He inclined his head. "It would be an honor, Your Majesty." Then he leaped up to his feet and whooped so loudly that Daire twitched against me, and Rik's fingers tightened on my shoulder. "Woo-hoo!"

Seeing our reaction, he laughed sheepishly, his cheeks turning beet red. "Sorry, sorry. It's just exciting. Granddad would be so proud of me that I'm making my own way and working into my own house. If it works out of course, Your Majesty. Regardless, I'm honored to assist you in any way that I can."

Gina lifted her large satchel onto the table in front of her. "Well, then, now that that's settled, let's go over the Isador sibling contract, shall we?"

Inwardly, I groaned. Daire took my cup and poured me more coffee. I was going to need it.

19

SHARA

We worked well into the wee hours of the morning, pausing only to eat sumptuous meals brought in by my team.

Gina had already drawn up a basic sibling contract based on the considerations we'd used with Zaniyah, though none of these siblings had their own nests, let alone heirs, to worry about. Kevin's eyes had just about bugged out of his head when he first saw my version that paid everyone double Skye's former contracts as well as allowing them to keep their own inheritances from their birth houses. Evidently, that was a rare allowance, which seemed ridiculous to me.

Why would I take away their birthrights, when I was already using them to solidify my power base? I said as much to him, and he shook his head. "It's the price weaker queens pay for protection. They need you more than you need them."

"I'm not in the mafia business. Nobody pays Isador for protection."

His eyes twinkled at my comparison. "Granddad would age a century if Marne Ceresa asked him to put such an allowance in her contracts. I feel that I should warn you, if Gina hasn't already. Once word gets out to other houses about Isador's favorable sibling arrangements, you'll be flooded with sibling requests. Most of the smaller houses never had enough of a legacy to tempt a house of Isador's stature, so they'll leap at the chance to align with you."

"That's not why I'm doing it, but I suppose that's a positive side effect."

He grimaced, shaking his head. "Not if the Triune objects to House Isador gaining too much strength too quickly. The houses are already balanced precariously, with a handful of large houses holding the power, and medium to smaller houses stacked underneath. These houses were never a concern to someone like Marne Ceresa. But even small pebbles stacked together can eventually topple a larger boulder if the balance shifts."

I smiled, but evidently it wasn't a nice smile by the way his eyes widened. "I'll deal with the Triune another day. I know how I want things done, and I refuse to strip birthrights from anyone who swears to Isador."

In the end, every sibling who'd stayed in the tower accepted my contract. Luckily, I only had to taste eight more queens' blood to solidify our alliances, assuming they all stayed too. My silver nails proved invaluable for making a small, tidy wound that didn't cause the same forceful climaxes as my bite.

Maybe it was petty of me, but I drank deeply from all the queens who wanted to swear to House Isador. For one thing, I hungered, though I'd rather have my Blood. But I also wanted to make a point. They'd all seen me drain Keisha Skye to death. I could drain them as easily. All of them. I chose to let them live, and I chose to pay them well to join my house. I didn't want to start out as their queen by making blatant threats, but I expected loyalty.

As the last queen approached me, pale and nervous, Kevin leaned down to whisper, "Daniella Thalassa, formerly a House Ceresa sibling."

So she carried Marne Ceresa's blood. Just the thought of tasting Daniella's blood, and taking Marne into my body, made me twitchy. "How did you come to serve House Skye?"

"The queens came to an agreement in a formal treaty," she replied.

Kevin offered a folder to me. The pages inside were hand-written in elegant, swirling strokes on what felt like some kind of antique parchment. The date in the upper left-hand corner gave me pause.

1480.

I glanced up at her again, unable to hide my amazement. She looked maybe thirty years old, not well over five hundred. Her complexion was smooth and glossy like a porcelain doll with big blue eyes and a delicate rose-bud mouth. Her gleaming brown hair was pulled back in an old-fashioned up-do with curls cascading down from the top of her head, though the short dress she wore was modern.

Despite the age of the document, the wording itself was simple to understand. Daniella Thalassa was an envoy to House Skye from House Ceresa and would improve relations and communication between the two houses.

Envoy. That seemed pretty clearly to mean spy.

"It was common for the queens to exchange envoys back in those days," she said quickly, noting the tightening of my lips. "It wasn't underhanded or sneaky in any way, shape, or form. I wasn't a spy or sent to betray Keisha in some way. I was truly supposed to bridge communication between her and Marne Ceresa. It was a mutually beneficial arrangement for several hundred years. I have Marne Ceresa's approval to make the same arrangement with you."

Fuck. She'd already been communicating with her former queen about me. I'd known that was a possibility. I just hated worrying that I'd said something or betrayed myself or my goddess without even thinking.

I tried to be as politically polite as possible rather than yelling *"fuck, no!"* "Please convey my appreciation to your queen for all the years of service you provided to Keisha Skye. Perhaps in the future she may wish to make a similar arrangement with House Isador, but until that time, I wouldn't dare offend her by taking one of her siblings into my house without personally agreeing to new contract terms myself."

Daniella inclined her head and curtseyed. "By your leave, Your Majesty, I'll return to Rome at once, then."

I nodded, trying not show as much relief as she was. She

probably thought I'd kill her, like I'd killed Alessandra. I closed my eyes a moment, fighting down a sudden wave of panic and reproach. She'd have told Marne Ceresa exactly what I'd done.

:*That's a good thing,*: Guillaume whispered. :*She'll respect it, because it was the right thing to do.*:

In my head, I heard too many other thoughts—and none of them were mine. Gwen was distracted, staring off into space as if she could hear something that no one else could. She mentally measured the distance between her and the Blood she'd called, trying to estimate when he'd arrive. Carys kept cooing what a good bird Winnifred was in cutsie baby-talk that was so at odds with her outward gruff appearance. The other queens were terrified, anxious, and excited, all at the same time, a dizzying mix of emotions.

My head felt so fucking cluttered now. All these new queen bonds made me feel stuffed and spied upon, even inside my own head. I could feel their emotions as my own. Could they feel mine? I didn't want them to know so much of myself. I didn't want them to know my heart. That was for my Blood alone.

:*Can I ensure they don't have full access to my thoughts, as I do theirs?*:

:*You're the more powerful queen,*: Rik replied at once. :*You can do whatever the fuck you want. Use them when you need to, but otherwise, shut them down.*:

Guillaume added, :*Just imagine them going dark, or silent, in your head.*:

I closed my eyes and blanked my mind. I wiped everything. I

just wanted a few moments of peace and quiet in my own head. Sweet, blissful silence.

Rik's fingers dug into my shoulders, grounding me. Though the pressure in his fingers told me he didn't like the silence much at all. Thinking of his bond was enough to let my alpha rush back into my awareness. His mind slammed up against mine, squeezing me tightly.

He fucking trembled, his fingers convulsing on my shoulders. :*Goddess help me, I couldn't feel you. It was like you'd completely dissolved the bond. You were fucking gone.*:

His bond settled in my head, laced with the scent of hot rocks and iron. :*I'm sorry. I had no idea.*:

I thought of Daire, and immediately his bond wound through me, just as frantic as a house cat who'd been locked out of the house all night by accident. Guillaume. His steel blade gleaming inside my head with a brutal, cutting edge. Xin, my ghostly wolf, howling mournfully until I opened to him. He pressed his nose against me and I fisted my hand in his ruff. I quickly opened the rest of my Blood bonds, not wanting them to be distressed another moment.

I could feel the other queen bonds, but I didn't touch them or let them come back up into my focus. I thought about Nevarre's Shadow, spreading over the window to block out the sun, and my sense of the queens faded even more.

Perfect.

Now that I had the bonds sorted, I wondered how different my power would feel, if any. I hadn't really tried to do anything since taking Gwen and Carys, and now I'd added seven others.

Some of them had taken siblings under House Skye, and some with Blood had also taken siblings. It was a complicated hierarchy of lives that now existed underneath my house name. My power base, ready for me to draw upon in times of need, would continue to grow as Gwen officially took her own Blood and siblings for the tower.

Remembering that Guillaume had said to try and pay attention to where I reached for my power, I closed my eyes and settled back against my chair. Rik still gripped my shoulders, but his touch was soft and steady not hard and desperate. I took my time sinking deeper inside myself. Thinking of my power... but not actively trying to call it up.

Night had fallen outside long ago. In fact, dawn was only a few hours away. I could feel the darkness now, though it was weakened by city lights that never went out. Blood trickled from the neat cut Guillaume had made for the queens. Just a few drops. I also sensed a large amount of period blood captured by the magical net I'd set so I didn't ruin all my clothes.

I'd been bleeding heavier than usual. Annoyingly so. I didn't know what it meant, if anything. Periods could change from month to month, and my Blood sure the hell weren't complaining.

Power flared to life inside me with a low, internal whomp like a gas stove or furnace catching flame. So much power, tossing me here and there like a tiny stick amidst a hurricane. Fuck, wave after wave crashed through me, lifting me higher. I had nowhere to go with it. Nothing to use it for. I wasn't in danger. I didn't need to grow another grove in the middle of New York City.

Thunder crashed and rolled in my skull, my ears roaring as if hundred-mile-an-hour winds rushed through me. My hands came up to my ears automatically, trying to quiet the noise. But it did no good. The noise was inside my head.

Finally, realization dawned on me. That endless thunder was the heartbeats of my new siblings. Several hundred lives thudded away inside my head, waiting to do my bidding. Using the Shadow again to distance myself from the pounding heartbeats helped. I still stood inside a raging inferno of rushing energy, endlessly searching for an outlet. A release. Power pummeled me, trying to bring me to my knees.

People always thought that great power was a fantastic gift, but in reality, it was a fucking nightmare. I had to figure out how to control it. With this much magic pulsing through me, I could obliterate New York City with a thought.

The power needed something to do. An outlet. Something big.

I had an idea. It might not work, but... What the hell. I'd try. The worst it could do was tear down my tower and kill us all. Not a pleasant thought.

Focusing my will, I pushed the power away from me. I could feel the crackling energy all around me, burning with my fire and Vivian's phoenix, softened by Isis' moon. A glowing magic sphere enclosed me, sinking down into the marble. Yes. I needed to go down. All the way to the ground.

One. Hundred. Stories.

I couldn't waver. I couldn't allow a distraction to break my concentration. I didn't think I'd survive the fallout if this power whipped back into me uncontrolled.

Distantly, I felt my physical body standing, my feet spread wide, my arms rising out on either side of me. Rik never let go of me. My anchor in the storm. His heavy palms on my shoulder kept me from getting sucked up into the maelstrom of power blazing through me.

I pushed the sphere's diameter out away from me. I needed to enclose this room. The hallway. My awareness passed through walls like a ghostly specter. Wider. I needed to hold the entire building. My arms trembled, strained wide as my sphere spread through the tower and out.

Into the night air.

I did it.

Relief made my heart pound, but I wasn't done yet. I took a couple of deep, forceful breaths, building up my strength. Then I shoved my power deep, down toward the ground. Falling. Wind blasted me as I picked up speed, almost like I was tumbling down an elevator shaft. Ground. I needed to find the ground. Not concrete and asphalt. I needed Gaia for this, the touch of Her life's essence. Not easily found in a skyscraper.

I smelled dirt and rocks moments before my power hit the packed earth deep beneath the concrete footings of my tower. I quivered, my legs trembling with strain. I held the entire tower in my sphere. I could feel the crisp, cool air on my face, even while my nose filled with the sterile, dark scents of dirt that never saw the light of day.

It was still alive, though. If I scraped some of this dirt up and put it into a pot, it'd grow whatever I gave it.

So I gave it my blood.

I released the magical plug holding my period blood inside

me. I felt the hot gush between my thighs. I smelled the raw iron and copper, mixing with the scents of cool earth and the darkness of night. My domain. Blood. Night. Dark.

Great Mother, please accept my offering and give me your protection on this place. Keep all who live inside this circle safe.

I shoved my blood deep into the earth, envisioning a giant blood circle snapping into place where my sphere touched the ground.

Land that had been neglected and misused for centuries lapped up my blood as eagerly as Daire. Tremors rocked the foundations of the tower. The building swayed, the floor shaking beneath my feet. Steel groaned, absorbing the stress of infinite power roaring up from deep in the ground and streaming hundreds of feet into the air like a geyser.

My blood circle. Complete. Without me ever stepping foot around it.

As the power ebbed, something called me. A whisper. A breath. I listened with my whole being, searching for that small, still voice.

Dried, dead lips whispered, *"Wake me."*

Panting, I opened my eyes. I'd fallen to the floor, though Rik cradled my head. My Blood were pressed in a tight circle around me, backed against me so they all touched me in some way.

Carys and Gwen both stood over Rik, glaring at me over his shoulders and clucking like angry chickens.

"A little warning would be nice, Your Majesty," Carys snapped. "You almost took down the whole building."

"We need you alive, not burned out into a shell," Gwen said only slightly less tartly. "What did you do, anyway?"

I closed my eyes a moment to be sure. The deep, red glow of my blood circle pulsed around the building, even up this high. Quirking my lips, I opened my eyes. "I laid a blood circle around Isador Tower."

Carys gasped. "No. That's not possible."

Gwen closed her eyes, and I felt her white light brush my power humming around the building. "She did. Goddess. I didn't know that was possible."

Rik stroked my cheek, his bond rumbling with worry. "You're hemorrhaging, my queen."

I didn't have to sit up and look to know a huge pool of blood was spreading around me. Grimacing, I rested back into his hands. "Brace yourselves."

I took a deep breath and released it, slowly, mentally preparing myself. Then I called my blood to me.

Super-charged period blood slammed into me, making me convulse. I felt the surge of release in each of my Blood, driven to climax by the feel of my blood sliding back into my power grid. All their pleasure simmered inside me, mixing and flowing with energy until my head wanted to float away.

I must have faded into la la land for a while. I opened my eyes and Rik was carrying me.

"Get the car ready," he ordered.

My eyes were heavy and sleep sang a sweet lullaby to me, but I wasn't wiped out like before. Tired, yes. Exhausted into a coma, no. Just high on pleasure and blood. The thought made me giggle. I had to concentrate fiercely to speak out loud. "Gina."

She stepped closer, her brow creased with concern as she looked down at me. "Yes, my queen?"

"Two. Things." I had to rest a moment, gathering my will. It was so hard to concentrate when I just wanted to drift away on piles of hard, sweaty muscle. "Ask Frank. Legacy."

Her eyebrows arched. "You want me to ask Frank to bring the legacy from your nest?"

I nodded jerkily, my head way too heavy to manage it gracefully. "I need it."

"At once, my queen. What else?"

I tugged on Vivian's bond. She stepped closer and touched my arm, her palm scalding hot on my skin. *:Tell her where we need to go to find Heliopolis.:*

Vivian gasped. "She says we need to go to Heliopolis. Surely you want to wait as long as possible, my queen? It's not a place that you can simply walk into and take what you want."

I might be bone tired and high on my Blood's pleasure, but my voice echoed with steel. "Indeed I will."

"Where?" Gina whispered, her voice shaking.

"Egypt, of course," Vivian breathed out. "Cairo. I can open the gateway there."

"When, Shara?"

I took a deep breath, trying to oxygenate my brain enough for clock math. I needed to rest. I needed to feed deeply. Frank needed time to fly here, though Gina probably already had him on a plane headed this way. And I had one important ritual to complete. I could only hope to find the clues I needed in the Isador grimoire. "Forty-eight hours, give or take."

"So soon," Rik said, his tone heavy with concern. He wasn't questioning me, not exactly. Just... worried.

"I must strike before he does."

He nodded, but his bond still weighed like tons of granite in my head. "What else, my queen?"

My eyelids fluttered, my words slurring. Hopefully they understood. "I need. To wake. Huitzilopochtli."

20

RIK

My queen slept on top of me like I was the most comfortable, airy mattress, rather than granite boulders. I kept a steady awareness on her bond, even though she slept deeply.

Those few moments where her bond had gone silent were the worst of my life. Worse than when she'd stepped into the Zaniyah nest and battled Keisha Skye's geas, while I was forced to stand outside. She'd at least had her other Blood with her, then. She'd had bonds to call upon.

This time, she'd had no one. And for one long, desperate moment, I'd feared that she might not let us all back in.

I couldn't blame her for wanting some peace and quiet in her head after taking so many siblings at once. Most queen siblings were added over generations, but in the span of twenty-four hours, Shara had taken nine.

Ten queens had sworn their lives to her. Gina said that accounted for nearly seven hundred former Skye siblings.

No wonder Shara had been able to lay a blood circle without tracing out its pattern. She'd already been formidable. Now, she had to be nearly unstoppable. Though that didn't mean I relished this trip to Heliopolis. At all.

Just thinking about it made me send a hard glare at Vivian through the bond. It wasn't her fault that our queen had decided to act sooner than later. Shara Isador would never stand aside and wait for someone else to help or protect another. That was only one of many reasons that I loved her.

Yet I still feared for her too. And I'd be a selfish asshole if I didn't admit that I was terrified I might be the one called to sacrifice his life for the red serpent.

I would do it. I wouldn't waver in my love and duty for my queen. Though I might wish such a terrible duty would fall to another, it was truly the alpha's place to make such a sacrifice for his queen.

She lifted her head, her eyes glittering dangerously. "Don't even think about it."

I kept my body easy and relaxed beneath hers, even though I wanted to clutch her desperately to my heart and beg her not to risk her life for any of us. "The goddess will choose. It's out of your hands."

Her head tipped slightly, her eyes taking on a knowing, all-powerful look of a goddess who couldn't be stopped. Surely very much like Isis must have looked while roaming ancient

Egypt. Though She'd been searching for Osiris's chopped-up body so She could resurrect him. "We'll see."

"What does that mean? You can't go against a goddess, my queen. Not even you."

One corner of her lips quirked briefly. "I know. But I feel a plan coming together. I don't know the details yet, but it's... building. The pieces are on the table in my mind and I'm sorting them. I'm constantly rearranging them. I almost see the picture."

I cupped her cheek and she rubbed her face deeper into the caress, making my heart crumble into a thousand pieces. "We're your pieces on the board, my queen. Move us to the position you need to ensure your victory."

She leaned down and brushed her lips against mine. "Checkmate."

"Yes," I breathed out, relishing every touch of her skin against mine. Goddess forbid that my days be numbered. That I might lose this. My queen, in my arms, looking at me like I was the northern star to guide the way, when she shone like the full moon and blotted out even the brightest star.

"I'm surprised you're not trying to talk me out of going to Heliopolis."

I huffed out a low growl, vibrating my chest against the softness of her breasts. "As if that would do me an ounce of good. My queen will do as she wishes. So it's been since the beginning."

"I can't stand by and wait, not when I know he's torturing women. I can't."

"I wouldn't expect you to."

She sighed, rubbing her cheek against my palm. "It's selfish of me. I don't want to hurt any of you. But sometimes, I miss the first days when you and Daire found me. When I didn't know about Ra and the Triune. When I didn't have so many people depending on me to make a plan and keep us all alive. The hardest thing I had to worry about was staying one step ahead of the thralls and wondering what kind of crap I'd have to clean up."

"That's not selfishness. I wish you could have the simpler life without danger." I glared at her, letting another growl rumble my chest. "Though my queen doesn't clean a fucking thing."

"I want that again. Just for tonight. I want it to be you and me and Daire, like it was in the beginning. In case..."

She couldn't finish that sentence, because I sealed my mouth over hers. I swallowed her words, as if I could erase her fears with a kiss. I didn't want her to be hurt or sad or grieve for any of us. Though I knew that was inevitable. The goddess had decreed it so.

Jerking her mouth free, she glared down at me. "Nothing is inevitable."

She sat up, straddling my hips. My cock was always at half-staff around her, and rock-hard every moment of the day or night when she was bleeding. But she didn't take me inside her. "I love you all, but tonight, I need to keep it simple. Everybody out except Daire."

"Lucky bastard," Ezra grumbled as he walked past, but everyone else did as she ordered without a word of complaint.

Daire rose to his knees, his palms loose on his thighs. He

stared at Shara, and though I couldn't see his eyes, I felt his emotion in our bond. Aching need. Tremulous and open and so damned needy. He wanted her to fuck him, sure. But more, he wanted her to lay claim to him. Take him. Use him. Make him hers for all time.

Yet our queen was always so careful to be sure of our wants and desires before she took us. She threaded her fingers in his hair. "What do you want?"

His purr dropped another octave, a rumbling bass that made my balls ache even more. "I want to feel those silver tips buried as deeply in me as Rik will be in you. I want you to hurt me, Shara. Hurt me until I forget that one of us is going to die."

She jerked his head back hard, twisting her hand deeper in his hair. Her voice quivered with fury. "No one's going to die. Not one of us."

"Who says so?" His voice was tight, his neck strained back under the force of her grip. But he didn't resist her. He never would.

"Me. I say so."

"Who?"

She forced him down to the mattress, sliding off me to pin him beneath her. "Shara fucking Isador."

Daire let out a rumbling chuckle. "Yes, my queen. Prove it to me. Prove it to us all."

DAIRE

I should die. It should be me.

That was all I could think every time I looked at my fearless queen and the rest of her Blood. I was good for cuddling and purring. I loved it when she allowed one of her other guys to push me around and fuck me. But in the end, what use was I, really? I wasn't alpha. I wasn't dominant. I liked to tease and test boundaries, but generally I was more annoying than anything.

I'd thought my warcat was badass when she'd first claimed me, but she had bigger and badder Blood now. If I could die so she could defeat Ra, I'd count that as a victory, especially if that spared Rik at the same time. Or Mehen. Or Ezra.

My throat ached and my eyes burned. I would not fucking cry. I refused to add another burden to the list of things she had to carry for us.

If I paid the price for the red serpent, I would know that I meant something to her. That—

She leaned down, nose to nose, and glared at me. "You're *everything* to me. Don't you know that?"

"No," Rik rumbled, his voice deep with reproach.

I closed my eyes, blocking out the sight of her. The love shining in her luminous eyes hurt too much. He was right. I wasn't everything to her. I couldn't be. She had too many Blood to deal with a bratty submissive cat, no matter how loudly I could purr.

Massive fingers seized my jaw and ground into my face, forcing me to open my eyes again. Rik scowled and gave me another good squeeze that made me wince. "He doesn't know, my queen. You'll have to remind him."

She pushed upright and opened her thighs, sliding down more fully over me.

Which put her bare, bloody pussy on my stomach.

I quivered. Every hair on my body stood straight up, like I'd just stuck my finger in a light socket.

She laughed softly and wriggled. Fucking smeared that hot, sweet blood on my skin. "You'll have to help me, Rik."

I groaned like she'd shoved her fist into my chest and yanked out my still-beating heart.

"Gladly, my queen, because he's everything to me, too."

"Don't fucking lie," I retorted, though my breathing was already ragged. "She's everything. I'm nothing. We're all nothing, as long as she lives. She can find another alpha. She can fucking take her pick of a dozen purring Blood right now from one of Skye's siblings. Her life above all. I learned my lesson, Rik, and you were right. You were fucking right."

Power flared to life, demanding that I look at her. That I worship her like the fucking goddess she was. Her bond weighed heavier inside me, crushing the life out of me. Until I surrendered. Until I finally met her gaze.

My heart stopped. Literally. Her power pulled on my will so hard that I couldn't breathe without her permission.

"I learned my lessons too." Her words fell heavily one by one, laced with power that throbbed through my body. "What this queen takes, she loves, and what she loves, she keeps for all time. I won't give you up. Not one of you."

"But—" Rik started.

She didn't move, but the force of her immense will snapped toward him, allowing me to breathe again. The biggest, baddest alpha ever to walk this earth immediately stilled. He didn't roll over and show his belly like I would have, but he gave up the fight before it could start.

He could have grabbed her face, like he'd done mine, and forced her to listen to him. But he would never touch a hair on her head in any way that was offensive. And to him, a giant smash-em-up rock troll, any gesture or word that was aggressive in any way to our queen would be as offensive as pissing on a goddess's shrine.

"I. Won't. Lose. You. Not one."

I couldn't help but drop my gaze to the red snake curled around her throat. Maybe it was a trick of the light, but I swore its head moved faintly, as if it was trying to free itself of her body and act. Now. Before it was too late and she missed her opportunity to end Ra's shiny ass once and for all.

She burst into laughter and the tension shimmering between us dissolved. "His shiny ass is definitely going to be eliminated."

"But how?" I asked softly, stroking my fingers up her thighs, unable to resist the temptation of touching her while she was so close. "If you don't use the snake, you can't kill him forever. He's a fucking god."

She nodded, her eyes deep, dark wells of mystery. "Oh, I fully intend to use it. I must."

I listened to her bond, trying to learn what she had planned. But either she didn't want us to know, or she truly hadn't decided how she would pull it off yet. I didn't know which one sucked more.

Rik blew out a frustrated sigh before I could. "Then you must pay the cost."

"I will. But it won't be one of you."

"One of the other Blood?" He asked hesitantly. "Nevarre was already dead—"

"No. *No.*" That one word resonated through me, heavy with her intent. "Not Llewellyn, even though he was my mother's. He's mine, now. I won't let him go. Not the headless knight. Not even Vivian. I won't risk her ability to regenerate herself as the phoenix. She's mine, and I'm keeping her too."

"Fuck it," I said, pushing my fear and emotion away. "Fuck Ra. Fuck all this bullshit. I don't know how you're going to pull it off, but I'm going to trust that you will. It doesn't do us any good to worry about what happens next, and this night isn't getting any younger."

She deliberately slid her pussy against me in a slow, delicious grind that made me grit my teeth. Lightly trailing those wicked silver nails across my chest, she chuckled. "Yeah. I think I will fuck it. And I'm going to ask Rik to fuck me while I do you. If you're lucky, he'll fuck me so hard that I'll tear you up with these nails."

My eyes rolled back into my head at the thought. "Sounds fucking good to me."

21

SHARA

I made my way down Daire's body with agonizing slowness, making sure to rub my blood all over him. He loved the exquisite torment. I could feel my blood burning on his skin, driving his need higher. Of all my Blood, he was the most open with what he wanted and needed from me.

Rik was stoic, alpha, and determined to always take care of me. He'd do anything I asked without hesitation, but he wouldn't ever allow his need to supersede mine. Even if I would enjoy it as much as I was enjoying Daire now.

I rose up enough to let his cock slide between my legs, dragging myself back and forth on his groin without actually taking him inside me.

Breathing hard, he clutched my hips, flexing his abs to curl up and get his mouth on my breasts. But he didn't try to get inside me. He waited, enjoying the torment. Hoping it would last as long as possible.

He sucked my nipple into his mouth, his tongue and teeth teasing the hard nub. The tip of his fang scratched over the tender flesh, making me moan. Now it was my turn to wait, to see how long I could endure his teasing before I put us both out of our misery.

Sucking on more of my breast, he inhaled me, gently pushing me deeper into his mouth.

I looked over at Rik, who still lay flat on his back, watching with dark, heavy eyes. One big palm lazily pumped his dick, though I didn't think he'd ever need to prime himself for me. My alpha was always ready, even if he'd already come just moments before. The only time I'd ever even thought about him not recovering quickly was when he'd licked my pussy.

"A feast," he rumbled like low, distant thunder.

Daire slid his fingers beneath me, smearing his palm in my blood. "I think he needs some lube. Don't you, my queen?"

Rik's jaw clenched, the muscles working across his cheek, but he made no protest as Daire reached over and wrapped his fingers around his dick, coated in my blood. His breath hissed out, his hips thrusting up restlessly into the other man's fingers. His dick swelled even bigger, thicker, calling me like the moon calls the tide.

Focusing on Daire, I braced the tips of my silver nails on his chest, just hard enough to get his attention. "Get that dick inside me."

He grinned, a dimple popping in his cheek. "His or mine?"

I pushed my nails slightly harder against him and slowly

scratched an inch or so down his chest. His teasing smile quickly faded to a groan. "You first. Rik will take care of his dick now that you've so nicely lubed him for me."

Daire positioned the head of his cock so I could slide down and take him inside me. Slowly. I teased just the tip, deliberately squeezing my muscles on him until he whimpered. He clamped his right hand over mine and pressed my nails harder into his flesh.

I smelled his blood and I couldn't tease him any longer. I took him to the hilt on one hard lunge that made us both gasp with relief. He wasn't the most well-endowed man, though none of my Blood were lacking in that department. But no one else had his purr. I pressed my pelvis harder against him, just to feel that vibration flowing through me.

"I could sit here like this and come all night," I whispered, letting my eyes drift shut.

"Goddess, that would be incredible."

Somehow, he managed to turn his purr into a ragged, growling rumble that made my clit throb with every beat of my heart. I pressed harder against him, holding my breath, letting him push me to orgasm.

My breath caught and my pussy rippled around him, but he didn't thrust. He didn't lose control. He didn't even come himself.

Opening my eyes, I stared at his expression, memorizing the dazed, raw look in his eyes. The soft pout of his full lips. The tawny fall of his hair around his shoulders like a wild lion's mane. I could get lost forever in his eyes. He gave himself over to me, his heart and soul an open book. He held nothing back.

No bit of pride or ego or fear prevented him from surrendering everything he had.

I dug my nails into him, relishing the way his pupils dilated and his nostrils flared. Eyes locked to his, I dragged my nails down his chest, leaving furrows in his skin. His blood coated the tips of my nails and my head fell back. My hips jerked, unable to stay still a second longer. Not when I could feel the rush of his blood hitting my system. I still couldn't believe that I could taste his blood, even though he wasn't in my mouth.

He buried his face against my throat and rubbed his bloody chest against me. I slid my arms around his waist and dug those brutal nails into the small of his back, pinning him close. Though he had no intention of moving away.

"Rik."

Immediately, my alpha wrapped me in his arms, his body hard and hot against my back. He slid his big palm along my right arm and grabbed my wrist, pulling my hand back toward his thigh. "What you do to him, I want you to do to me too."

"You're not into pain. Not like him."

"I am for you."

His words made me pause and really listen to my own desire. I liked that vulnerable, ragged look in Daire's eyes. I liked hearing the way he gasped. Those delicate sounds of pain that I swallowed from his mouth as eagerly as his blood.

It wasn't his pain that turned me on, not the way it cranked his lust. For me, it was the knowledge that he trusted me so completely that he'd allow me to do anything to him. Literally. He put his life in my hands, knowing my hunger. Knowing my power. He allowed me to feed on him so deeply that he passed

218 | JOELY SUE BURKHART

out, to the point where a few more swallows could actually endanger him.

He'd seen me drain Keisha Skye to death, but still never protested as darkness closed in.

"Fuck her hard, Rik," Daire rasped. "Make her shred my back with those nails."

"Gladly."

22

RIK

My dick was so hard I could cut diamonds with the tip. Her blood sizzled like acid, eating away at my control. I wanted to be inside her, feeling that rich, sweet blood on my flesh. Though I'd gladly take her ass too. I'd take anything she gave me. Every single fucking time.

Hell, I'd be perfectly happy to simply lie there and watch her come. I didn't need to come myself, not when I could feel her pleasure pouring through our bonds. The only thing better was coming inside her, and feeling her pleasure singing through the bond at the same time.

Her blood. Fuck. I could smell her heat, and every muscle in my body ached with the need to sink into her and empty my balls so hard and deep that an Isador baby would be inevitable.

Stupid. It wasn't the time. She wasn't ready.

But I couldn't stop that thought from sprouting in my head.

I could see her with a daughter. Goddess, they'd be so beautiful. She'd be an incredible mother, fierce, protective, a fucking unstoppable force of nature. She loved so easily, so openly. She didn't have to love all of us. She could take a hundred Blood—and might need that many to stand against the Triune—but she wouldn't. Because she wanted to love us.

She wanted this. Every night. Her body pressed between us. Hands sliding over her skin, hot flesh against hers, driving her need higher. If she wished it, she could have the rest of the Blood pressed against her. Hard dick and muscle for miles. Endless pleasure. Our focus entirely on her. Our queen. Our forever.

Yet she'd chosen to share this night with only me and Daire. Her original vampire knights.

Goddess, let this never end, I prayed, not ashamed of the sudden hot ache behind my eyes. *Protect her, please. Keep her safe. I'll pay the cost if I must, but I would rather love her for all time.*

She must have picked up on my grim thoughts in the bond, because she stabbed her nails deeper into my thigh. The small pain cut through my aimless worry, scattering my fears. All that mattered was her.

Straddling Daire's legs, I rubbed the tip of my dick down the crevice of her ass. Lower, so I could feel him inside her, and more importantly, her blood.

The future of House Isador. Everything her mother had sacrificed to bring about.

Daire slid his thumb though her dark curls and found her clit. I felt the jolt of her body between us. The immediate surge of her desire as he rubbed methodical circles around swollen, sensitive flesh. I pushed the head of my dick against her asshole, but I didn't force my way in. We had time. Even though my balls ached and a fist the size of my rock troll's blazed at the base of my spine.

Clutching my thigh, her sharp nails breaking my skin, she pushed back against me, pushing my dick inside her. Like Daire earlier, I simply froze, letting her use my dick, my body, for her pleasure. Her blood helped me slide deeper. So fucking tight I could feel the rub of his dick so close. Both of us moving inside her.

She claimed us both. Taking our hearts all over again.

I suddenly wished I'd been the one on the tree in Mexico. That she'd sacrificed my heart instead of Itztli's. My chest burned, my ribs creaking, as if the organ wanted to leap out of my body and do her bidding.

"Harder," Daire whispered raggedly. "She's not hurting me enough yet. Rik, please."

My blood hit her, sucked up by those silver nails, and I shuddered. I felt her thirst as my own, a burning, gnawing ache that would never be satisfied.

A thirst for me. For Daire. Forever unquenched.

I closed my hands around her waist and shifted her forward slightly, changing my angle inside her. I felt Daire's dick sliding inside her and I swore that sparks clashed between us, a combustible explosion waiting to happen. I filled her ass until my balls hung heavy against her, rubbing in her blood, and I was lost.

I sucked in a hard breath and hauled myself out of her so I

could ram home again. She dragged her nails down Daire's back and he pitched beneath us, pushing her higher. Pushing me deeper. Her nails blazed in my thigh like red-hot pokers. She gasped and tore at Daire's back. Again. Her fingers slipping in his blood.

I wanted it to last forever. I didn't want to come. I'd rather she drain me dry and keep us inside her as long as possible. If I came, I'd lose this. I'd lose this connection with them both.

We rocked together, pinning her between us. Smearing her with our blood. Our skin soaking up hers. Every breath made my lungs catch fire. Sweat poured off me like I'd run a marathon. But I couldn't stop. I didn't want to stop. My head pounded with my heartbeat, so rapidly that the constant thudding blanked out my eyes and ears. There was only her scent, the feel of her skin against mine, the tight, wet heat of her body, and the luscious haven of her blood.

The fist in my spine tore through my stomach. Fire licked my vertebrae. I tried to hold back the climax, but she sank her fangs in Daire's throat, and he roared with release. The savage, desperate howl brought my rock troll to the surface. It was all I could do not to shift as the first spasm hit me.

My balls clenched hard, my cock jerking inside her. For a moment, it felt like I'd picked up Ezra's hook. My dick felt massive, swollen, too large to move inside her any longer. But then the hot spill of my semen spurted deep inside her and I felt her body absorbing me. My sweat, my heat, my blood, my come.

My queen consumed me.

Her bond exploded in a brilliant spinning rainbow that obliterated my last conscious thought.

Panting, I forced my eyes open. We were tumbled together in a heap on her bed. She made a low, sated purr of pleasure that sure as fuck made my dick twitch all over again. I groaned, Daire laughed, and my queen nuzzled my throat.

"This was better than the first time," she whispered, lifting her head to see my face.

I brushed her heavy, sweaty hair back from her face and tried to slow my breathing down. "Practice makes perfect."

Her lips quirked. "You didn't shift and destroy the entire room."

"It was a near thing," I admitted, shaking my head. "You took me to the very edge of control. If I ever shift while I'm inside you..."

She brushed her lips against mine. "Don't tempt me."

As big as my rock troll was, I couldn't imagine the horror of what I'd do to her body. Shuddering, I clamped my fingers on her nape and put as much command in my voice as I dared to give my queen. "Don't even joke about such a thing."

She laughed softly, and I eased my desperate grip. "At least I didn't die this time, right?"

When I'd taken her virginity, she'd died in my arms. Coming into her power that first time had not been easy. I couldn't let myself remember the lifeless, heavy weight of her body in my arms without wailing like a lost, inconsolable child.

If I lost her now...

If someone didn't kill me quickly, I'd go absolutely raving

mad. I'd kill everyone and everything in my path until someone managed to put me down like a rabid dog.

"You can't die," Daire retorted, burrowing into us both for comfort. "You can't, Shara. Do whatever you need to do to save yourself. That's all we care about."

She combed her fingers through his hair and shushed him with a low hum, but her bond hardened in my mind. Tempered steel, a sleek, unbreakable blade crafted by a master swordsmith for one purpose.

Death.

23

SHARA

I'd forgotten what it was like to be able to sleep for a few hours and still function like a normal person. I'd never been a morning person per se, but I loved being able to roll out of bed after six or eight hours of sleep and not feel like death warmed over.

Poor Winston was shaken to see me downstairs before noon and didn't have anything ready for breakfast. Despite my assurance that I wasn't going to dry up and blow away from starvation, he insisted I sit at the kitchen island with a cup of coffee and toast while he quickly whipped up a masterpiece omelet.

Nevarre strode in and handed me a cellphone. Sliding my arm around his waist to keep him from leaving, I answered, "Hello?"

"You've rattled everybody with this new schedule," Gina

replied tartly, though I heard the amused grin in her voice. "Frank came here instead of the house. Should I send him over or would you rather come here?"

I didn't have to think very hard. "Please send him over here, and if you're free, I'd like you to be here too."

"Of course. We'll head over straight away."

"No rush, unless you haven't had breakfast yet."

I disconnected the call and handed it back to Nevarre. "I'd forgotten I even had a phone. Have you had it the whole time?"

His lips quirked, and he nodded. "We thought it would be easier if one of us was responsible for it. Only Gina ever calls you, and since she's usually with you, you shouldn't need it very often. I'm happy to keep it charged and ready for you, my queen."

He even made managing my phone sound dirty. Which I liked, very much indeed. I trailed my fingers down over his buttock playfully. He wore his kilt, tempting me to reach underneath and see exactly how charged and ready he was.

His voice deepened. "I'm always ready for you, my queen."

My fingers found bare skin and I started to make my way up his thigh, pushing the hem of his kilt up with my wrist. "Where do you even put a phone? Does your kilt have pockets?"

Winston coughed politely. "Your omelet is ready, Your Majesty."

Regretfully, I allowed the material to fall back in place. "You need to show me later, Nevarre."

He bowed formally, bending at the waist, which sent his shiny black hair waterfalling over his shoulder to brush my arm. "With pleasure, my queen."

I'd barely taken a bite, when I heard Gina talking with Magnum as they headed to the kitchen. They stepped inside, and Gina gasped. "Miracles do happen! She's awake before noon!"

"Haha, very funny," I grumbled with a blush.

The marble island went on for miles, so there was plenty of room for Gina to take a seat beside me. Frank carefully set a box covered in white linen in front of me and then backed away slowly, like it'd bite him if he startled it.

"Thank you, Frank. Sorry to drag you all the way out to New York City."

He started to blush too and waved off my appreciation. "It's an honor, Your Majesty. Besides, this gave me the chance to check on the new hires. I hope they've been doing a good job for you so far?"

"Yes, a definite improvement over the guards Keisha Skye had. I love the uniforms too."

He wore the black Isador shirt, though he wore black cargo pants rather than khakis. "A team always seems to perform better when they have a uniform they can be proud of. If it's alright, I'll head back over and make sure they're following procedures."

"Of course. Thanks again."

"Should I give you some privacy, Your Majesty?" Winston asked.

"Don't be ridiculous." I pulled off the white linen cloth and set it aside so I could look at the box itself while I finished my breakfast. Daire refilled my coffee cup before I was ready to open it up.

I'd put off looking at its contents since that first time in Kansas City. I knew what was inside. I'd seen it before, or at least glanced at it. Four ancient clay jars and a thick, leather-bound book that had been hand-stitched and painstakingly copied by my mother from all the Isador queens before her.

A compilation of my family's entire history. Hopefully, it also included some hints on how I was supposed to defeat Ra. Without dying.

Dread tightened my stomach and I had to push my plate aside. I couldn't eat another bite, not with my stomach in knots. Those four jars represented pieces of the goddess, Isis. Her gifts that Her daughters had inherited over thousands of years. Since I was the last daughter of Isis...

She'd given me *all* Her gifts.

I'd already transformed into a giant cobra queen and enven-omed Rik. I'd sprouted wings in Venezuela when I freed Leviathan from his prison and added Mehen to my Blood. As the wyvern, I'd saved us both when he shifted back to his human form after centuries of imprisonment and tumbled out of the sky.

In Mexico, I'd gained the new form of a winged jaguar, partly Isis' gift, and also partly my new queen sibling, Mayte's, whose gift was calling jaguars.

All wonderful gifts, but also dangerous creatures. Monsters.

I'd seen a cat head and a cobra on the jars. I couldn't remember what carvings the other two jars had, but one of them had to have something to do with wings. My instincts insisted that whatever was on that fourth jar—whatever gift I had yet to receive—was terrifying. Something inside me lurked for the right time to come crawling out of me to fight a god.

But if it helped me save us, then so be it.

A mosaic Isis held a tiny golden bowl in her hands, lifting it up like an offering. Only the blood of Isis could open the box, and I was the last.

It was a sobering thought. If I died, these gifts that were incredibly ancient and powerful would simply fade away.

I pressed my thumb into the tiny golden bowl on the box's top. A small hidden pin punctured the pad of my thumb, drawing my blood. And even though I was still on my period, my Blood smelled that tiny drop and went on full alert. I held my thumb out to Nevarre and let him lick the small smear of blood away.

Fine cracks appeared around the box, showing me the lid. I lifted the wooden top and set it aside. I took my time, letting my eyes settle on the familiar first. The closest jar's lid was a black hooded cobra with a red diamond on her hood. I picked the jar up carefully, surprised that it wasn't heavy at all. The lid came off easily, and I verified there was nothing inside.

The next jar's lid was a gorgeous tawny sphinxlike cat head wearing a blue lapis lazuli collar. I didn't open it to check its contents. I knew I'd already received the gift of my jaguar. The third jar was topped with large black wings that arched up and crossed at the tips. That explained why both my cobra and the jaguar could fly.

I took a deep breath and focused on the fourth and final jar. Its top was cone-shaped and colored a murky green. I picked it up and had to shift my grip, because it was extremely heavy.

Whatever was inside pulled my hands down hard, as if giant magnets were trying to suck it down into the ground.

I set it on the bar in front of me so I could study it without straining to hold it. It had scales on the lid and the top ended in what might be a blunt nose with a hint of teeth where the jaws would open. A crocodile? Goddess help me. I had dreamed about having crocodile teeth before.

But the bottom of the jar didn't seem to go with the top at all. If the jar was a crocodile, the bottom was more like a hippopotamus. With a weirdly long tail.

"Does anyone know what this is?" I asked softly.

"Ammit," Gina whispered hoarsely. "The Devourer. Eater of Hearts."

Oh shit. I shivered, and Rik immediately enfolded me in a hug, pulling me back against his chest.

"To understand Ammit, you need to understand ancient Egyptian religion," she continued. "I hope you can find more answers in your mother's book, because my knowledge is limited."

"Do you mean like the *Book of the Dead*?" Guillaume asked.

"Exactly. When an Egyptian died, the body had to be prepared correctly, so that the person could stand before Anubis for judgement."

For once, Daire wasn't purring. "Is this the heart and feather thing?"

Gina nodded. "Yes. The heart is weighed against Ma'at's feather. If your heart was too heavy, or in other words, carried too many sins, it was given to Ammit."

My stomach clenched so hard that it hurt to breathe. "Ammit ate the sinners?"

"So they say, which is why she was feared. She's represented as part crocodile, lion, and hippo, the three most deadly creatures of the Nile."

I closed my eyes, fighting down the bile that burned my throat. I seriously regretted eating now. Even though the mushrooms browned in butter had been delicious. "Let me get this straight. I have to fucking *eat* Ra's *heart?*"

24

SHARA

I'd done and seen some weird and fantastic shit since I discovered my heritage, but *eating* hearts wasn't something I'd ever thought I'd face. Drinking blood, sure. Pulling a still beating heart out of Itztli's chest...

Burying my face in my hands, I groaned miserably.

Ezra let out a disgusted growl. "If she's going to kill Ra by eating his fucking heart, why the fuck does she need the red serpent?"

"Ra's immortal, asshole," Mehen retorted. "Have you ever tried to eat a god's heart? It's not like she can just walk up to him and say, 'Pardon me, Lord of Sun. Could I please have a bite of your heart?'"

I laughed. I couldn't help it.

Which was exactly why they did it.

Lifting my head, I reached out with trembling fingers to touch the jar again. The lid was solidly locked shut. The gift was still inside. I had no idea how to get it out, but I hadn't done anything to bring the other gifts to life. Isis sent me what I needed just in time. It'd be foolish to fear She wouldn't do so again, when I'd been born for this purpose.

My mother had prepared the way for me before I was even born. She'd visited my future queen sibling, Mayte, in dreams. She'd compiled centuries of notes into one place for me. What I needed was here, in the legacy, and wrapped around my throat. I just had to figure out how to use the gifts I'd been given and keep everybody alive.

Every. Single. One.

"Do you need me at the tower for anything today?" I asked Gina.

"No, Gwen and I can handle everything. She's been working her way through the siblings and organizing who's staying and who's leaving. We'll compile a list of things we need your input on, and we can go over it tonight. Maybe a late dinner?"

I nodded. "That sounds good. How's Kevin working out?"

"Excellent so far. A very quick mind, amiable to work with, eager to dig in and help, which of course is a concern if we can't trust him. So far, I have no reasons not to be suspicious, but it's early yet. I asked him to make a list of everything he'd been suspicious of while working under Madeline so we can go through those files with a fine-toothed comb." She hesitated a moment, her eyes crinkling with worry. "Do you still want to go to Cairo?"

My mouth was as dry as the Sahara. "Yes. Soon. I won't risk

Xochitl a moment longer than I must. We don't know who else in the Zaniyah nest he might have corrupted. Mayte said she'd keep her inside, but you know how kids are. I'm terrified one of his followers will cause a distraction, and within moments, she runs outside the blood circle to pet a horse. Or goddess forbid, he figures out that she loves unicorns and conjures one to tempt her outside. She'd go in a heartbeat."

Gina nodded grimly. "I'll have the jet standing by."

"Winston, I need a place where I can sit quietly for hours to read and think. With lots of tea, coffee, and snacks."

Turning around with a platter already loaded with exactly that, he stepped toward the door. "Right this way, Your Majesty."

As we walked down the hallway, I marveled again at the size of this house. There had to be at least ten rooms on this level that I hadn't even seen yet. Plus, the bedrooms upstairs for guests, and the very top floor for the winged Blood to come and go easily. It was beautifully decorated and well maintained, but... cold. Empty. The only room that held any hint of my mother's personality was the one bathroom where she'd delivered me. Otherwise, anyone could have lived here.

He paused outside a door, and Magnum stepped around us to open it for him. "Your mother's library, Your Majesty. I took the liberty of lighting the fireplace. If you're too warm, please let me know."

"Thank you." I followed Winston inside. Expecting the room to be large and spacious with wall-to-wall books, I was surprised to find it small, cozy, and dark, like we were tucked up beneath the stairs. In front of the fireplace were a couple of easy chairs, with lots of cushions and pillows on the floor. On the opposite side of the room was a high work table with stools. Modern track lights hung over the table for targeted lighting, though they weren't turned on now.

There were shelves all around the room, but only a few actually held books. The rest held antiques and collectables, though there were several cabinets behind the work table with shelves and doors that could have hidden anything.

"This room has no windows, so it's safe for any spells you wish to work," Magnum said.

Startled, I looked around the room as it dawned on me. This was my mother's *magic* room. A place of darkness, hidden from Ra, so it was completely safe. She must have plotted how she would conceive me here.

As I walked around the room trying to take it all in, my throat ached. How many days and nights had she come here to shut out the world outside? How long had she worked and plotted and suffered to make sure that I would stand here, now, and see the things she'd left behind for me?

"Countless years," Llewellyn whispered beside me, his voice raw. "Sometimes she refused to allow me inside, but I could feel her pain, and her joy. She would have done anything to make sure you could stand here now."

It made me remember the writing on the wall upstairs where she'd delivered me. *Lo, Father of Monsters, look down from Heaven and see what we have wrought.*

What *she* had wrought. She'd dedicated countless years of planning and careful manipulation to ensure her—and my—success. She'd sacrificed everything for me, including her life.

Which was why I was sure that whatever information I needed for this final battle with Ra would be here. Either in her room, or in the book she'd left for me. The pieces were on the board. The puzzle was ready to be solved. The game, won. I could feel the threads vibrating closer, straightening, ready to snap into place.

This time, I would be the hungry spider at the center of that web.

25

RIK

We held our queen for hours while she read in front of the fireplace. I lay on my side behind her, so she could use my chest to support her back. Daire was wedged partway between us, his purr a steady drone. The rest of her Blood came and went quietly, taking turns to refill her cup, bring her something to nibble on, or answer a question.

The latter was mostly Mehen and Guillaume, her oldest Blood who'd seen more than I could even begin to comprehend. Mehen, especially, had a wealth of knowledge about the ancient world, as if he'd accumulated the memories of every person he'd ever eaten. For all I knew, maybe that was exactly how he knew so much, though the man also loved books almost as much as he loved our queen.

The questions were so varied that I had no idea what she was planning. Once, she even asked Nevarre for her phone so she could call her queen sibling in Mexico.

"What do you know about Huitzilopochtli? Even stories that you might not think are important."

"Hold on a moment, my queen." Mayte was silent for several moments before continuing. "I'm sorry, Shara. I needed to make sure no one overheard this discussion. Several years ago, when I wanted to find Tepeyollotl and have a child of my own, Grandmama finally told me about how Mama conceived me. I don't know for sure, but we suspect that he's my father."

Fuck. I didn't like that at all. Now Shara had not one, but two people in her house that were descended from sun gods.

Shara didn't seem to be bothered by it. I could only hope that Isis' blood in her was strong enough to combat anything Ra or Huitzilopochtli's blood might throw at her.

"I suspected," she replied softly. "You were the last Aima queen born in recent memory. That's why my mother talked to you in dreams, isn't it? To be sure she could replicate whatever your mother did to have me."

"That's how I knew to find a god of my own to have Xochitl, but I've been careful to try and never even say his name, especially outside my nest, just to be safe."

"Tell me everything you can."

"You remember how my brothers were conceived, right?"

As a young queen, Mayte's mother had been fostered in a larger house, where the unspeakable happened. She was raped by their queen's Blood.

I couldn't comprehend how any Blood would even consider

such an evil act on any woman. Let alone a queen, even a queen not his own. Our queens were so rare. Even five hundred years ago, Aima numbers had been declining rapidly.

If Shara ordered me to rape another woman, I didn't think I'd be able to do it, even with her bond compelling me to complete her orders. Perhaps I was naive, but I couldn't believe that our goddesses would have ever allowed such an atrocity to happen. I couldn't be Shara's Blood, let alone her alpha, if she would ever command me to do something like that.

It wasn't in me. It wasn't in her.

"Mama wasn't ever right after that," Mayte said. "She rarely talked and often just... existed. One bright sunny day, a hummingbird was flying near her, like she was playing with it. When Grandmama came back, Mama was gone. Even Grandmama's alpha couldn't find her. It was like she stepped outside the nest and disappeared. She was only gone two days, but when she came back, she was incredibly happy and better than she'd been in decades. She told Grandmama that he was coming back for her on the summer solstice, but he never did."

"Did she know why?"

"Not at all. Mama fell into a deep depression, and Grandmama worried every day that she'd lose me. Weird things started to happen. Horrible storms. Giant spiders coming out of the jungle. Mama was terrified of them, but few people would know that."

"Why was she scared of spiders?"

"House Tocatl, where she fostered, was dedicated to the Great Goddess of Teotihuacan. Even Grandmama doesn't know much about Her, but She's always pictured with spiders.

Since few people would know that, Grandmama assumed that meant he was trying to kill Mama before she could deliver me."

Shara didn't reply, and I felt the turmoil in her mind. She didn't want to give Mayte false hope, or worse, alarm her, but she didn't want to deceive her either. Would she want to know about the mummy we'd found? Or how Shara intended to use him? Because her bond hardened with a cutting edge when she thought of the sun god hidden away in the basement of her building.

"If the attacks were targeted at me, wouldn't they have continued all these years? Wouldn't I have sensed him watching me? Hunting me?"

"Not necessarily," Shara replied softly. "I found him in Skye Tower. He's been here for a long time as far as we can tell, and very much dead."

"Dead?" Mayte whispered. "But he's a god."

Through my queen's bond, I felt Mayte's shock and sorrow. She'd feared her father, but she'd also wanted to know him. She'd hoped that maybe…

Maybe he would love her.

Even two-hundred-year-old vampire queens still mourned for parents she'd never known.

"He's been mummified and his body is definitely dead. Though I'm sure I can bring him back."

Mayte gasped softly. "But should you? What if he really was trying to kill me? Would he go after Xochitl too?"

"Nothing is certain, but I think he must be a part of how I will take down Ra. In fact, some of Ra's human goons broke in last night and tried to burn the mummy. I think Ra is just as scared that I'll resurrect Huitzilopochtli as you are."

"But why?" Mayte's voice rang with bewilderment. "He's a sun god. He joined Ra as far as we know."

"Exactly. As far as *we* know. I won't know why he's mummified and locked away in a queen's nest until I wake him. Keisha was definitely scared of him and had put every protection she could think of on his prison, even though he's dead. That tells me a lot about why he might have been there. I might not have tried to resurrect him, until they tried to destroy him."

"But maybe that's exactly why they tried."

Shara sat upright rather than lounging back against me. "Maybe. Though when I laid the blood circle, I distinctly heard his voice telling me to wake him. He's part of this, as surely as you are. That's why I need to know as much about him as possible."

"Well... Let's see. He was one of the patron gods of Tenochtitlan. He was the god of war too. His mother was Coatlicue and according to the legends, he loved her dearly. There's one story where he even killed his sister to protect his mother. They found a huge stone carving at the base of the Templo Mayor that shows her body cut up into pieces in his rage."

Something clicked inside of Shara's mind. It made me sit up quickly, alert for any danger, though she didn't otherwise react. "Coatlicue must love him very much too. She gave me the red serpent so I could kill Ra and avenge Her son. She wants me to free his soul so he can return to Aztlan, whatever that is."

"Archeologists think it's the place where the Mexica people

originated, but let me tell you that I spent twenty years searching for the location, and it's not a place on a map. Aztlan is more than that. It's like an entirely different realm."

Another click in Shara's head reverberated through our bond, like a thief methodically cracking a safe. "Through a portal."

"Yes. I used an obsidian mirror to reach Tezcatlipoca, my jaguar god's other aspect. Humans have lost their souls after touching Aztlan. Mama drowned in the cenote trying to reach her lover, and that golden bird Ra sent to attack us almost took my daughter through the same portal."

Shara's breath sighed out softly, her mind racing from ideas and scenarios so quickly I couldn't keep up. Tension hummed in our bond, as if she was on the verge of something momentous. "Vivian."

The new female Blood immediately dropped down to her knees in front of us. "My queen?"

"You said Ra's priests are constantly trying to cure him."

She nodded. "There's a poison in his blood that burns, driving him into a frenzy."

"Do you know where the poison originated?"

"There was a story whispered in Heliopolis, but I don't know..."

Shara nodded impatiently. "Even if it's just gossip, I need to know."

"When I was still a fledgling, the oldest captive queen said he was bitten by a snake."

Shara flipped through the Isador book on her lap, quickly turning pages until she came to one near the beginning of the book. "The mighty sun god walked the land, proud of his creations, but the heat of his passing began to damage what he had wrought. The ground dried and cracked in misery. The Nile withered to a modest stream. Crops failed. Crocodiles and leopards hunted the people, desperate for food as their prey died.

"Thus Isis decided to persuade Ra to move aside and allow the people to flourish. She made a snake out of Ra's essence and sent it to lie in wait for the sun god. When it bit him, the snake made him very ill. Ra has power over all things of sun and day, but he couldn't heal himself since the snake was part of him.

"Isis promised to heal him, but only if he agreed to tell her his secret name of power. She knew that if she asked him to distance himself from the world, that he would refuse. He was too proud. He wallowed in his achievements and the adulation of his people. They couldn't praise him enough. He would never willingly lose their worship.

"Finally, the pain forced Ra to agree to her bargain. He disappeared to a secret place, and took her heart to heart, so her body would know his secret name. Now, the mighty sun god's power was hers, and Isis stood equal to him in power. She commanded him to withdraw from the world.

"And so he did'"

Mehen let out a disgusted huff. "Took her to a secret place and held her heart to heart? You know what the fuck that means, right?"

Shara laughed, shaking her head. "I suppose the gods and goddesses all took turns with each other, wouldn't they?" Her laughter faded, and she read through the next page to herself. "Though I don't get the impression that it was an experience she ever indulged in again. Whoever wrote this passage says that Isis believed that Ra helped Set murder Osiris to punish her."

"He definitely holds a grudge," Vivian said. "But that doesn't explain the poison that still burns in him."

I'd been silent for so long, that when I spoke behind her, Shara jumped a little. "Maybe it's like your venom in me. You healed me, but your venom is still in my blood. He probably still carries the antivenin from that snake's bite."

Shara turned slightly to face me, her fingers cupping my cheek. "And when they lay heart to heart, he fed on her. Or she fed on him. Or both. Now he hungers for more Aima blood, but especially an Isis queen."

My jaws ached from clenching too hard. "Then he will especially hunger for the last Isador queen."

I didn't like the look in her eyes. Sadness. Regret. That heaviness in her eyes had me pulling her closer, as if I could shield her.

She blew out a sigh. "Now I know what bait to use to gain access to Heliopolis."

SHARA

I wasn't sure which one was more furious, Rik or Vivian.

"No," they both retorted at the same time.

"I won't let you out of my sight," Rik growled, his shoulders bulging like towering cliffs of granite.

"You don't know what he's like," Vivian added. As her rage blazed higher, Smoak burned hotter. If she wasn't careful, I had a feeling she'd light my sweater on fire and torch the fragile papers of the Isador history. "I know you're strong, my queen, but his power is literally painful. It hurts to even be anywhere near him, and the closer he gets, the more it hurts."

"If he lays one finger on you..." Rik trembled with the force of his fury.

I said nothing, allowing them each to vent their emotions. Even Mehen practically frothed at the mouth at the idea that I might go in alone to deal with Ra.

When that was exactly what I'd done to bring Leviathan to heel.

"That was entirely different and you know it." Mehen's eyes glittered like green fire, his words snapping between us. "I only wanted to eat and kill you to win my freedom. I would have made it quick. He'll want to fuck you first and deliberately torture you as long as possible before maybe someday you die in horrible agony."

"And that's exactly why I must go, so that I can stop him."

"How?" Rik's neck and shoulders corded, veins standing out in stark relief against his skin. "How will you stop him?"

I didn't say anything, but only touched the scales embedded in my throat.

Mehen seized my arm and whirled me around to face him. He leaned down into my space, each word quivering with fury. "And how close will you have to be to that monster to use the serpent? This close, Shara? What will stop him from blasting you into smithereens as soon as you put one dainty toe on Heliopolis soil?"

I leaned in and pressed my forehead to his. He crumpled

against me, hauling me tightly against him. "I'll have to be close, of course. I'll need a distraction, or at least a reason for him to not kill me right away. And that's where Huitzilopochtli comes in."

I'd dropped the phone, but I heard Mayte calling my name. I picked it up, though I was still smashed against Mehen. "I'm here."

"You can't trust him, Shara. At all. If he would kill his lover, why wouldn't he kill you too?"

"Even if he did indeed try to kill your mother before you were born, I don't think he could kill me if he tried. He's mortal. He's mummified. I can resurrect him by calling his soul back to his body, but he won't be the Aztec god of war and sun any longer. He'll be... Well, I'm not sure. More than human. But not a god."

"Are you sure?" Mayte's voice quivered and I felt her in the bond, clutching Xochitl as tightly as Mehen held me.

Tears burned my eyes. I felt her dread and absolute terror. I couldn't blame her for fearing for her daughter. "As sure as I can possibly be. I swear to you that if I have any reason to distrust him, I'll put him right back into the grave. Isis gave me Her power over life and death for a reason. I won't need the red serpent to suck his soul out and leave him an empty shell again. He won't hurt you or Xochitl."

I didn't say, unless something happens to me first. Everyone was already upset enough.

Rik fisted his hand in the neck of my sweater, picked me up, turned me around, and dropped me into his lap. I wrapped my arms around his neck and buried my face against his throat, content to hold him until some of his worry for me eased.

"Tell me." His rock troll wanted to start tearing shit apart to reach me, even though I was still right here, in his arms. "Tell me your plan."

I ran my hands down his back and slipped my palms up beneath his shirt so I could feel the heat of his skin. "I don't know yet. I need to wake Huitzilopochtli first. I need to know why he's imprisoned, why he's mortal, and if there's anything left of his power that I can use."

"And then?"

I stayed soft and easy in his arms, my hands stroking up and down the long muscles of his back. "We go to Cairo. Vivian will open the portal to Heliopolis. And I go inside."

A tremor rocked his body against me like a massive earthquake had just dropped California into the Pacific Ocean. "Alone?"

"No. I don't think so." I breathed slowly, still stroking him. "Like Mehen said, I'll need a reason for Ra not to blast me into smithereens as soon as I show up. He needs a reason not to fear me, or suspect me of being capable of bringing him down. If I try to walk into his palace with the open goal of killing him, he'll just attack me before I can get close enough to use the serpent."

"Mehen's right." Rik's voice rumbled like rocks grinding into dust. "You'll have to be very close to use it, unless that snake can fly."

"Then I get close. I'm the bait. I can't change that. Ra wants a queen, and he'll want one of Isis' lineage even more. Maybe he hopes I can heal him, like Keisha wanted me to heal Tanza."

"Or more likely, he wants to foul Isis' line by siring a queen on one of her daughters," Vivian said grimly.

I shuddered, and Rik almost popped my ribs squeezing me harder against him. "I won't fuck him. I'll die first. But I may have to allow him to think that I'm open to the idea. I may have to allow him to believe many things that I hope you all know aren't true."

Daire pressed his face against my flank, wriggling beneath my sweater to find my skin. Mehen smashed me against Rik. Vivian braved the other men and hugged me from the other side. My other Blood stood close, Guillaume on one knee, a hand braced on the floor, his head hanging down as if he'd been stripped of his honor.

"I've never assassinated a god before," Xin said, his voice cold and hard. "Send me through the portal. Allow me to get him first. Even if he's immortal, I can at least provide a distraction."

"What if your power of invisibility doesn't work against him?" My voice was faint, because I couldn't breathe. But I didn't ask them to loosen their hold on me. "What if they kill you immediately, and I'm incapacitated by the pain of losing you? He's God of All Things Light and Day. For all we know, all our powers will be useless against him, or surely others would have succeeded in killing him already."

"The Morrigan's Shadow can stand against him," Nevarre said, his baritone ringing. "The Phantom Queen sent me to you for a reason. You need my darkness to fight his light."

"Vivian, is there more than one portal to access Heliopolis?"

"Of course, some more guarded than others. I know them all."

"How are they opened?"

"The blood of Ra opens portals. His foul blood burns in my veins."

I lifted my head from Rik's neck and focused on her. Solemnly, I asked, "Would you be willing to allow a few of my men to feed on you, only so they may carry that same power and open extra portals?"

She stared at me, her lovely face glowing with inner fire. Her eyes so fierce they pierced my soul. "For you, my queen, I will do anything. Anything at all."

26

SHARA

The dusty basement room was crowded with all my Blood, Gwen, Carys, and Gina. Though I didn't ask any of them to leave.

My rat friend sat on my shoulder, her tiny paw locked in my hair. Through her, I felt hundreds of other rats nearby. If the worst happened, and Huitzilopochtli tried to kill me or escape to kill his daughter and granddaughter, they would clog the tunnels with their little bodies and prevent him from reaching the surface. Hopefully by then, one of my Blood could kill him.

Guillaume had brought out his heavy Templar sword for this job. He stood at the mummy's head, ready to chop him in half at the first sign of trouble. Xin, Ezra, Nevarre, Llewellyn, and Daire all stood at the door to prevent his escape.

Clutching the Isador grimoire in my arms against my chest, I turned to my twins. "Is there anything else you can tell me about him? Signs of his power? Anything?"

"His calendar day is One Flint." Itztli's face was grim and hard, though his black dog's mournful eyes looked back at me. "The first day of the calendar to symbolize his founding of Tenochtitlan."

"He was the god of human sacrifice, war, and the sun," Tlacel added. "War captives were most often sacrificed to him, but every year, a handsome young man would be chosen to take the god's place. He would live in luxury as Huitzilopochtli until he was sacrificed during Toxcatl. Warriors who died in battle were transformed into hummingbirds and flew to his side. Also, women who died in childbirth. They were considered great warriors for battling to bear a child and received honors at his side."

Itztli lightly gripped the hilt of his obsidian blade on his hip. "He was always pictured with Xiuhcoatl, a weapon that was made to look like a fire-breathing dragon. It might have been a spear thrower, though I also saw a picture once with Xiuhcoatl stuck in his sister's chest."

"The one who tried to kill his mother?" I asked.

He nodded. "He chopped her up and threw her head up into the sky, which became the moon. Xiuhcoatl was sometimes thought to be a representation of the fire god, too. He supposedly threw it during battles like lightning bolts."

Handing the book to Gina for safekeeping, I stepped closer to the mummy. I held my hands out over him, palms down, though I didn't touch him. Closing my eyes, I listened, not with my ears, but with my magic.

I sank slowly into the mummy. I felt the rasp of brittle wrappings around the body. Dried and shrunken flesh. Cords of muscles that had tightened to thin strips of leather. Bones. So ancient my mind couldn't comprehend exactly how old he must be. As old as Isis, surely. Would I someday find the Great One's body like this? Lost and forgotten, dried up in some dingy basement?

Or my mother's?

I felt a cold wisp brush my nape, sending chills trickling down my spine. I had a feeling that my mother would never have left her body behind. She wouldn't risk me trying to find her so I could resurrect her.

:My time is over, daughter. It is your time to rise.:

Deep inside the mummy, I felt the cavity where his organs should be. In true Egyptian fashion, they'd been removed. That told me it had to have been done by Ra, or at least ordered by him. It didn't make sense that Keisha Skye would have attempted to mummify an Aztec god.

The emptiness didn't feel right, though. There was an echo. A greater hole that felt wrong. It took me a moment to realize why, but I had to check the book to be sure.

Opening my eyes, I lowered my hands. "Gina, can you find the page where the mummification ritual is covered? It should be fairly close to the beginning."

She flipped carefully through the pages. "Yes, here it is. What do you need?"

"Is the heart removed?"

"No," she replied. "It must be kept with the body. The heart was the seat of thinking and emotion for ancient Egyptians.

That's why it had to be weighed against Ma'at's feather of truth before they could continue their journey to paradise."

"Bingo," I whispered, smiling. "That's why he's trapped as a mortal. Ra had his heart removed. It's not here."

"Can you resurrect him if there's no heart?" Rik asked.

"I'm not sure, but I think so. I can bring his soul back to the body, but he won't be Huitzilopochtli the god until he regains his heart."

In the bond, I felt an immense wave of relief from Mayte, who was holding on tightly to our bond, watching everything I did. I could almost feel her pressed against my back, even though she was at least a thousand miles away.

I closed my eyes again, but this time, I wanted to ground myself. I concentrated on the earth beneath my feet, still separated from me by concrete, but closer than when I'd been in the top floor of the tower. I felt the hum of my blood circle singing around me, brilliant energy streaming up from the ground to the hundredth floor, blocking all attempts—human or supernatural—to break my protections. Powered by my period blood, this circle could not be broken.

Not until my death.

I reached deeper inside myself and found my heart tree hundreds of miles away in Eureka Springs. My heart ached for my nest. My manor house. My trees. My hot spring bubbling up from the ground. I'd suffered and died to grow the heart tree, its thorns piercing my body, puncturing my heart. My blood flowed in the tree, powering the sacred grove that our goddesses had helped me grow. The Morrigan, Nevarre's goddess, had even sent Her crows to live in my grove.

With that thought, I saw my crow queen in her nest, her shiny black feathers fluffed up against the cold. *Soon*, she seemed to say in mind, and I felt the promise of warm eggs beneath her breast. In a few months, she'd lay her first eggs.

All of them would. Birds had flocked to my nest. Mostly crows, but I sensed blue jays, cardinals, owls, even a bald eagle in the trees.

The queen sent another image to me, the skies dark with countless flocks of birds flying to her from across the country. Birds chirping and singing, telling her of things they'd seen. Some brought her tokens and gifts. Shiny coins, bits of ribbon, strands of hair. I touched a delicate silver locket, and I could suddenly see the owner.

A woman. No, a queen. I knew it beyond a shadow of a doubt. Alone, she wept, silently, staring out into a vast darkness. I had no idea who she was, or where she lived, only that she'd once owned the locket now in my crow's nest.

The crow cocked her head, showing me piles and piles of trinkets. Goddess. So many. If they all had images of owners, bits of secrets attached to them...

:*Eyes*.: She chirped in my head. :*Ears*.:

Yes, of course. The birds were my eyes and ears in the world.

I was going to have a huge hoard of shiny treasures to sort through as soon as I went home.

I started to pull back to the mummy, but hesitated, lingering with my crow queen. How had she been able to communicate directly in my head? I hadn't tasted her blood.

An image filled my head of a large thorn puncturing her in the side, just below her right wing. :*Blood. For you.*:

She'd bled on my heart tree that flowed with my blood and power. Now she could talk to me directly. Implications flickered through my mind. Reaching up to my rat, I scratched her lightly under the chin. *:Would you be willing to offer your blood on the heart tree?:*

She squeaked and touched her nose gently to my cheek. I took that for yes. If only I could figure out a way to travel between the tower and my grove quickly without having to get on a plane. I pushed that thought away and focused on the mummy lying before me. My heart tree pulsed inside me, tying me to the earth and the sacred grove. I was as rooted to my power as possible.

I punctured my index finger on one of my sharp nails and traced a pattern on the mummy's chest. I didn't know what it meant, only that it needed to be done. The magic dictated that symbol. That word. It meant...

"One Flint," Itztli whispered. "His calendar day."

"Huitzilopochtli, Hummingbird on the Left, Lord of Sun and War, patron god of Tenochtitlan, I call you from beyond the grave. By the blood of the Great One flowing in my veins, I command your soul to return to this body."

My hair lifted around my head briefly. Something fluttered past my head and landed on the mummy. A hummingbird, bright blue with an emerald-green chest. It paused a moment, wings outspread, and then they blurred, releasing the trademark buzz of a hummingbird in flight. With a loud pop, it disappeared into the mummy's chest.

I traced my still-bleeding finger over the bandages covering his mouth. "Huitzilopochtli, your queen calls you to rise. I call you to glitter and shine as in days of yore. Rise."

In the distance, I heard a tinging sound, as if someone played a harp or chimes far away, almost out of hearing. His chest rose on one deep breath, and then he released that breath on a furious, heart-rending bellow.

Rik shoved me behind him, while the twins took up position on either side of him. Through the bond, I felt Guillaume raise the sword over his head, poised to slice off the mummy's head.

"Wait!" I commanded them, pushing Rik's arm over my shoulders so I could see, though I didn't make him move out of my way. I was already asking much of my alpha. While I could, I'd allow him to protect me as carefully as he wished, because all too soon, there would be nothing he could do to save me.

The mummy thrashed on the table, rending cloth and scattering centuries of dust. His body swelled beneath the wrappings, shredding them more to reveal blue skin. Strips of cloth fell away, stained with the same blue, so it must be some kind of paint or dye. He reached up and dragged the cloth from his face. Too quickly, because I could see the white bone of his skull before his flesh knitted together over the top, filling in over the cavity where his nose and mouth were.

His eyes gleamed golden like the sun. Beneath the blue paint, his skin was nearly black. His hair hung in twisted plaits from a high ponytail on the crown of his head. He jerked upright and promptly lunged toward me.

Rik pushed me back with a warning growl, and the mummy fell to the ground. He crouched, eyes gleaming like molten gold, and threw his head back to roar again. Not like a beast or a jaguar. To me, it sounded like rage. Pain. Unimaginable grief.

He spoke, but I couldn't understand the words.

Tlacel translated for me. "Where is she? Where is my love?"

Huitzilopochtli threw his head back and roared again, this time a name that I recognized. "Citla!"

:Oh, Shara,: Mayte cried in our bond. :He's still looking for my mother.:

27

TLACEL

In the five hundred years and more of my life, I'd never thought that my affinity for the ancient language of Mexica would be of use to anyone. Yet here I sat between my queen and the god of Tenochtitlan, acting as interpreter.

Something even my mighty older twin could not do.

I'd grown up used to being second place. It wasn't Itztli's fault that he'd been born first. In fact, I was incredibly lucky that Grandmama had decided to ignore the old ways and allowed me to live. It wasn't uncommon in those days to kill the weaker twin, and I had never been as powerful as Itztli. Given our heritage and how we were conceived, it was a miracle that either of us had been able to hold on to our sanity long enough to find a queen.

Shara had moved us all back upstairs to a private room.

She'd offered food and drink to the ancient god, but he'd refused everything, other than a blanket that he'd casually wrapped around his hips.

"What happened to you?" She asked the man who'd once been the most important god of Tenochtitlan.

Huitzilopochtli didn't look at me as I repeated the words for him. He couldn't look away from our queen. Not that I blamed him in the slightest. "After the fall of Tenochtitlan, I slumbered off and on for centuries. I hoped that Mexica would rise once more, but as the years passed, I realized we were doomed. We would never again build our temples. Our ways were lost, corrupted, and destroyed, our temples torn apart to build the Spaniards' churches. Mexica was no more.

"But then another god began to whisper to me. He promised to bring us back to our full glory. He promised golden temples would bear my name once more. Sacrifices would be offered to strengthen me again. Our cities would rise on the earth and we would destroy any who stood in our way. All I had to do was eliminate the last few witches that lived in my ancient country."

Pausing, he tipped his head to the side, looking at Shara. "Queens. Like you."

"So Ra woke you and asked you to kill the last few queens in Mexico?"

I repeated Shara's words and Huitzilopochtli grunted acknowledgement. "There were so few left. I thought it would be easy. But then I found Citla Zaniyah and she conquered me with her gentle spirit. I felt great pain inside her. A great darkness. She'd endured much, but she still carried a sweetness in her that called to my hummingbird. I watched her from afar, and then I sang to her as a bird. She heard me. She answered me. I knew, then, that she was mine."

He stared off into the distance, a pained smile on his face. "I took her from her family for a time. It was only days on this earth, but in Aztlan, it was a lifetime. She told me about the evil she'd endured in House Tocatl. I sensed the other sun god's touch in that foul deed. He would revel in such a thing. He wanted all the queens dead, yes, but he wanted them to suffer, too. He would have laughed with glee at the thought of a young, powerful, beautiful queen being ruined by men who were supposed to protect and nurture her power."

He focused on Shara, his face hardening. "I couldn't bear that I had participated in the spread of his evil. I had not tortured young queens, but I had caused others to die. I knew that if he could find my love, he would destroy her. So I took her back to her home and set out to correct my misdeeds."

Shara leaned back against Rik in her normal seat, though our alpha vibrated with urgency. If Huitzilopochtli so much as moved an eyelash in a way that Rik didn't approve, he'd have her up in his arms. The last Templar knight casually stood behind Huitzilopochtli's chair. He didn't have to have the sword unsheathed to make his threat known. A whisper from our alpha, and the former god would be dead.

"I was the sun. I was invincible. I took Xiuhcoatl in my left hand and went to defeat the Egyptian Lord of Sun with all the love burning in my heart. Only to be batted down like an annoying insect. He is so strong. I've never seen his like. Even at the height of my glory in Tenochtitlan, I don't think I could have defeated him."

"I told you," Vivian muttered beneath her breath.

Shara ignored her. "What did he do to you?"

Huitzilopochtli stared back at her, his gaze unwavering. "He hung me up by my ankles, slit my throat, drained every drop of my blood from my body, and drank it while lounging on a throne made of gold, while his priests cut my belly open and took my organs, including my heart. I was aware the entire time, though I couldn't move or defend myself. He wears my heart with others around his neck. As long as he has my heart, I cannot return to Aztlan."

Huitzilopochtli jerked his head to me, his eerie golden eyes blazing with conviction. "You. Tell her. She cannot defeat him. She cannot face him. Because what he did to me will be nothing compared to the horrors he will do to her."

SHARA

Tlacel threw himself against my knees and buried his face against my chest. "Please, my queen. He says you cannot go. There's no way you can defeat him."

I stroked his straining shoulders, but I didn't say anything to soothe his fears. I couldn't. I was scared shitless too.

But what choice did I have?

"Do you have any powers remaining?" I asked Huitzilopochtli.

Tlacel translated my words in their language, his words muffled against me.

The former god closed his eyes, as if he was looking inwardly. A hummingbird appeared on his shoulder. Grimacing, he opened his eyes and shook his head. "Without Xiuhcoatl, my fire serpent, this is the most I can do. Other than indulge my immense thirst for blood, which may increase my power somewhat."

Mehen snorted. "Sounds familiar."

Tlacel explained to Huitzilopochtli, and the grim man actually smiled. "You have an immense thirst as well? In my height, I reveled in the blood of sacrifice."

"She fucking drinks it," Ezra said.

Huitzilopochtli's eyes gleamed with interest. "Citla drank from me and said my blood gave her great power and pleasure. Is it the same for you?"

"It is," I said, trying not to sound embarrassed. I wasn't. It was just strange discussing my thirst for blood with a relative stranger.

He licked his lips, his eyelashes fluttering. "I still taste you. That's how you woke me."

"Yes."

He averted his face. I wasn't sure why, until I noticed the way he gripped his thighs. Hunger. While I'd given him enough blood to raise him from the dead, that would have only been a tantalizing taste for a man of his appetite.

"You have a question," he said suddenly, turning back to face me. "Ask, lady. I know all things that deal in blood."

I thought a moment, and then nodded. Yeah. I did have a question. I gestured to my Blood gathered around. "When I drink, I can drink from them all. Where do I put that much blood? Where is the power stored?"

For once, Huitzilopochtli didn't seem alarmed at how many I

could drain at once. "If I may see you feed, I can better answer your question."

Tlacel lifted his head. "Feed on me, my queen. I beg you."

He tipped his head to the side, baring his throat. My fangs throbbed, but I didn't want to indulge in pleasure, not with this stranger watching. Mayte's father. Though I wouldn't tell him that until I knew for sure that we could trust him.

Instead, I pressed one of the silver nails to Tlacel's throat and carefully punctured his skin down into the vein throbbing so invitingly. I locked my mouth to the small wound before removing my nail, so the blood spurted directly into my mouth.

The taste of him made my eyes roll back in my head. Rich green growth of a wild, untouched jungle. The green-blue feathers of Quetzalcoatl flowed through me, a soft whisper of magic deep inside me.

"He says to focus on the flow of blood," Tlacel whispered. "Feel it slide down your throat. Watch where it goes. Ask it to show you its secrets."

I closed my eyes, trying to do as he said. It was hard, because I wanted to focus on the taste of him, the surge of power flooding my system. And yes, my desire. I wanted to push him down on the floor and mount him while his blood poured down my throat.

Down into my stomach. I felt it there, heating my blood. Stirring my lust. Deeper. My core, as if the blood was no longer in my digestive tract at all.

:Your root chakra,: Guillaume said. :That makes sense. Blood and desire are tied together for most queens.:

I focused deep in my lower abdomen, pushing through the layers of arousal and need that tried to distract me.

And suddenly I slid into Daire. I was inside him. Flowing through him like an energy current.

"He says," Tlacel gasped. "Root to root. You pass the energy to your surrogates. We store it."

I didn't try to control the flow, but watched as my energy crackled up Daire's spine. He seemed to absorb it without even noticing, though he felt me sliding around in him now. I sucked harder on Tlacel's throat, taking more blood.

I felt it this time, flowing down my throat, my stomach, down through my root chakra to Daire's, and back up his spine. It was like his bones were giant batteries, gathering my power.

Lifting my head, I met Huitzilopochtli's gaze. "Are they all surrogates? They all hold my power?"

Tlacel repeated my question and the god nodded. "The more surrogates you have, the more power you can store. That's why they're all so big and strong. You power them. You build them to house more energy. Their frames can take the load because of your stores built inside them. When you need the power, it will snap back to you immediately."

I sat back, stunned. I didn't have massive reserves inside me. My reserves were in my Blood. I'd been pumping them up with my power this entire time. After the last huge feeding...

I touched each of my Blood. Now that I knew what to look for, I found my power humming inside them, stored along their bones. Mostly around their spine. Root to root.

An idea sprouted. A way I could appear weak and defenseless, to gain access to Heliopolis without alarming Ra. But still have access to my power stores, thanks to my Blood.

"Are you willing to join me in one last fight to destroy the Lord of Sun?"

Huitzilopochtli stood, his chin inching up proudly, shoulders wide and eyes blazing. "One last battle, lady, aye. Hummingbird flies on your left to defeat our common foe."

I turned to Gina and before I could ask, she inclined her head. "The jet stands ready, my queen."

28

SHARA

Egypt, the land of my ancestors. I'd never imagined what it would feel like to stand on the ground that Isis must have walked Herself thousands of years ago.

I stared out over the sprawling city, wondering what She would think of Cairo now. Modern houses and high-rises had been built on top of the ruins, though here and there, hints of the ancient city remained. I couldn't see the Great Pyramid from here, reinforcing the size of the ancient city.

To be safe, I waited past midnight before stepping out of the jet. I didn't want Ra knowing that I was here until I was ready. On the flight, Vivian had plotted the portals out on a map and we'd spent the trip arguing over who should pair up and come through which portal. Rik insisted that everybody stay with me, which I knew was impossible.

Grudgingly, he agreed that if my distraction was *with* me… it wouldn't be much of a distraction.

I didn't tell them exactly what I planned until we were on the ground in Cairo. I needed time to prepare myself mentally, to run every option over and over through my head. I had whispered each option one by one to Carys and watched her flinch and sweat and shake her head vigorously over and over.

Each idea was worse than the last.

"You can't do it," she moaned, mopping her face with a handkerchief. "Every avenue sets you up for failure."

Winnifred looked like a frazzled feather duster from all her queen's frantic pets. I wasn't overly worried, because I hadn't even told her my real plan yet. I'd already gone through each of those options and discarded them. They didn't feel right. But with her probabilities, I'd at least devised the best placement of my Blood to attack through different locations.

I met my dragon's glittering emerald gaze. "Do you think your hide can stand up to some demon acid fire?"

"Fuck yeah."

Vivian said there was a portal in Giza, but it led directly into the sunfires' lair. "Then I want you to head to the Great Pyramid and access the portal there. Cause as much damage as you can before the sun demons can come after me."

"A pleasure, my queen."

"Guillaume, I'm hoping your hell horse will be just as impervious to Ra's power. I want you to come through the portal near the citadel."

"If the fires of hell can't burn me, I should be fine."

Vivian made a low sound of disgust. "You'll see, knight. Hellfire and sunfire are very different things."

I focused on her. "I want you to get to the breeding grounds and get out any queen you find there. Start with the youngest first, but I'm counting on you to get them out."

She narrowed a hard look back at me, her blue eyes piercing straight to my heart. "And then I'm coming to you, wherever you are. It won't take me long. I don't even know if he has any queens held captive any longer."

"I hope not. I hope it's a quick trip for you to check." I took a deep breath and scanned the rest of my Blood. "I don't know how well you'll be able to withstand sun demons and Ra's power, but I need at least Rik and Nevarre to come to me as quickly as you can. Ra's palace lies beneath the obelisk. That's where I'm going in."

Vivian's breath hissed out. "The fucking front door? Are you mad?"

Rik said nothing, but I felt his body hardening against me into solid granite. His rock troll was not amused with my plan.

Carys moaned. "Twenty five percent chance at best, my queen."

Something creaked oddly. I looked up, worried that we might be under attack. The plane moved and jiggled. Then the chair Rik and I were sitting in exploded. He only fell a few inches, but enough to jounce me on the boulders of his thighs.

Daire snickered. "I guess even fancy jet seats aren't impervious to a rock troll's weight."

Unbothered, Rik gathered me closer, his massive hands even

larger now. Cold stone touched me everywhere. "Who goes in the front door with you, my queen?"

"Huitzilopochtli," I whispered, braced for Rik to start tearing apart the jet around us. Or maybe his massive weight would crumple the floor and we'd just tumble down onto the runway.

Carys focused on me, her head tipping slightly. "How?"

And now the part that none of my Blood would like. "I want him to feed on me to the point where I'm barely conscious. I'll appear weak and defenseless. He can take me to Ra like an offering and demand that Ra make him immortal again."

Rik's voice crashed and rolled like boulders tumbling down a mountain. "You'd be his prisoner."

"Yes."

Huitzilopochtli wisely said nothing, but his golden eyes blazed. He was all too eager to indulge his legendary thirst.

"He's not Blood," Rik growled. "You can't trust him."

"He's not my Blood," I agreed, keeping my voice light. "And that's why this will work. Ra knows enough about Aima queens to be suspicious of our bonds and blood exchanges. I think he'll be able to verify that Huitzilopochtli has taken my blood, but that I haven't taken his. That makes me weaker in his eyes. He will trust I'm actually a captive because of it. He shouldn't be too alarmed by Huitzilopochtli, either, because he's already defeated him once."

"That's true," Vivian said, though her lips twisted sourly. "I've seen his vizier touch a queen and even burn out her bonds. It's extremely painful, and one of the first things he does to new captives. He can't risk their Blood finding a way to track them down."

The plane shifted beneath us again, metal groaning.

"Rik," I said warningly. "We can't fly to safety if you damage the plane."

The creaking stopped.

"What about *our* bonds?" Ezra growled. "You can't fucking let him burn us out of you."

"I won't," I agreed.

Rik's chest heaved against me like massive bellows. "No. You can't. I can't bear it."

Teary-eyed, Gina looked from Rik to me and back. "What? I don't understand."

My heart ached so badly that I couldn't breathe. I didn't try to answer her.

"She can shut our bonds down." Each word that Rik said crunched like rocks bursting under immense force. "It's like she's gone. Even to me."

I turned in his mighty arms and cupped his stone face. My hands looked like a child's on him. "I need to get close to him. Close enough to kill him. I must appear weak and defenseless. As soon as I can, I'll open our bonds and access my power stored inside each of you. I'll blast through the reserves if I must, deploy the red serpent, and then we leave. All of us."

"Thirty-five percent probability," Carys whispered.

I nodded, not turning to look at her. "That's the best number you've given me all night."

"Those numbers fucking suck donkey dicks," Ezra retorted. "You can't risk your fucking life on thirty-five percent!"

I didn't look away from Rik's granite eyes. "I can, and I will, because I know I will win. I know it beyond a shadow of a doubt. I can't fail because I love you too much to let you down."

He lifted me up higher in his arms. "You could never let me down."

I pressed my lips to the cold stone of his. "Because I'm Shara fucking Isador and what this queen loves, she keeps for all time."

"You will have to order me to leave your side. You will have to compel me to your will. Because nothing else will keep me from you. I love you too much to allow this without your power forcing me to do so."

I swallowed my tears and nodded. "I know. I'm sorry. I love you."

"And I love you, my queen. Give me my orders."

I reached within myself and tapped the power humming deep inside me. My hair sparked, electricity shooting through me like a live current. I'd been bleeding for days and my period had made no signs of decreasing. Perhaps my body knew I'd need every single ounce of blood and power to defeat the Lord of Sun.

"Alrik Hyrrokkin Isador, I command you to depart from me. I command you to lead the rest of my Blood to attack through the palace portal. You may find me on the other side and come to me, but not before I reach the throne of Ra and have deployed the red serpent to its task."

His jaws worked beneath my fingers, a low groaning rumble deep inside him as if the plates of the earth collided and crashed inside him. "I hear and obey, my queen."

29

SHARA

I sat on a bench in front of a red-granite obelisk that marked the heart of the ancient city of Heliopolis. Ra's earthly temple had once stood here. The Isador book said it had once been Egypt's most radiant temple. The floors had been polished so well that the evening sky was reflected on its surface. Two giant pillars had marked the entry to the temple. Like two scales, they represented balance and order.

It was fitting that only one obelisk still stood. Ra had lost his balance long ago. His extreme order and fanatical drive to wipe out the goddesses' children would be his downfall.

I was here to spread chaos in his own backyard.

I'd chosen to wear a simple, light cotton dress in white, the color mankind had come to associate with virginity and innocence. Plus, it'd show the blood well. I had to look weak. Defenseless. Defeated. Nothing showed that better than a pretty woman in a torn, dirty, stained white dress, and I'd play to every single one of Ra's biases to defeat him.

The sky lightened on the horizon. It was almost dawn. I felt my Blood approaching their locations across the sprawling city. Far to the south and west, my dragon flew toward the pyramids. The rest of my Blood were closer, though still miles away. All except Xin, who stood silent behind me.

Rik hadn't said a word to him as he left. Xin knew full well that he was the only one close enough to help me with Huitzilopochtli if I had any issues with him.

The former Aztec sun god sat beside me as silent as my invisible Blood. One of my guys had lent him some jeans and a simple black T-shirt. He sat easily, his hands relaxed on his thighs. I had no idea what he was thinking. He hadn't made a single objection to my plans, even though coming back to Heliopolis might mean his death again. Or worse. Ra would certainly enjoy torturing us if I failed.

"Before I was captured, Citla used to sit in the noonday sun and tell me things," he finally said softly. At least we could understand each other now, though I wasn't sure if I was drawing on Tlacel's gift with language, or if the former god's power had returned. "She told me she carried my child. She couldn't wait for me to return and take her back to Aztlan. The thought that she died, believing that I had abandoned her, is a worse torment than anything Ra ever did to me."

I touched Mayte's bond. *:Do you mind if I tell him about you?:*

I felt her half the world away, her daughter clutched in her arms, with her Blood pressed tightly around her. They lay in a dark place. The basement of her house, I thought, where she'd hidden Xochitl from me when I'd first arrived. Good. A place of darkness would be best. In case…

I refused to even allow the thought to cross my mind. I couldn't fail. Xochitl would never know about the breeding grounds and sun demons. Never.

:*It's alright if you tell him,*: Mayte replied, her voice trembling with emotion. :*Will you close my bond too?*:

:*Yes, I must. If I fall, I don't want him to have any way to reach back to you.*:

Aloud, I whispered, "Citla did carry your child. A daughter. Her name is Mayte."

Huitzilopochtli jerked his head toward me, his gleaming eyes wide with shock. "She lives? Citla lives?"

"No," I replied quickly. "But she did live long enough to deliver your daughter. She believed in you right up to the end. She tried to reach you through the cenote."

The light died in his eyes to grim sorrow. Lines bracketed his mouth. "My poor love. My Citla. Perhaps she waits in Coatepec for me with the Mother of the Gods."

I hadn't seen anyone but Coatlicue at Snake Mountain, but that didn't mean Citla wasn't there, waiting for him to return. "You accomplished what Ra could not."

His head tipped slightly. "Oh?"

"Mayte is a queen, and she has also delivered a queen of her own. You rejuvenated her house's line."

His face softened, and he laughed quietly, though I could hear the heaviness of sorrow still in his voice. "Two queens with the blood of Hummingbird walking the earth. Ra was right after all. Tenochtitlan rises once more."

As we waited for the sunrise, I told him about my queen sibling and her daughter, the princess of unicorns. But all too quickly, the sun peeked above the horizon. Vivian said the best time to open the portal was when the first rays of light touched the top of the obelisk.

It was almost time.

Dawn waited for no queen.

Tears trickled down my cheeks. I sent one last surge of love through my bonds, straining to reach them all, even Frank back in New York City. My rat. My crow. My beloved grove.

:I will return.:

And then I closed myself off from them all.

Silence filled my head, blanketed by Nevarre's gift of Shadow. Soft and cool and dark.

I stabbed the silver-tipped nail of my index finger deeply into my wrist and tore a nice deep slash. Huitzilopochtli quivered slightly, a quick inhale telling me he smelled my offering. But he didn't move. Not until I lifted my wrist toward him.

"Forgive me, lady. This won't be pleasant after so long."

I nodded, already numb.

He locked his mouth over the wound and drank. At first, I only felt minor discomfort. I'd forgotten what it was like to bleed from an injury and feel nothing from it. He wasn't my Blood. I felt no enjoyment or pleasure in his mouth on my wrist. His human teeth dug into my skin, tearing and gnawing at the wound impatiently. My breath hissed out. Pain, yes. But nothing I couldn't manage. Certainly not worse than the aching hole in my heart where my bonds belonged.

As he drank, his power rose. He warmed, as I chilled. He leeched my power from me, and yes, that hurt. Terribly. It felt like he was stripping off my skin, layer by layer, stealing my energy with every drop of blood. My queen instincts screamed with alarm, demanding I fight back. My bonds were there. If I commanded the fog to dispel, I could find Rik. I could tap my reserves. I could save myself.

It took everything I had to surrender and allow Huitzilopochtli to drain me. Exactly why this would make a convincing story for Ra. No queen wanted to be drained to death. Especially a queen as strong as me.

I thought of my Blood, one by one. The way they smelled. Tasted.

Mayte. Her daughter. For Xochitl, I could do this. I could let myself die. *I must.*

He ripped tendons and muscles from my bones. Smashed my organs. My lungs. My chest caved in and my heart throbbed with agony. Burning. I couldn't breathe.

Something moved in my line of vision, making me blink to focus. I'd fallen across Huitzilopochtli's lap. Xin hovered at his shoulder, silver eyes burning ice cold. A blade in his hand rose toward Huitzilopochtli's throat. I tried to reach for Xin's bond, but his bond was gone.

All my Blood were gone.

I concentrated fiercely, commanding my lips to move. "No. Xin."

I wasn't sure that I made any sense at all, until he lowered the blade. The last thing I saw as darkness claimed me was the red track of tears down his cheeks.

30

GUILLAUME

I had found myself in some shitholes over the years, but never a place as bad as this.

With the phoenix's blood still burning in my stomach, I'd easily passed through a portal that wasn't apparent to the mortal eye, directly into Heliopolis.

A mockery of lavish luxury.

It was the kind of place where slaves shit on golden toilets and wiped with gold-leafed paper and died for a twisted god's amusement.

Goddess preserve me, I will never again admire anything that glitters like gold.

Empty hovels the size of prison cells still stank of misery and pain despite the grandeur. Golden walls were streaked with old blood stains. Rotted corpses lay where they'd fallen. Delicate skeletons. The size of which told me they were women. Children.

Queens.

Tortured and dead. The sheer waste of such power and blessings from long-gone goddesses appalled me at a level deeper than even Desideria had ever been able to do. The thought that my queen had come to this place...

Deliberately weak.

Captive.

My blood boiled, and I galloped down golden streets filled with refuse and death. Even my burning hooves couldn't leave a mark on the streets of gold, but centuries of bodies stacked and tossed carelessly like garbage marred my soul for all time.

There was no honor here. No hope. No love.

This wasn't a place that my queen could survive unscathed.

In the distance, two shining obelisks stabbed the sky. Ra's primary temple lay beyond. As I neared, I worried that the clatter of my hooves would alert the sentries to my presence, so I shifted back to my human form. I'd rather creep quietly through the streets naked and silent than gallop into a squad of armed skeletons. Surely Ra would have his Soldiers of Light guarding the temple. I'd battled them in Kansas City shortly after hearing my queen's call, and they weren't easy to fight.

They were already dead, the best of the best warriors over thousands of years.

I could make out a line of golden columns marking the temple entrance, when a geyser of fire shot up into the sky on the opposite side of the city. A high-pitched shriek made me duck down against a low wall. Hopefully that was the dragon's fire blasting the sunfires' lair, and not the demons roasting a dragon on a spit.

Without my queen's bond in my head, I had no way of telling where the rest of her Blood were. Rik was supposed to be approaching from my left. Vivian was going to search the breeding grounds to the east. I shuddered at the thought. Could those buildings be any worse than what I'd already seen? I didn't want to know.

I found a fallen skeleton soldier, his bones scattered across the road like he'd been plowed over by a tank. Hopefully a queen had succeeded in escaping, though the bones were so old and brittle that I couldn't tell if it'd been recent, and the skeleton was simply that old, or if it'd been lying here, drying out like sticks for centuries. He'd carried a fine set of blades. Golden chainmail made me wince at the ridiculous opulence, but even malleable rings were a better protection than bare skin. Though I'd give up my favorite spine sheath for some plain, tightly woven steel chainmail.

I crawled the last few feet to a low wall that marked the outer boundary of the temple grounds. There was no shadow. No place to hide. My skin felt tight, my nerves jittery. I hated being out in the open like this unprotected. It felt like eyes watched my every move, though I saw and sensed nothing.

Carefully, I peered over the top of the wall. My eyes watered trying to make sense of it all. Glittering lights flashed in all directions, painfully bright. Blinking tears away, I finally realized I had indeed found the Soldiers of Light, dressed in their shining armor and armed with every sword, shield, and gold-tipped mace imaginable. They lined the columned aisle at least five deep. Easily one hundred dead, expert soldiers.

Not something I could fight singlehandedly.

A flash brighter than ever made me duck down. Even through clenched eyelids, the light roasted my eyeballs. I winced, waiting until I was sure the brilliance had faded, before I carefully peeked over the top of the wall.

My queen. Bloody. Apparently dead. Her eyes stared sightlessly up at the burning ball of light in the sky without a single tear.

Huitzilopochtli still gripped her wrist against his mouth, feeding on her blood. He'd doubled in size from when I'd seen him not even an hour ago at the plane. Our queen's blood had worked a miracle in him, bringing him back closer to his former glory as a god of sun. He rivaled even Tepeyollotl now, the biggest man I'd ever seen.

Clutching her wrist in both hands to his mouth, he snarled at the soldiers, whirling away from them, a starving wolf fighting to keep his kill. He dragged Shara like she was a lifeless rag doll.

And I quivered. Enraged. At the dishonor.

My hands ached on the sword hilts.

My head throbbed with the fury of my heartbeat.

Yet my queen's command rolled through my head. She hadn't commanded me directly, only Rik, but my alpha carried her authority and had directed me to approach only once she was close enough to Ra to ensure the red serpent would kill him.

I hadn't even seen the motherfucker yet and I wanted to kill them all. I wanted to gallop between the columns screaming a challenge and trample them all into the dust.

Panting and fighting myself, I almost missed Huitzilopochtli's words.

"Tell him Huitzilopochtli brings a sacrifice worthy of Lord of Sun."

Typical soldiers. They milled around, unable to make a decision for themselves. Maybe Huitzilopochtli knew that, or maybe he was just lucky, trying to buy us all time to approach. At least the soldiers were all focused on him, now, which allowed me to work my way along the wall to the side of the temple.

Vivian said there was a small niche on either side of the temple for observers. Nothing fed Ra's vanity like having people watch his atrocities. If he still held any living queens captive, they might be commanded to watch, though Vivian thought it unlikely.

Finally, a ranking officer marched back down the aisle toward the main temple. I heard the heavy thud of his boots and the jingle of spurs. Former knight, I thought. He sounded like he carried a full set of armor.

I was close enough to hear him call out, "Greatest of Seers, one of the Lord's conquests has returned with a sacrifice he claims worthy of Lord of Sun."

A man stuck his head out from a royal purple curtain. He wore pristine white robes and a heavy gold and lapis lazuli collar around his throat. "Which conquest? What sacrifice?"

Huitzilopochtli heard the man and raised his voice, "Behold, Tenochtitlan shall rise once more! Hummingbird on the Left returns with a queen descended from Isis herself!"

Dragging Shara by her arm, Huitzilopochtli pushed through the soldiers with the ego of a former sun god. Miracle of miracles, they allowed him to pass unscathed. Or maybe they were too stunned by the dreaded word.

Isis.

The Great One's name seemed to hang in the air like a massive charge of lightning, building until the hairs prickled up and down my arms.

"Who dares utter her vile name in my presence?" A deep voice bellowed through the curtains, making them dance and shimmer as if a mighty wind had blown through the temple.

I started to creep forward again, but something sharp jabbed me between my shoulder blades.

"You have too much meat on your bones to wear the golden wings of Ra." The sword jabbed harder, ready to slip between my vertebra. A quick twist of the blade, and my spine would be a jumbled mess. Shara could heal it, sure, but not if she was dead.

With a sigh, I let the weapons fall from my hands and stretched out on the blistering gold stone.

Perhaps she could still make use of me yet.

31

SHARA

Something was burning. It took me an embarrassing long time to realize it was me.

I was sure that I screamed, though I couldn't hear anything. The pain was too great. Light burned into me, charring everything it touched. Nothing would ever blot out that light. It was too bright. Too hot.

I tried to flee. I tried to reach for help. Someone. If I could reach him—

Cool, dark Shadow enfolded me, and I sighed with relief. Emptiness. That was a good thing, though I couldn't remember why.

"I told you. No bonds."

I recognized that voice but I couldn't place it immediately.

The light dimmed slightly, enough that the pain went to from excruciating death to merely sharp agony.

"Where did you find her?"

I didn't know that male voice. I tried to remember what I'd been doing. Where was I? Where was...

My Blood.

The cool Shadow whispered back to me.

Shara fucking Isador.

"She was stupid enough to resurrect me after you gave me to the Skye witch."

Huitzilopochtli. So that other voice had to be... Ra.

But it didn't sound magnificent and awe-inspiring, let alone terrifying.

He didn't sound like a god.

"No bonds, hmm? Then what's this?"

A body thumped down beside me. But I couldn't see. A body? Goddess help me. If one of my Blood were dead...

"Pardon, High Lord. We found him outside the wall trying to worm inside. He surrendered peacefully enough."

Who was it? I fought down the sobs. I couldn't react. I couldn't betray myself. I couldn't have bonds or Ra would blast them out of me.

I needed my bonds to remain deep in the Shadow. Until it was time.

The light faded another notch and I blinked furiously, trying to get my eyes to work. They should be watery, teary, right? After that brightness? But every movement hurt, as if I was ripping my eyeball apart. I smelled blood, and realized it was my own. I bled from my eyes. I tasted blood in my mouth. I swallowed it, willing that small amount of blood to heal my eyes.

I had to see which Blood they'd captured.

First, I took in the three men standing over me. High above me, so I was on the ground. Huitzilopochtli was almost unrecognizable. My blood had pumped him up to rival my alpha's rock troll. His dark skin was painted blue again, his eyes flashing like twin suns in a brilliant sky. Green and blue feathers rose from his ponytail in a high crest, and he wore a leopard skin around his waist. Definitely not what he'd been wearing on the other side of the portal.

The man beside him was dressed like a high official in a pristine white linen sheath complete with collar, but no crown. A recently-healed scar cut across his eye. The other man was dressed very similarly but his sheath was shorter, and he wore more gold. His eyelids were painted blue with dark kohl outlining them into a bold point, giving him a sinister look.

The first was bald, the second was not, but he wore a crown.

Something told me it wasn't Ra, though. The crown wasn't dramatic enough. Surely the Lord of Sun would bedazzle with his clothes.

But who'd hurt me with the light? Did his priests have the same power?

I closed my eyes a moment, even though the simple movement felt like razor blades slipping into my skull. I sank deep within myself, centered in Shadow. Whoever it was, I couldn't react. They couldn't know he was my Blood.

Or all would be lost.

We'd all die.

No one else could stop him.

Someone nudged me with their foot. "Look, witch, and tell us which Blood this is."

Groaning, I opened my eyes and forced my head to turn. An inch. Two.

Guillaume.

Oh G. My poor Templar knight. What are they going to do to you?

I rolled my head back around and to look up at the three men. Huitzilopochtli wore a convincingly arrogant sneer. The bald one had to be a priest. The other man with the jewelry…

I wasn't sure. He wasn't Ra. Other than that, I didn't know.

I swallowed painfully, trying to get my mouth to work. "No. One."

The man with the jewelry smiled with a strangely benevolent look on his face. "He's no one you know? Is that what you're trying to say, witch?"

He said witch like a slur. I wasn't a witch. At least, I didn't consider myself a witch. I was a motherfucking badass vampire queen who also worked some magic thanks to the Great One's blessings.

Something told me all women were witches in his eyes. We all deserved to be burned at the stake. Boy, was he in for a big surprise when I torched his ass instead.

He leaned down and I noticed a golden disc hanging about his neck, marked with the rising sun. It started to glow, and I tried to avert my face to save my eyes. But he seized me by the hair and forced me to look into the burning orb that grew on his chest.

My eyes. They were bleeding, melting out of my skull.

Panting, I curled up in a ball. I didn't know how long he'd blazed into me. If I had any eyes left.

I heard their low voices whispering several feet away. I couldn't follow the conversation, only that the evil one said, "no bonds," but doubtfully, as if he didn't believe what he was seeing.

Please, Great One, help me. Help me hide my Blood until it's time. Help me to keep them safe.

I heard their footsteps nearing. Shivering, I curled tighter, seeking the Shadow once more. The balm of endless night filled me, taking away the agony in my eyes. But they wouldn't let me rest in the Shadow. That would be too easy.

They seized me, wrestling me up to my knees. I was sure one of them was Huitzilopochtli. He touched me like a warrior with grim, unwavering hands that were calloused and hard. No priest would have hands like that. The other man was probably the priest. I didn't hear any golden chains sliding or tinkling as they dragged me up.

"If this man is no one to you, then it should be easy for you to feed on him and kill him."

Don't react. Don't betray us.

I didn't dare open my eyes. Not until the fires stopped burning in my skull. I could only hope that Guillaume didn't react too. He was the most honorable man I knew. He couldn't possibly betray us.

No. *I* would betray *him.*

"Heal yourself, witch. You're in no shape to entertain His

Imperial Majesty until you drink. You're easy meat right now. He likes a little fire and spunk in his whores."

I reached out a hand, blindly feeling for my knight. He snagged my hand, drawing me near.

I needed to make this convincing.

Feeding on him alone wouldn't be convincing.

His gentle hands pulled me to him. Hands that had been twisted and broken in torture.

His body welcomed me. He told me without words that he understood. He made himself available to me, to use however I wished. He would endure with honor, proudly, regardless of my need.

I would have cried, except my eyes were a ruined mess.

I tore into his throat like a savage beast. I didn't spare him my fangs or my ravaging hunger. I let my cobra's thirst drive my instincts. They thought me a witch, something less than human. Then I would play the part.

His blood immediately soothed the agony burning inside me. He let out a roar of release for me, holding nothing back. He knew we played a game. He thrashed hard against me, appearing to fight, struggling against me.

When he cradled me to his torn throat and welcomed the coming darkness.

Hissing and snarling, I hauled him closer, rising up over him as he sank to the floor. He lay on his back, twitching slightly as I drained him. I could see him now. My beloved knight. His blue eyes stared up at me with the softest, most beautiful look of love on his face.

Goddess. I willed him to understand. I willed him to forgive me.

Then I lunged up toward the skeleton guard who'd dragged him in. I seized his sword, lifting it over my head with both hands.

And brought it down on my headless knight's old scar to cleave his head from his body once more.

32

RIK

Something was wrong. I knew it. Her plan wasn't unfolding as she'd expected.

Or worse, it was going exactly as she'd expected, and now Carys's probabilities were coming true despite our queen's best efforts.

My skin twitched like Guillaume's hell horse trying to dislodge a fly. Since my skin was solid granite...

That wasn't an easy feat.

I had a feeling that Guillaume was in trouble. I wouldn't have normally thought of his horse. Not now. Not when our queen's bond was dead.

I met Daire's worried gaze, and I couldn't feel him. After decades of sharing a bond with him, I had no idea what he was thinking.

Fuck that shit. I did know. I didn't need a bond to tell me we were fucked.

"I'm not waiting a fucking second more," I growled.

Daire breathed a sigh of relief. "It's about fucking time. Let's go get our queen."

I reached for Xin's bond automatically to check his location and muttered a curse beneath my breath. I couldn't feel him. I had no idea if his gift of invisibility worked here or not. I could only hope he was still alive and making his way toward Shara.

Something crashed behind us, sending me whirling around, boulder fists raised, ready to pummel the threat into dust.

Leviathan, king of the depths, huffed smoke into my face. I didn't need her bond with him to know what he was thinking, either. *What's taking you so fucking long?*

He shifted back to his human form as we ran toward the temple. Tlacel, Nevarre, and Llewellyn led from the air, keeping watch for those skeleton soldiers that had tried to drag her through a portal in Kansas City.

Fuck, that seemed like a lifetime ago. Not just a few months.

I tried to keep up with Daire and Itztli, but they easily outpaced my rock troll's lumbering pace. Only Ezra and Mehen hung back with me. I wasn't sure why Mehen had even shifted, until he started telling me what he'd seen.

"The sunfires are fucking impervious to just about everything I could think of." He shook his head grimly. "They didn't care about my fire. I tried to smash them with my tail, shred them with my claws, bite them in half. Nothing worked. Finally, I just knocked a giant wall down on top of their lair. That did the trick, though I don't know how long they'll be pinned."

"It's not the rocks blocking the lair," Ezra panted. His shaggy hair was plastered to his face. I could see why he didn't want to shift to a furry grizzly here. The sun was merciless. "It's the fucking darkness."

"Yeah," I said slowly, my mind racing. "Nothing here will like the darkness. That means the temple will be open to the air, right? We should be able to see everything. But if they know we're coming…"

Mehen grunted. "I'll shift and go tell the other fliers to stay high and quiet. If I see the chance to grab her and get her the fuck out, I will."

I grabbed him by the scruff of his neck, squeezing hard enough he cursed at me. "Don't interfere unless you must. She knows what she's doing."

He grimaced and nodded, so I released him. He leaped and shifted into the dragon in mid-air. For a moment, his wings provided a tiny bit of shadow. Such a relief. Then he raced ahead to flag down the other winged Blood. They'd have to fly very high to avoid casting shadows on the ground and alerting the guards.

My blood pounded in my veins as mercilessly as the sun. I had to reach her. I had to find her. Before it was too late. Every instinct I possessed told me she was in desperate need of assistance.

Daire and Itztli came trotting back to me. The black dog's tongue was lolling and Daire's fur was streaked with sweat. At this rate, we'd all be dead from dehydration and sun poisoning before we even found her.

It was the strangest goddess-damned place. Buildings with

no roofs. Was it ever night here? How did people sleep? I knew the answer.

There was no sleep in Heliopolis. No rest. No safety. Unless you were a sun demon or a minion of Ra.

I had to do something, though, before the Blood keeled over. I finally knocked a wall over and propped it up enough to provide a modest amount of shade. We all crammed inside in the blessed shadow. I shifted to make more room for the others, and Daire and Itztli shifted so they could talk.

Not having our bonds was damned inconvenient.

"Soldiers," Daire panted, dripping with sweat. "Skeletons. They guard the temple avenue."

"Blood," Itztli said in between breaths. "Smelled it. Some our queen's, but mostly Guillaume's."

I slammed my fist down on my thigh. "I knew it. Something went wrong. Any sign of Xin or Vivian?"

They both shook their heads.

"How many skeletons?"

"A hundred. At least."

"What the fuck is this skeleton shit?" Ezra said. "Can't you just tear them apart?"

"They're Soldiers of Light," I told him grimly. "The best soldiers down through the ages who came to Ra's call. They're nearly impossible to kill. The last time we faced them, it was three of us to ten, maybe twenty, and we nearly died. Daire took a wound to the chest that would have killed him without Shara, and the rest of us were injured. Even Guillaume, though he held his own way better than me and Daire. She had to shatter the portal to destroy them."

"Fuck me sideways," Ezra gasped, shaking his head. "I'm not a fighter. I mean, I'll hold my own against anything a grizzly would fight. But I don't know a fucking thing about weapons and warfare. I'll be fucking useless in hand-to-hand combat."

I needed to come up with a way to even our odds. Shara depended on me. They all did. I could wade into the battle and let the soldiers break their swords on my rock hide, but eventually, they'd avoid me and go after the rest. They didn't have the same protection, and I wouldn't be able to hold off a hundred. Not alone. Even if the dragon could help from the sky...

Vivian popped her head down over the side, startling us. "I have an idea. If you don't mind a few humans dying, I think I know a way we can get most of the skeletons out of our hair."

"Fuck humans," Ezra growled as he climbed out of the troll-made cave. "Let's go get our queen so she can get us the fuck out of here."

SHARA

"Most impressive," the man with the golden disk on his chest said. "That's much better. His Imperial Majesty will enjoy you very much. Do you know your lineage, witch?"

Licking Guillaume's blood from my lips. I slowly straightened. I refused to cry. I refused to show any weakness, regret, or indecision. I'd been blessed by the Great One Herself so that I might stand here, now, and put an end to Ra's self-righteous bullshit. I wouldn't flinch now.

Though it hurt something deep inside me to step over Guillaume's lifeless body like he meant nothing to me at all.

I drew myself up proudly, shaking my hair back from my face. "First of all, it's queen, not witch. You may refer to me as Your Majesty, or even Shara Isador, but not witch."

The bald one gasped, his hand darting up to touch the vivid scar over his left eye. I had a feeling he'd gained that scar when he'd attacked me through the portal in Kansas City.

I gave him a slow, feral smile. "You recognize me. Good. You know my power."

The other man narrowed a hard, suspicious look on me. "You know this witch?"

"She's the one who detonated the portal," the bald man whispered.

Bingo.

His eyes widened. "So it's true. You are descended from... *her.*"

"Yes." I looked around the temple with disdain, as if every golden ornament offended me. Because it was true. I'd never seen a tackier, more self-indulgent display of ridiculous opulence in my entire life.

He backed up a step, before catching himself. He grabbed his golden sun disc and held it up at me.

It took every drop of Isis' blood in my veins to keep from flinching, or quickly averting my gaze.

"Cooperate, witch. You know what I'm capable of."

"Queen," I said firmly, refusing to look away. "And you know damned sure what *I'm* capable of."

"Not without your Blood."

I let one corner of my mouth quirk suggestively. "I can find new Blood, though I tend to go through them rather quickly.

Who are you people? Where'd Huitzilopochtli go? I have a few things I'd like to say to him," I finished with another snarl, as if I was pissed at him.

They looked at each other, as if trying to decide whether to indulge my curiosity or not. I ignored them and slowly walked around the temple like I was an invited guest.

Massive golden pillars soared overhead, draped with white linens. But no ceiling. A single glance up at the sky, even with my hand shading my tender eyes, made me want to recoil into a dark room for a year. Ra's power blazed overhead like a sun that hung entirely too close to the earth.

The floor was polished like a golden mirror, making the sunlight radiate right back up into my face. My exposed skin was red and hot, as if I'd been sunbathing for hours.

The bald one finally answered me. "I'm Greatest of Seers, High Priest of His Imperial Majesty. This is High Lord Vizier Amun. Per the Hummingbird's request, he was given leave to worship Ra and beg for a boon."

Amun-Ra. Another name for Ra after the sun god had absorbed Amun.

The vizier smiled again, that indulgent fatherly smile that pretended to care about me, a complete stranger, whom he hated with every fiber of his being. I smiled back at him. I was going to be sure to kill him too. Though I didn't think I'd need the red serpent for it. "Take me to His Imperial Majesty."

He chuckled, shaking his head. "Why in heaven above would I do that, witch?"

I allowed the smile to slide away into a flat stare. I didn't say anything immediately, but only stared back at him. In ancient times, the vizier had been second only to the pharaoh.

I didn't fucking care who he thought he was.

When he averted his gaze to the priest, frowning like it was his fault, I finally answered. "Because I'm breeding, and I intend to bear Ra a queen."

33

SHARA

I'd never seen a pompous windbag move so quickly. The vizier stared at me, his mouth falling open, for a count of three. Then he whirled around and strode toward the rear of the temple. "Prepare her. I'll inform His Imperial Majesty."

Greatest of Seers, the high priest, stared at me like the heavens had opened up and dropped an angel at his feet. Only this angel was coated in feces and smelled like death warmed over. I was everything his god yearned for and hated at the same time. No wonder he didn't know how to talk to or act around me. He was terrified of refusing or insulting me, if I might truly become his god's mistress, or concubine, or whatever the hell Ra would deign to call me.

His hand started to rise toward his scar again, but he caught himself and gave me a glare. "I have powers you can't possibly comprehend. I won't be as kind as the High Lord."

I threw my head back and laughed. "Sure. Go ahead and kill the last breeding queen to walk the earth. I'm Ra's last shot at siring a queen and you know it. So shut the fuck up and take me where I need to go."

Despite a dark scowl, he led the way after the vizier. At the rear of the temple, we stepped through what seemed to be wispy white clouds or fog.

The three giant pyramids of Giza shot up to the heavens, only these were surely two or three times as high. It was hard for me to guess, since I hadn't seen them in person yet, but I could barely see the golden triangle at the top of the largest one's peak. Bloody tears tracked down my cheeks again from trying to look up beneath the punishing sun.

The priest led me to the smaller pyramid. I couldn't suppress a soft sigh of relief as soon as we stepped inside.

Dark and cool, the pyramid was a relief after the blaring sun outside, though everything was still solid gold and luxurious. Gold and purple curtains hung on the walls to create separate rooms. The walls themselves were painted with intricate hieroglyphs. At a glance, I made out enough to recognize the "Adoration of Ra," an ancient poem dedicated to him that often appeared in the *Book of Coming Forth By Day*.

Otherwise known as the *Book of the Dead*.

Slaves rushed forward, beautiful young men and women that were mostly naked, their skin marred with whips and burns like Vivian's back. I clenched my jaws, fighting down my rage. Many of these marks were old, and these were young people. Mostly human, I thought, though I sensed a spark in them that spoke of a goddess's heritage. They probably contained enough Aima blood to see and know things most humans couldn't. Just enough to attract the attention of Ra's minions.

Who'd snatched them up young and brought them here to live a life of misery.

A young man bowed low before me, lifting up a pitcher of water. I grabbed it and drank my fill of sweet, delicious water. Maybe I was doomed now, like Persephone after she'd eaten the pomegranate seeds, but I couldn't help it. My body's physical reserves were shot. I could easily regain my strength and power if I tapped my bonds...

But I couldn't. Not yet. So I had to deal with burned skin, dehydration, and sun poisoning, without my power to heal myself.

I allowed the slaves to bathe and tend my tender skin. They removed my torn and stained dress, slipping me into an Egyptian white sheath so thin and diaphanous that it hid nothing beneath it.

Especially the dark blood smearing on my thighs. My stomach cramped and ached, my period still flowing like one of my heaviest days. Maybe it was stress. Or maybe I really was trying to breed Aima style, rather than enduring a very normal human period.

I had to see Dr. Borcht again, and soon. Hopefully she'd be able to tell me something conclusive about my reproductive cycle. Assuming I lived to return to our world.

My hair was still damp from the bath when the high priest clapped his hands and shooed the slaves away. "This way...

Your Majesty." He said the last grudgingly, as if the very idea that he must show me any respect at all was salt in a wound.

We stepped back outside, and my hair instantly dried in the vicious sunlight. My burned skin throbbing with pain. I hurried after him, eager to get to the next pyramid, but a shriek made me pause and look back.

Toward the temple.

I kept my face smooth, though I willed my Blood to wait. To give me time. I wasn't close enough yet. They couldn't attack. Not until I was in sight of Ra.

A skeleton soldier went running past toward the larger pyramid, and the priest yelled after him. "What is it? What's happening?"

"One of the obelisk portals has failed. His Imperial Majesty's sunfires are crossing to the human plane at will."

The priest moaned, shaking his head. "Great Lord above, he will not be pleased. Heads will surely roll."

He scowled at me. "It was probably that Hummingbird idiot. I bet he didn't use the portal correctly and now it's failing. The vizier will be beside himself trying to explain this debacle to His Imperial Majesty."

I gave him a tight, small smile. "But His Imperial Majesty will surely be pleased to know that Huitzilopochtli has brought him such a worthy gift. What are a few humans in the end? They're merely cattle for gods and queens."

He grunted sourly and dared to seize my arm, tugging me along after him to the larger pyramid in the middle. "Let's hope you really are breeding. Then much will be forgiven. Who knows, His Imperial Majesty might even name you God's Wife."

Oh goody. I could hardly wait, though I had to admit that God's Widow had a much better ring to it.

XIN

My wolf hated this place. Henceforth, the smell of gold would always remind me of decay.

I padded quietly along beside my queen, though even she couldn't see me. Not without touching her bonds that lay hidden deep inside Nevarre's gift of Shadow. The priest stank of fear as he hurried Shara to the next pyramid, craning his neck to look back over his shoulder worriedly.

Evidently even the High Priest was afraid of the sun demons. Hopefully the dragon had decimated their numbers, or we had no hope of fighting them off.

The skeleton soldier raced back to the temple, shouting orders ahead. "Soldiers of Light, deploy at once to the earthly plane! We must contain the sunfires at any cost!"

It was all I could do not to release a howl of glee. Surely my fellow brethren had a hand in releasing those demons, which had also served to draw the skeleton soldiers away from the temple. Hopefully that meant they were close.

Because as we entered the large pyramid, I had a feeling we would need every weapon at our queen's disposal, no matter how small, just to keep her alive.

This pyramid was as lavish and orate as the other, but there was something wrong here. The gold was... melted. Soft. It still moved beneath my paws. I stuck to the carpeted areas to avoid leaving telltale wolf tracks in the malleable floors.

Brilliant light sparkled off the golden surfaces, compromising the wolf's sharp vision. Shafts had been built into the pyramid, acting as giant sun lights to allow the punishing light to reach even inside a pyramid the size of a mountain. We seemed to walk forever, slowly making our way deeper into the bowels of the pyramid.

A tomb? That was all I could think of.

A molten gold river bubbled up from a crevice in the ground, making a liquid glittering lake. Streamers rose from the surface like solar flares. The air simmered with heat. Boulders rose up from the flowing gold, giving us places to hop and step. Otherwise it was like a lava fountain slowly flowing up from the heart of the pyramid.

Something moved beneath the surface of the lake. A head broke through streams of gold, then shoulders and torso as a giant rose up out of the molten lake. He waded through the golden river like it was a pleasant mountain spring, slinging droplets of liquid gold with every step. His massive erection jutted up like a golden log, and I feared greatly for my queen. I couldn't see how any woman other than a goddess could take such a cock and live.

Beneath a large shaft of sunlight, he sat in a golden throne facing us. Rivulets of molten gold streamed down his face and body, spreading across the throne to drip on the ground. He wore a heavy, lumpy necklace around his throat, but coated in gold, it was impossible to tell what the objects were.

The High Priest began to chant in a sing-song voice. "Oh mighty Ra, Lord of Sun, Radiant Majesty of Heaven, Maker of—"

"Silence." His rich voice oozed with dulcet tones that should have been pleasing to the ear. But there was something so... off about him. Like a beautiful poem marred by one misplaced rhyme, or a masterful rhapsody that crashed on a single discordant note.

He gleamed painfully bright. Gorgeously gold. His body was carved like the finest sculptures of the world. Perfect.

Yet he was rotten to the core and ruthlessly insane.

He might turn on anyone, even his High Priest, just because it amused him.

He leaned forward on his throne, puddles of gold pooling at his feet. He glared at my queen like the sun blasting a single snowflake that had been careless enough to fall on the brightest day of the year. "You. Smell. Like. Her."

I loved my queen more than anything in this world, but even I was awed at the way she slowly inclined her head in a graceful move that belied the terror she must feel. The god was fully capable of rape and destruction. She'd known that, even before seeing him the flesh. If he touched her, he could melt the flesh off her bones with the heat of his golden form. How was she even supposed to survive his attentions?

Yet she showed no fear in the face of his immortal glory.

"I'm Shara Isador, last daughter of She Who is All that Hath Been and Is and Always Will Be."

He threw his head back and laughed, showering droplets of gold up into the air that coated the sides of the pyramid in another layer of gold. "The last, huh? Then my desire has at last come to fruition."

Shara waited for his mirth to quiet. Another few seconds for him to focus on her again. And then yet another deliberate pause to be sure she had his full attention. "I thought your desire was to sire your very own sun queen."

He leaned back in his throne, sprawled carelessly in all his grandeur. Yet for all his casual positioning, his erection grew even larger. The tip started to whiten, as if thousands of years ago, Isis had touched that massive organ with the tip of Her finger and cursed him to always remember Her despite his roaring solar power. "I'd rather see *her* line dead than sire a queen of my own."

"As you will, my lord." She lowered her head and said nothing else, but shifted subtly, her hand slipping gracefully down the front of her body, between her breasts, to rest low on her stomach where she'd carry a child. Drawing the god's gaze to the darkness between her thighs. The blood that pooled between her thighs as surely as gold puddled at his feet.

"Why have you come to me?" His words sharpened, shards of glass to rip and tear at our senses. "Your kind know to fear me. Yet you allowed the Hummingbird fool to drag you here. Don't tell me that was an accident. Surely, you aren't that stupid."

She kept her face down, her lustrous hair shining like black silk in the cruel light of day. "All queens are stupid. Isn't that what you think? Where is Huitzilopochtli? What have you done with him?"

His eyes narrowed dangerously. "Why do you care?"

I knew she was deliberately tugging on his pride and ego by pretending to care about the other man, but it was like playing with matches on top of a mountain of explosives.

"If you have no interest in giving me a daughter, then perhaps he will do."

He laughed again, but there was a darker thread running through his mirth that made the wolf's hackles rise. "Oh yes, I remember having this conversation with another witch desperate to conceive."

Shara didn't lift her head but peeked up through the cascade of her hair. "I'm not desperate, my lord. I know what Keisha Skye did not."

Ra didn't immediately respond, but finally raised his hand and gave a careless twitch of his fingers. A molten lump of gold moved from against the sloping wall. My nose worked hard, trying to discern who or what it was, but I couldn't smell anything beyond the metallic stench of gold. The lump seemed to stagger under its weight but finally came to stand near enough for Ra to lay his hand on it.

The gold dripped away, pouring off the shapeless lump to reveal Huitzilopochtli, his blue paint smeared and melted away. His body quaked beneath the god's palm, but he locked his knees and stood firm despite the pain of being encased in molten gold.

"How could a lesser sun god give you a child?"

Shara blinked up at the mighty god, tilting her head quizzically. "He's done it before. Surely he can sire another queen for me."

34

SHARA

A fresh wave of gold spilled down over Huitzilopochtli's head, melting his face. He screamed, gurgling on liquid gold. I refused to react. I couldn't. The game was too deep for me to show any regret or fear now.

When a queen played chess with the Lord of Sun, she couldn't feel anything remotely like remorse. Or worse, pity.

For Ra would certainly never show pity to me.

Mentally, I counted the thousands of humans who'd been sacrificed to Huitzilopochtli. Innocents. Warriors. Women. Children. I couldn't be sure.

The list was longer than I could imagine. Citla would have been on that list, if he hadn't fallen in love with her. Mayte would never have been born. Neither would the princess of unicorns. House Zaniyah would have been decimated by him without regret.

Finally, he fell to his knees, and that seemed to satisfy Ra enough that he ceased the fresh flood of hot gold.

"Lies," Ra whispered.

I didn't leap to defend myself. I didn't need to. Though sweat trickled between my breasts as I waited, barely breathing, for the confirmation I needed from another source. One that Ra would actually believe. Had the priest left the pyramid? I didn't dare look behind me. Any reaction at all could tip my hand. No doubts. No fear. No hesitation. I couldn't crack my calm, confident reserves.

The red serpent tightened on my throat, reminding me of its presence. Urgency coiled its scales into my flesh. I had to get closer. I wouldn't have a second chance.

The High Priest finally stepped forward several paces to my left, his hands clenched tightly together. "Your Imperial Magnificence, I'm afraid the witch speaks truly. We did find a child queen in Mexico recently. We lost her only thanks to this one's interference. But the avatar did taste the child enough to recognize Zaniyah."

Ra's lips twisted as if he'd smelled something vile. "The house I sent him to destroy centuries ago."

The High Priest bent low at the waist, not meeting his god's eyes. "The very one, Lord."

Ra looked back at me, his eyes whitening, the solar brightness sheeting over like glass.

"Then it's a pity that Hummingbird is no longer immortal. He will be of no use to you."

I inclined my head in a single, measured nod, but I didn't break eye contact with Ra. "A pity, my lord."

"What do you know that Keisha Skye did not?"

Now I did allow my gaze to slip from his, but only to settle on his cock. He made Guillaume look like a pony, and that was a terrible thought that almost shattered my cool reserve.

My poor knight. What have I done?

I swallowed, trying to use any emotion that had flickered on my face as one he'd recognize, and appreciate, as a man with his particular lusts.

Fear.

Dread.

And yes, shame. All things he wanted women to feel at the prospect of sex. Goddess forbid a woman fucking enjoy her sexuality and revel in it.

Ra chuckled, arching his hips up in an air thrust. "Ah, yes, she enjoyed staring at my rod, too. All queens do."

Carefully, I reminded myself. *Slowly.*

Pretending nervous shyness, I flicked my gaze back up to his as I sidled a single step closer. "Did she find pleasure in your arms, my lord?"

He thrust again, deliberately drawing my gaze back to his dick. The same frost spread down his shaft as in his eyes, as if he'd already jizzed and it had frozen on the tip. "The better question is how well did she please me?"

"Did she, my lord?" I whispered, running my gaze down his legs to his ankles. Had the book said which ankle had been bitten by Isis' snake? I couldn't remember. It might not matter. "Did she please you well?"

"No." His voice sharpened, slicing my skin like razor blades. Blood dripped down my cheek, and cuts on both of my arms oozed blood. "She did not."

A hint of something not gold flashed on his left outside ankle. A trick of the light? Or a scar from a snake bite that had never fully healed? I took another step and jerked to a halt. I curled my arms around my waist as if I'd had second thoughts. I looked back to Huitzilopochtli, braced on his hands and knees, head hanging as he coughed and vomited up chunks of gold stained with my blood.

Was he my pawn, a sacrifice moved to distract the king? Or could I count on him to be my bishop and protect my flank? I couldn't be sure.

I stepped closer. I could feel the heat rising off of Ra's body. My skin prickled, uncomfortably dry. He was too hot to even make me sweat. I didn't want to touch him. I didn't want to melt.

The snake coiled tighter on my throat, a faint quiver of antic-ipation. A spring waiting to launch it at our target.

Ten feet. Nine. It wasn't enough, and the High Priest watched me suspiciously.

"Keisha conceived her daughter, my lord, but Tanza was not a queen. She certainly wasn't *the* Sun Queen." I added empha-sis, a stroke to his ego. "She failed you, my lord."

Ra flicked a finger at me, scattering an arc of gold droplets in the air. "Disrobe."

My fingers shook as I pushed the single strap of the linen

sheath off my shoulder and allowed it to slide down my body.

"Inspect her," he said to his priest.

Greatest of Seers bowed even lower. "I did, Your Imperial Majesty. So did the High Lord Vizier."

"She has no Blood bonds? A queen of this strength? I deem it unlikely."

"We both examined her and found her empty of bonds. The High Lord searched her twice, pushing deeper than any queen has endured before."

Ra made a low sound of distrust, eyes narrowed on me. "And what of this snake on her throat? Have you examined that?"

The red serpent on my throat didn't move, locked in place like a tattoo.

"We did, naturally, Your Imperial Majesty. Given your history with snakes—"

"Silence!"

The priest fell down on his knees and bowed forward to press his face against the golden floor. "I beg your forgiveness, Oh Mighty Sun of Radiance!"

Ra sneered at me, his eyes whitening to solid ice. "What is the significance of the snake, witch? And remember that when I touch you, I can sense a lie. I'll split you in half on my cock and feed you to my sunfires if you try to lie to me."

What could I say that wasn't a lie? I hoped my face wasn't as panicked as I felt. House Isador didn't lie, even to kill the god of light. But what could I say to buy myself some time?

I was still too far away to launch the serpent. I didn't need Carys's probabilities to tell me the serpent would fall short. And then what? What would become of me? My Blood?

I'd already killed Guillaume.

I had no idea where the rest of my beloved Blood were.

I couldn't feel them. Anywhere.

I was desperately, hopelessly alone.

Fighting down waves of panic, I dropped my gaze to the floor, my mind racing.

And I saw one delicate print in the soft golden floor. A print I recognized.

My wolf. Xin.

My eyes burned, but thankfully I was too dehydrated to worry about tears.

"A gift," Huitzilopochtli rasped as if every word shredded his throat. "From my daughter."

I dared a quick breath. So he was to be my bishop and partner in this match, not the sacrificial pawn. Good. I couldn't wait to tell Mayte how much her father had helped me. How much he must have loved her mother and would have loved her.

Assuming we ever escaped Heliopolis.

Ra dropped his hand on his head again, but at least this time, he didn't try to drown him in liquid gold. He listened a moment and then nodded.

"No wonder you're so strong. You've formed a coven with his illicit daughter."

My knees quivered faintly but I didn't otherwise react. It wasn't a lie. Mayte had given me the snake, through her goddess. "I love her dearly."

"Love." Ra slammed his hand down on Huitzilopochtli's back, knocking him down to sprawl on his stomach. "A ridiculous weakness that brings a man to his knees quicker than anything else. Better yet, come to me, witch. Show me how much you love my dick, and I'll let your pet Hummingbird live another day."

35

SHARA

It shouldn't have surprised me that Ra was so dismissive of my coven, as he called it, with Mayte. He was dismissive of all women. Naturally, the friendship and love, sisterly or carnally, between women wouldn't alarm him in the slightest.

If only he knew that was the main reason I was here. To protect other women, but specifically, Mayte's daughter.

I would die before I'd allow him to take another child from her mother and torture her, like he'd done to Vivian and countless others.

I'd even suck the giant dick he was so proud of, if that meant another woman would be spared. But it wasn't going to come to that.

Shara fucking Isador loved sucking dick. But only the dicks she loved.

This bastard would rot in hell before I'd ever love him.

I paused, giving him another sly, playful look beneath my lashes as I slipped my right hand down over my pelvis. I watched his face as I slid my fingers deeper, stroking myself just enough to bloody my fingers.

Lightly, I trailed blood up over my stomach. His eyes burned blizzard-white. His mouth tightened in grim disapproval. His nose wrinkled, his lips turning down with disgust.

Though his dick surged toward me, seeking my bloody heat.

"Was Keisha breeding when you fucked her?" I whispered, sidling closer.

"No. I fucked her until she started breeding. I made her come into heat."

"Did you taste that blood you made her shed for you?"

He closed his eyes in a one long, deliberate blink. He looked blind, his eyes completely white, but I was sure he saw everything. "A necessary evil for your kind, but nothing I would ever indulge in otherwise."

"A pity," I whispered, holding out my bloody fingers out toward Huitzilopochtli.

Braving Ra's wrath, he lunged up and sucked my fingers into his mouth.

Ra was too disgusted to react. He stared at me, too appalled to even pretend otherwise. My actions had completely shaken the foundations of his world.

I tossed my head, throwing my hair back over my shoulders

to stand proudly naked in front of God of All Things Light and Day.

But he was not the god of me.

I was darkness. I was chaos. I was death, destruction, and finally, rebirth. I carried the bloody proof between my thighs.

"Did you love her?"

He blinked again, dragging his gaze up from my pussy. "Why would I love a witch?"

"No, I meant did you love She Who Is and Always Will Be?"

He seized me by the throat, sealing my neck in liquid fire. My fangs shredded my lips, but I didn't scream. I refused to give him the pleasure.

I was close enough now. I could use the serpent.

But it was trapped beneath his fist.

Don't move, I whispered frantically to the snake in my flesh, hoping it would hear. *Wait. I will get you free.*

"She Who Lies and Cheats the Light of Day?" He roared, shaking me so hard that something popped in my back. "Why would I love her? She healed me, so she said, but then left me to fuck Osiris. The poison of her touch remains. She burns in me to this day!"

I couldn't breathe, but I wasn't panicked. Yet. The pain was terrible, yes, but not nearly as bad as what the vizier had done to my eyes. I had sense enough to shove my other hand between my legs, and then I wrapped bloody fingers around his cock.

He dropped me like I was the one burning him. I fell against his thigh and the throne, which sizzled against my skin like a branding iron. But I held on to his dick, refusing to let go.

Huitzilopochtli leaped to his feet and shoved both of his hands into the molten gold streaming down the pyramid wall. I could smell his flesh burning, but he didn't howl with pain.

No.

The one howling was Ra.

Neck and shoulders straining, head back, he gripped both arms of his throne and bellowed like I'd cut his dick off. The frosted white of his eyes spread across his cheeks, and his dick felt like a giant icicle in my hand, though the spurt of his seed was hot on my flesh. He came so hard I felt droplets landing in my hair and on my shoulder, burning like acid. I couldn't imagine taking that come inside me with the hope of bearing a child. It must have felt like icy-hot pokers stirring Keisha's insides.

Only to fail. Even the God of All Things Light and Day had not been able to give her a daughter. She'd resorted to dark magic, trading a life for a life in the process.

His roar of release turned into a deep, rumbling chuckle. "You waste the gift of life."

His hand came to my head and he petted me. Almost fondly. Before he seized a handful of my hair and pulled me up on top of him.

I didn't fight him. Not when I now had him exactly where I wanted him. His skin didn't even burn me any longer. The molten gold had run off his body, revealing more of his true features. His head was bald, but he had a long prince's lock at the base of his skull that hung down his back, probably to the floor. He wore a chunky necklace, the chain heavy enough to hold at least a dozen large charms. I fingered one of them, trying to make out what it was. Gold had settled over the carvings, blurring the image, but it looked like a scarab.

A heart scarab. The amulet that was worn over the deceased's heart to protect it on its journey through the underworld.

One of these probably belonged to each of the sun gods he'd absorbed. Including Huitzilopochtli. I didn't look up to see what he was doing. I didn't want Ra to realize he'd moved.

He gripped my chin, a little too firmly, as if he was out of practice. Staring into my eyes, he gave my head a tiny shake. "Tell me. If you're her true daughter, then you know what I want to hear. What I've yearned to hear since the beginning of time."

I nestled closer to him, pressing my breasts against his chest.

And he took her heart to heart, so her body would know his secret name.

Smiling up at him, I reached up and cupped the back of his head, pulling him down closer to me. As if I would kiss him.

"What makes you think that She could ever love a monster like you?"

His eyes bled back to molten gold. His skin started to sizzle against mine. With a fierce scowl, he gripped my waist so hard it felt like he was bruising internal organs. But he couldn't dislodge my hand on his neck.

I closed my eyes and whispered, *"now."*

The red serpent tore from my flesh and sank fangs into his face, directly over his left eye.

He erupted from the throne to his feet, tossing me aside.

Molten gold sprayed from his mouth like a geyser rather than any sound. It poured from him, a flood of liquid sun, dimming his harsh brilliance.

The High Priest screamed, "Witch!"

Something brushed past me, invisible fur, a whisper of death. My ghostly wolf materialized as he tore out the priest's throat.

Ra still stood, screaming out liquid gold like I'd punctured the sun itself. I needed my power to finish him. All of it.

I touched the Shadow buried inside me and commanded it to dispel. Thousands of wings fluttered through me like rushing winds. My ears roared as my bonds blazed to life inside me.

:Rik!:

36

RIK

I waited.

My head braced against hot golden stone. Sun beating down on my head and shoulders. Barely breathing. Waiting.

She would call me. She would.

When it was time.

Not before.

I could endure. I could wait as long as it took. She would be enduring far worse.

That thought didn't help in the slightest.

Rock crumbled to dust beneath my grip.

Yet I waited.

My queen's bond slammed into me so hard that she knocked

my rock troll over on his back. I stared up at the brutal sun and
fried my eyeballs, but I didn't care.

:Rik!:

I shoved up and leaped toward her like a deadly rock slide.
:Go! Get her out!:

Her Blood responded immediately. A fireball shot out of the
sky, followed by a dark, massive dragon, a shrieking gryphon,
and a giant crow.

They flew past the temple, guided by her bond, and disappeared through a wispy veil.

Goddess. It felt so good to have her bonds in my head again.

Itztli's black dog reached the temple first, followed by his
brother. Tlacel wheeled over the temple and sent me an image
of a body on the ground.

Guillaume.

Panting, the rest of us finally reached the scene. The knight
sprawled on his back, mostly naked, except for a golden chainmail vest he'd picked up somewhere. Blood pooled around him
and his throat gaped open in a horrible, vicious wound that
bared the white of his spine.

It took me a moment to realize the flesh was knitting back
together. He wasn't slowly dying from a neck wound—but
rather slowly growing his head back to his body. His eyes met
mine, his hand flopping beside him. Reaching.

For a weapon. Even in death, he was ready to kill for
our queen.

I picked up one of the swords and pressed it into his palm.
"Join us when you can."

:We need the lighter Blood,: Mehen roared in our bond. *:We can't*

fit through the door. A handful of skeletons guard the pyramid, but we'll have them finished before you get here.:

The twins were already racing that direction with Daire on their heels. Ezra and I hurried after them, though my mind was locked on Shara.

I pushed into her bond, invading her mental space, but I couldn't help it. I needed to feel her. I needed to access her health and ensure she wasn't too badly injured. She could have locked me out, but thank the goddess, she let me in.

She was naked, had a few scrapes and cuts, and burns in half a dozen places, but she was otherwise unharmed. A golden giant loomed over her, head tipped back as liquid sunlight poured out of him. A red snake clung to his face.

Good. She'd done it.

I refused to think about the cost.

I will pay it. In a heartbeat. Please, just let me hold her one more time.

Yelling in his language, Huitzilopochtli raced toward Ra and launched a heavy turquoise spear. It struck him directly in the chest.

The golden stream slowed, and Ra lowered his head. It took me a moment to realize he was laughing.

"You fool. Your Fire Serpent lost all its power when I took your immortality." He pried the spear out of his body and tossed it aside like it was a toy. Then he reached up and jerked away the serpent dangling from his eye. "And you, witch. Did you honestly think a snake could end me, when *she* failed exactly the same way?"

He seized her in both hands and held her out in front of

him. My queen began to scream as liquid gold poured over her head.

SHARA

Blistering agony. Liquid fire. My flesh melted. I screamed and fought mindlessly a moment, before remembering what I was.

Who I was.

I was more than this screaming, flailing creature. Let him roast me alive. Goddess help me, I'd take him with me.

I drew hard on my bonds, calling my reserves to flood me with power. Eleven Blood bonds emptied a bottomless well of magic directly into me.

I wrapped my body in the Morrigan's Shadow, and the agony ceased immediately. With a thought, I healed my burned flesh. I hung suspended in a flood of liquid gold and stared back at the god who'd hurt so many.

My voice echoed through the Great Pyramid, rising with power. "I am Shara Isador, last daughter of Isis, She Who Is and Was and Will Be. Lady of Heaven, Queen of the Gods, hear your daughter's prayer. What You began, allow me to finish in Your blessed name."

I shoved my fist into the hole that Huitzilopochtli had made with his spear and closed my hand around Ra's heart. With a shout, he threw me aside, but I clutched his beating heart in my hand and took it with me.

I fell into solid granite that clutched me like I was a baby kitten. Rik. He cradled me in his arms but didn't try to stop me. He knew, as I did, that my greatest work yet remained.

Lifting my hand into the air, I held Ra's thumping heart above us. "The red serpent made you mortal, Lord of Sun. It gave you a heart." I paused, watching the horror slipping across his face like a frosted glaze of ice. "A heart that can be judged."

He fell to his knees. "No. It cannot be. The Lord of All Things cannot be judged. I am immortal."

A gong echoed through the Great Pyramid, resounding off the golden walls. A set of scales appeared before me. Whispers flowed down from above, though I couldn't understand the words. I looked up, and the top of the pyramid was gone. People looked down from a balcony on all sides, watching the proceedings. From the Isador book, I knew they were the forty-two judges.

Beyond them, where the peak of the pyramid had been, I saw only clear, blue sky, shining like a single eye.

Something drifted down from the upper level and came to rest on one side of the scale.

Ma'at's feather of truth.

Ra crawled on his knees closer to me, hands rising beseechingly.

Rumbling with fury, Rik braced against me. My wolf and black dog both crouched in front of us, hackles rising. My warcat pressed against Rik's leg and roared. Ezra rose up on his hind legs, all nine feet tall of sheer bulk and vicious teeth. My gryphon let out a piercing shriek.

Tlacel and Nevarre streaked in above us, circling on silent wings. I didn't turn to look behind me, but I felt the heat of Leviathan's fire and smelled the burning cinnamon and myrrh of my phoenix.

Tears flooded my eyes, my throat aching. The only Blood missing was Guillaume.

Last Templar knight, made headless by my own hand.

Had this death been final because I dealt it to him? Was his life the price for the red serpent? *Please,* I prayed, closing my eyes. *I can't. Please don't take him.*

:What the fuck took you so fucking long?: Ezra retorted.

:You fucking made her cry, asswipe,: Mehen growled. *:Fucking headless knight.:*

Beloved hands cupped my cheek. Fingers once broken and twisted, now made whole, wiped my tears away. "My queen. Take me. I'm yours."

I didn't open my eyes but flung my free arm around his neck. My knight. Fully healed. I hugged him so hard he grunted, but my joy was short lived.

I still had to lose someone.

But first, I had to finish Ra.

I pressed a soft kiss to Guillaume's lips. Rik set me on my feet and I stepped closer to the scale.

"Begin the Declaration of Innocence," a deep voice boomed from above.

I laid Ra's heart on the opposite scale, and for a moment, it balanced perfectly with Ma'at's feather. Until he began to recite the required script.

"I have not done crimes against people…"

The heart tipped heavier. A tremor shook Ra's shoulders, almost completely white now. His sun power leeched away, draining into the golden lake.

"I have not done any harm. I have not blasphemed a god or goddess."

With each sentence, the heart tipped the scales and the whispers above grew louder.

I lost track of his declaration. We all knew he was guilty. We knew he deserved eternal damnation.

But the one to deliver that justice... was Ammit, the Devourer.

Me.

In my mind, I saw the legacy box open once more with the four jars inside. As soon as I focused on the one with the conical top that looked like a crocodile snout, the jar tipped over with a clink, and the lid fell off.

My heart pounded, waiting for the gift to swell inside me.

"I am pure," Ra said.

Something rumbled deep inside me. Claws clacked across my ribcage. Scales slithered up my spine.

"I am pure! I am pure! I am—"

Fury welled inside me. This man, this god, had been a creator. He was supposed to represent hope and light, the promise of a new day and new beginning. Instead, he had destroyed entire houses of our goddesses' children. He had raped and tortured countless women. He had tortured his own children. He had corrupted the lives of humans and destroyed the natural balance of the world. He corrupted everything he touched. He spread hate and vileness throughout the world.

I opened my mouth to tell him to shut the fuck up, but a roar came out instead of words.

"Please," he whispered. Perfect crystal tears glistened on his cheeks.

Even that pissed me off. He wasn't allowed to fucking cry. He couldn't possibly be sincere. He only cared that it was time to pay for all the horrible things he'd done. He'd wallowed in pain and suffering for countless millennia. Did he honestly think a few tears were enough to wipe away those sins?

"I only wanted her to love me."

Of fucking course. Rage pounded in me. So many lives destroyed. Magic wiped from the face of the earth forever. Because this man's ego was bruised when a woman he fancied chose another man over him.

I shot forward and hit the scale with my snout, knocking his frantically pounding heart up into the air. It was a fucking pleasure to chomp on that foul meat and swallow it whole.

Wailing, Ra began to puddle in his gold, losing his form.

Ezra huffed with disgust. :*If I ever see another fucking gold leafed anything, I'm going to puke. At least our queen is smart enough to only eat the heart, huh, dragon?*:

Leviathan huffed a plume of noxious smoke over us that made my crocodile eyes water. :*I hope he doesn't give her indigestion.*:

I wanted to laugh. I wanted to feel relief. I'd done it. Ra was dead. Xochitl was safe.

But one of my loved ones still had to die.

I turned my head and Ra's golden monstrosity of a throne was replaced with a jade throne. Two serpents rose above the goddess's head, facing each other with their fangs bared. Two jaguars, one black and one golden, sat on either side of Her feet.

Coatlicue. Mother of the Gods.

My heart thudded heavily, aching as if the Great Pyramid had suddenly collapsed on top of me.

I stepped closer to the waiting goddess, not surprised that I'd shifted back to my human form. Diaphanous linen flowed around my legs and my head felt heavy. I reached up and felt Isis' crown on my head, the sweeping horns holding the red sun disc. Good. I would need all the help and authority I could get.

The whispering witnesses were gone. My Blood gathered around me as they shifted. Their hands touching me, assuring me that they were all here with me.

One last time.

"Well done, daughter of Isis." Coatlicue looked the same as I remembered from the dream. Full, heavy breasts. Stomach rounded from carrying many children. Kind, loving eyes, gleaming with sadness and joy both. She wore a living skirt of snakes like the one She'd given to me to use on Ra.

Turning her head, She held out Her hand. "Thank you for returning my most beloved son to me."

Huitzilopochtli stepped closer to his mother and dropped down on one knee before her. He laid the turquoise spear on the ground in front of him. "Forgive me, Mother, but I've lost Xiuhcoatl. He breathes fire no more."

She laid Her hand on the back of his head. "All that matters is you, my son. Now you may return to Aztlan, where your beloved star awaits."

He lifted his face, hope burning in his golden eyes. "Citla waits for me?"

"She always has."

He laughed with joy, settling back on his heels. "Thank you, Mother. Thank you."

My Blood knelt around me. Rik beside me, his right arm around my waist. Daire pressed against my other side. My first two knights. Losing them would destroy me.

Losing any of my Blood...

"Great Mother." Rik's voice rang with authority, drawing Her gaze to him. "As alpha, I ask that you take me for the cost that must be paid."

"No," I whispered, pressing harder against him. "No! I won't allow it."

Coatlicue nodded. "Very well, child. Which would you ask me to take in his place?"

I trembled. Tears choked me. I opened my mouth, but I couldn't. I couldn't say a single name. I wouldn't. I wouldn't ever choose just one of them. Not to love. Not to kill.

I loved them all.

I needed them all.

"It's as I thought," She said, not unkindly, but as a weary mother who had lost many children in a long lifetime. "It's never easy to choose."

She plucked one of the writhing serpents from Her skirt and gave it a gentle toss in my direction. It plopped in front of me and rose up several inches, scanning us all. Its tongue flicked out, as if trying to decide who might taste better.

"The oldest Blood?" Coatlicue asked as the snake slithered closer to Mehen. Emerald eyes glittering, he gave the snake a sardonic bow. "He's certainly had plenty of lifetimes already, but so few days with a queen he loves."

"The headless knight has already paid a cost for your love," She said as the snake bypassed Guillaume. "The bear's grumpy attitude is needed to help you laugh. I think I should not take him. This time."

The snake passed to Nevarre and hesitated, its head swaying back and forth.

"Ah, now, this one is quite interesting," Coatlicue said. "He was already dead, but the goddess of life and death returned him to you. He's a likely choice."

I squeezed my eyes shut. Nevarre. My Celtic raven. *No, please, Great One. Not him.*

Daire snorted. "You can't take him. She'd miss his kilt too much, and he has the best hair."

"I beg your pardon," Vivian retorted, slinging her fiery red hair over her shoulder. "If anyone should be taken, it's me. I'm her greatest enemy's daughter."

"No," Llewellyn said roughly, pushing to the front of my Blood. He dropped down beside Huitzilopochtli. "I'm the logical choice. I served her mother faithfully for hundreds of years. Send me to her side and spare her daughter any pain of losing one of her own Blood."

I pushed free of Rik and Daire and hurried to Llewellyn's side. "No."

Coatlicue didn't even look at me but stared sadly at my mother's Blood. "I'm afraid that your former queen does not wait in paradise for you. Instead, you must go ahead and prepare a place for her, because her spirit refuses to leave her daughter alone in this world."

"Very well."

"No!" I cupped his face, turning him to look up at me. His eyes were dark, the red-gold falling stars already extinguished. "You have too much to tell me. You haven't shown me any of the scenes with my mother. You haven't had the chance to tell me anything about her. How will I ever know her if you're taken from me?"

"She walks with you," he whispered, his face ravaged with sorrow. "You will always know her."

I pulled his face against my stomach, wrapping my arms around his head. "No. I can't bear it. Please, Mother of the Gods, please don't take him."

"Mother," Huitzilopochtli waited until she looked at him. "This queen resurrected me. She saved me. How can you cause her such grief when she returns a beloved son to you?"

Coatlicue shook her head. "She has not returned you to your former glory, my son. Your heart is missing. She has breathed life into the shell of your body, but your soul will depart once this body fails."

His heart was missing. Of course.

I released Llewellyn and scanned the ground, trying to remember where Ra had melted. Buried in the malleable golden floor, I found the necklace he'd been wearing. I pulled it up out of the gold. Frantically, I scanned each glyph, trying to tell which one was Huitzilopochtli's. I didn't know his language. I couldn't read the glyphs like I could Egyptian ones, but there was only one with a bird on it.

I jerked the scarab free of the chain and stepped back to Huitzilopochtli. I held it out toward him, and the scarab started to glow. It thumped in my hand. Once. Twice. Faster as it neared his chest.

Pulling my hand back, I gripped the amulet fiercely in my fingers and held my fist up. "His heart. For my Blood."

She jerked back in Her throne as if I'd slapped Her. Eyes narrowed, She gave me a long, hard look that spoke of a maddened mama bear protecting her cubs. "One of your humans, then."

"No. Not one. What this queen takes, she loves, and she loves for all time. I love them all. I won't give them up."

She leaned forward, the snakes on Her skirt hissing furiously. The jaguars on either side of Her bared their teeth, braced, ready to pounce. But I refused to back down. "We. Had. A bargain."

I squeezed the amulet harder. It was some kind of stone. I could crack it into pieces without much effort. "Yes. And I gave you exactly what you wanted."

Rik stepped up and wrapped his hand around my fist, stroking my fingers until I slowly loosened my fierce grip on the scarab. "My queen, Great Mother, I believe I have a solution that will please you both."

"Yes?" We both retorted.

"Take all of us." I started to open my mouth to retort, *are you fucking crazy?* But he gently laid his fingers against my lips. "When one of us dies, take us all. Especially if it's our queen. We'd all rather go with her when she dies anyway."

"Aye, yes, take me," echoed around me, my Blood stepping up to join us.

"You Aima live a very long time," Coatlicue said, though Her furious glare faded. "How long must I wait to collect on this bargain?"

"As long as it fucking takes," Ezra retorted. Gulped. Then added, "Great Mother. Sorry."

She laughed, shaking her head. "Ah, child. What a collection of interesting creatures you've called to your side. How about this. No matter how many Blood you call in the future, they will all die at the same time. Not one will be left behind to mourn the others."

I closed my eyes a moment, concentrating on settling my emotions so my voice didn't crack. "Even me?"

She nodded, her eyes gleaming with amusement. "Even you. Few would stand against the Mother of the Gods to fight for what she wanted. I'm satisfied with the price of my red serpent, *if*," She hardened her voice. "You give my son back his heart."

"Done," I said faintly and quickly pressed the scarab to Huitzilopochtli's chest. The stone fell away and the glow disappeared into his flesh, though I heard the rapid beating as it sank inside his ribcage.

Huitzilopochtli stood, towering higher and broader than ever, fully restored to his former glory as the god of sun and war. He bowed low to me and took my hand to press a kiss against my knuckles. "Lady, I thank you."

I inclined my head to him. "Thank you, my lord."

"Huitz," a sweet voice called to him. He looked toward his mother, and a young woman stood beside the throne. Her face gleamed with joy, her eyes shining with happy tears. With her long brown hair and delicate cheekbones, I recognized her easily as Mayte's mother, Citla.

He swept her up in his arms. "My star."

I blinked, and they were gone.

"Let's blast this shithole," Mehen growled.

I threw my arms around Rik's neck and burst into tears.

37

SHARA

We flew down the freeway in the middle of the night. Stars twinkled in a perfectly clear sky, with a crescent moon rising. Freshly fallen snow made the world clean and perfect, reflecting the pearly moonlight so well we didn't use headlights.

Rik's chest was warm against me, his mighty arms braced on either side of me with his hands on the handlebars. Daire rode close beside us, and Ezra's muddy Ford truck paced us in the other lane.

Mehen and Guillaume had raced each other for awhile, enjoying the purring rumble of their engines, but all too quickly they dropped back to ride near us.

Near me.

The rest of my Blood hovered near, either protecting from

the rear or flying overhead. Their banter and jokes warmed my heart until my eyes overflowed with tears. Not with sadness this time. But with so much love that I couldn't contain it all.

A tiny squeak drew my attention down to my shoulder. My rat curled against my neck, her tiny paws tight in my hair.

"What did she say?" Rik asked against my ear.

"She wants to go faster."

He grinned, and we shot to the head of the pack. Wind in my face. My love all around me. A quiet, perfect night.

Once upon a time, I'd been afraid of the dark. I'd been alone, on the run, hiding from monsters.

I lifted my hands and arched back against Rik, trusting him to keep me safe.

I would never be scared of the dark again.

The End

But Joely…! This can't be the end.

Shara still has to deal with the Triune. You never gave each of the guys their own one-on-one scene. We never got to see the challenge on the green. Who's the Dauphine and is she a friend or foe? What about Leonie? Can Shara trust Kevin, or will he betray her to Marne Ceresa?

All very valid points. Certainly, I've left several questions unanswered.

Which is why Checkmate is NOT the last book for Shara.

In the beginning, part of my decision to only have five Shara books was the cover art. We only had five images of the same model in the same bloody series to use. So I planned five books. However, when it was apparent that I was running out of space, and that many of you weren't ready to let Shara go, I reached out to Marisa and she's going to use the same model, but a new (less bloody) series of images. If needed, there are at least a couple of more usable images of Shara.

This book is already the longest book in the series so far. I couldn't possibly fit the Triune details into the same book. So QUEEN TAKES TRIUNE will continue Shara's less bloody, but no less deadly, political dance with the Triune. I have a few shorter projects to wrap up before it, so don't start looking for this sixth book until December or January.

I hope you liked Gwen. She gets her own novella QUEEN TAKES CAMELOT, which will be included in an all Reverse Harem boxed set in February, 2019.

If you love the steam, be sure to pick up Between the Sheets for "Queen Takes Alpha," and Halloween Between the Sheets for "Queen Takes Twins." Both are standalone, ultra-hot sexy scenes with Shara and a various assortment of Blood. These scenes are exclusive, meaning they're not available anywhere else until the anthologies are closed.

I still plan to write a spinoff series for the Skolos court. I'm sure Shara will continue to appear in those books, even if Queen Takes Triune is her last book. (I'm honestly not sure. It depends on what she tells me when I get there.) Targeting 2019.

I'm also planning a prequel of short stories for each of her Blood that captures the moment they first felt her call. Guessing early 2019, though I may tackle it before Queen Takes Triune. It depends on how cooperative the Blood are. You know what an asshole Mehen in particular can be.

And of course, our beloved princess, Xochitl, still has unicorns to take. I just need to grow her up a little, because a child/young adult author I am NOT.

Lastly, thank you. From the bottom of my heart.

Thank you for trusting me to keep Shara and her Blood alive. Thank you for welcoming her into your hearts, even when MM or FF isn't your usual reading fare. Thank you for encouraging me to keep writing at all. Because a year ago, I was on the verge of quitting entirely.

Shara has taken me on an incredible personal journey that I never would have imagined possible.

You made that possible. By picking up this series and leaving your reviews and joining the Triune. By telling me your favorite Blood and asking interesting questions like these characters are real, living and breathing people.

That's the greatest honor of all. Because they are real, at least in my head.

Shara fucking Isador loves every single one of you.

What she takes, she loves, and what she loves, she keeps for all time.
Long live House Isador!

ALSO BY JOELY SUE BURKHART

Their Vampire Queen, reverse harem vampire romance

Free in Kindle Unlimited

QUEEN TAKES KNIGHTS

QUEEN TAKES KING

QUEEN TAKES QUEEN

QUEEN TAKES ROOK

QUEEN TAKES CHECKMATE

QUEEN TAKES TRIUNE

QUEEN TAKES JAGUARS

Mayte's story available in Realms & Rebels boxed set

August 21, 2018

"Queen Takes Alpha"

Exclusive short story in Between the Sheets

"Queen Takes Twins"

Exclusive short story in Halloween Between the Sheets

QUEEN TAKES CAMELOT

RH Boxed set Feb 2019

Crimson Arcana, fantasy/paranormal Reverse Harem

CONJURING SHADOWS

Available in What Goes Bump in the Night

Blood & Shadows, erotic fantasy

Free in Kindle Unlimited

THE HORSE MASTER OF SHANHASSON

The Shanhasson Trilogy

A Complete Reverse Harem Epic Fantasy

THE ROSE OF SHANHASSON

THE ROAD TO SHANHASSON

RETURN TO SHANHASSON

Keldari Fire

SURVIVE MY FIRE

THE FIRE WITHIN

Mythomorphoses, Paranormal/SF Romance

Free in Kindle Unlimited

BEAUTIFUL DEATH

The Connaghers, contemporary erotic romance

Free in Kindle Unlimited

LETTERS TO AN ENGLISH PROFESSOR

DEAR SIR, I'M YOURS

HURT ME SO GOOD

YOURS TO TAKE

NEVER LET YOU DOWN

MINE TO BREAK

THE COMPLETE CONNAGHERS BOXED SET

Billionaires in Bondage, contemporary erotic romance

(re-releasing in 2017 from Entangled Publishing)

THE BILLIONAIRE SUBMISSIVE

THE BILLIONAIRE'S INK MISTRESS

THE BILLIONAIRE'S CHRISTMAS BARGAIN

Zombie Category Romance, paranormal romance

Free in Kindle Unlimited

THE ZOMBIE BILLIONAIRE'S VIRGIN WITCH

THE MUMMY'S CAPTIVE WITCH

The Wellspring Chronicles, erotic fantasy

Free in Kindle Unlimited

NIGHTGAZER

A Killer Need, Erotic Romantic Suspense

ONE CUT DEEPER

TWO CUTS DARKER

THREE CUTS DEADER

A Jane Austen Space Opera, SF/Steampunk erotic romance

LADY WYRE'S REGRET,free read prequel

LADY DOCTOR WYRE

HER GRACE'S STABLE

LORD REGRET'S PRICE

Historical Fantasy Erotica

GOLDEN

The Maya Bloodgates, paranormal romance

BLOODGATE, free read prequel

THE BLOODGATE GUARDIAN

THE BLOODGATE WARRIOR